## RETREAT INTO PARADISE

City girl Hannah Stockton writes histories as her day job and family histories in her spare time. Needing a temporary escape from a violent boyfriend, she takes up an advertised position as a live-in caretaker 'with light duties' at a country retreat outside Melbourne. The owner, Philip Boulton, is a hunky high-flying banker who visits on weekends to attend to his small herd of cattle.

Hannah is dismayed to discover that Philip has been taught all he knows about farming by his next-door neighbour, who lusts after Philip and resents Hannah's presence. Hannah can't tell whether Philip is 'more than friends' with his guru.

Philip has recently discovered a family secret. Given his profession, he's sensitive about this fact becoming public. Fearing Hannah's skills as a family history researcher, he keeps her at a distance while he processes his secret.

Meanwhile, as her 'boss', he helps Hannah to overcome her fear of cattle and she learns to love country life … and Philip.

# RETREAT INTO PARADISE

LOUISA VALENTINE

Retreat into Paradise

Copyright © Louisa Valentine 2021

First published in 2019

Republished by Louise Wilson, South Melbourne, 2021

www.louisewilson.com.au

ISBN 978-0-6450741-1-6 (digital)

ISBN 978-0-6450741-2-3 (print)



Cover design by Bookcoverology

Cataloguing-in-publication data is available from the National Library of Australia.

CHAPTER ONE

A swirl of dust enveloped her car as Hannah jammed on the brakes, skidded to a halt on the dirt road and surveyed an impressive gateway. A large sign saying *Wallumatta Farm* adorned the right-hand gatepost. Etched into the gate itself was the number *301*.

She checked the directions scribbled on her scrap of paper. Wiping her dashboard clear of the dust with a tissue, she peered at the trip gauge. She'd been told that in the country a street number indicated the distance from the turn off. She'd reset the gauge when she'd turned left from the bitumen road, the road leading to the small town where she'd stopped for a morning coffee. Now she was 3.01 kilometres from that intersection. She rechecked the number on the gate. *This must be the place. WOW.*

Her jaw dropped as she contemplated the very antithesis of an average farm. Where were the corrugated iron sheds and lean-tos? The old cars and tractors, overgrown by grass and weeds, abandoned until the day when they might be required for spare parts? She'd passed a few farms like that, a short distance back along the dirt road.

That parade of real estate had lulled her into a false sense of security, consistent with her expectation that here, in this little backwater of modest people living modest lives, she could hide away from the world. She could fade into its unpretentious country lifestyle and immerse herself in her writing without the painful distractions of the world she hoped to leave behind … for now, anyhow.

As she gazed at the numbers 301, Hannah grappled with her acute disorientation. Her heart sank. A gateway like this could only belong to someone with serious money. What was she doing here? She shook herself, trying to reconcile anticipation with reality. *Darn, I had no idea this place would be so upmarket. The owners of this property won't want someone like me as caretaker. I don't focus on fashion. Even my car lowers the tone of the place.*

After a few seconds of hesitation, she took her foot off the brake and nosed into the gravelled driveway. No point scuttling away. Seize the day. Might as well keep her appointment. An avenue of crab apple trees led her towards an impressive country mansion, overlooking a broad sweeping valley.

A twitch of the curtains betrayed the presence of someone watching her drive towards the house, probably alerted by the scrunch of her tyres on the gravel. Hannah bit her lip as she pondered the thought of that hidden judge, no doubt agreeing with her own summation that her old car belonged to another time and place.

Scanning her environment, she drove slowly past a four-car garage complex close to the house. The two central bays could be locked up. An extension of the garage roof, supported on posts, created the two outer bays. The raised garage door on the right-hand side revealed a silver, late model Mercedes, albeit a very dusty Merc. An old ute was parked under one of the open bays. This surprising lack of perfection reassured her.

Hannah entered the circular drive in front of the house, pulled up at the front door and scrambled out of the car. As she stepped onto the broad verandah, the front door opened.

Out strode a man, the very opposite of the type she'd been expecting at *Wallumatta Farm*. She sucked in her breath and forgot to release it for a second. This was no hobby farmer needing help or an old-timer needing a break from a burdensome routine. A man to be reckoned with, late thirtyish, he looked like he'd be much more at home in a powerful head-office boardroom. She reminded herself to start breathing again as she absorbed his height, his confident posture, the superb cut and snug fit of his jacket, his tailored pants and the pair of storm-grey eyes that scrutinised her, head to toe.

'You must be Hannah Stockton,' he said in a voice as commanding as his appearance, as deep as he was tall, and resonant. Curt and business-like, his face did not carry a welcoming expression. If anything, he looked quite stern.

'I am.' She tried to smile politely but couldn't. He rattled her. Triggered all her insecurities and preconceptions. He exuded the brisk attitude of a businessperson who expected people to turn up for appointments on time, with a clear agenda in mind and no time to waste on small talk.

Her confidence ebbed away as she retreated to her back foot. Did he think she hadn't noticed his silent assessment of her approaching car, was unaware of his cool appraisal of *her*? Like her car, she'd seen better days too. Her clothes had, that's for sure. Her emotions too. Stale and dowdy, not yet quite thirty but in a rut; that was her. By contrast, he probably had a glamorous wife stashed away inside the house, all style and gloss, inspecting her from behind the curtains as he'd done.

'Philip Boulton.' He interrupted her self-doubting thoughts. He extended his hand for the customary handshake.

She reciprocated for the briefest possible moment. His hand was warm and firm, but she detected no warmth in his greeting. His born-to-rule aura rubbed her the wrong way. If anyone ever asked, she'd have to confess to succumbing to prejudice created by media coverage of the big end of town and its goings-on.

A sinking negativity crept over her. She'd intended her decision to look for a writer's retreat in the country to be a positive step, aimed at removing her from contact with Alex —that troubled, demanding and energy-sapping man she'd somehow allowed to encroach on her life. She wanted to recharge her batteries, refresh her outlook on life, and bolster her self-image. The man standing before her sapped her fragile self-confidence, battered by Alex.

Her brain kicked in again, chasing those emotions away. She chastised herself and stiffened her spine ... no way would she allow this unexpected encounter with a man like Philip Boulton undermine her hard-won resolve to refocus her life. Surely an alternative caretaking option would present itself, in a spot less intimidating than this.

The awkward silence continued as she contemplated the

best way to withdraw gracefully. He stared at her, as if he could see right inside her. She stared back, biting her lip, her hands clenched with tension. A mesmerising spell stopped her from blurting out "I think I've misjudged the situation here. Sorry to have wasted your time".

'Did you have any trouble finding the place?' He kept his gaze on her but sounded as indifferent as an old policeman taking a routine statement from an unimportant witness.

'No, your instructions were very precise. Thanks.' As her manners kicked back in, on automatic, she managed a half-smile.

'No wrong turns, then?' His raised eyebrow suggested he'd expected her to lose her bearings.

'None whatsoever. I'm good at finding my way round. I carry a mental map.' Hannah had no need for electronic instructions from her phone—she was proud of her orientation skills.

'Impressive.' The corner of his mouth ticked up. Briefly. His eyes held a glint. Briefly.

Was he teasing her? Did he have that dry sense of humour which so appealed to her? Hannah relaxed her guard. She might have to reconsider her assumptions about him.

'Have you driven up from Melbourne this morning?' She'd have to give him credit for quickly moving to safer conversational ground.

'Yes, I have.' Her enthusiasm for the district's scenery overcame her lingering discomfort in his presence, so she added, 'It's a beautiful drive.'

'One of the best in Victoria.'

Being a city girl, Hannah didn't have much experience of the Victorian countryside. She nodded.

He solved her dilemma about what to say next. 'Did you eat before leaving? Need a coffee or a cold drink?'

Her apprehension waned further with this evidence that, unlike Alex, her potential employer possessed a few social graces. 'No thanks, I had coffee in town a short while ago.' She needed to help this awkward conversation along a little. 'I found a very nice café.'

His expression softened, but his lips did not curve upwards. 'I hope you mean Zuzu's. Some of the other places in town are a bit dodgy.'

'Dodgy?' She frowned. Did this explain why he'd advertised for a caretaker? It didn't look like that kind of town.

'The Greasy Joe's kind of dodgy. The operators are mostly salt-of-the-earth types.'

'Oh. Right,' Hannah mumbled. What was wrong with her? Small talk struggled to form in her brain, let alone reach her mouth.

After another awkward silence he said, 'To business, then. A quick tour of the premises, before we talk about possible arrangements.'

She knew she radiated uncertainty.

He tried another tack. 'Would you *like* to see the place?'

Instead of making the excuse she'd planned before escaping, unaccountably she heard herself say the words, 'Yes please, I would.' Her above-normal heart rate warned her to be cautious. Would she want to work here?

His matter-of-fact words belied his continuing and penetrating evaluation of her. She wondered, did he happen to wield a spotlight or a microscope on weekdays? His silent appraisal unnerved her but, regardless of the outcome of this unusual interview, she was definitely curious to see the property. She was keen to view the life of the moneyed class first-hand, rather than reading about it in books. A twinge of disappointment flashed through her brain ... she'd never be able to impress *him* with her dazzling lifestyle. Not even a teeny bit.

He strode along the shady front verandah and Hannah hurried behind him. This man was like a panther on a leash, his restless energy radiating off him in waves, in total contrast to her hesitant caution.

Around the corner, a swimming pool sparkled in the late morning sunshine. Hannah's intake of breath betrayed her astonishment at the impact made by a patch of clear blue water in a dry landscape. 'I didn't expect this,' she said.

Philip had turned to watch Hannah's reaction as she discovered the pool and a moment of gratification flashed across his face. 'It's a good place to cool off when it's over 40 degrees, where it's heading today.' He was so unrelentingly no-nonsense.

Her breathing had confirmed the low humidity level and she responded, 'At least it's a dry heat.'

He nodded as they walked on. 'Ah, but that's what creates the perfect conditions for raging fires on a windy day. It's another reason for the pool ... it's a fire-fighting defence. Plenty of water here for fire-hoses in case they're needed.' He stared out across the dry paddocks.

Hannah couldn't detect any actual bush for kilometres, just grazing land dotted with some large old trees, but she assumed this was a necessary precaution. 'A good plan.'

His onward stride faltered, and he turned to her again with his eyebrows slightly quirked. 'You swim, I hope.'

'Sometimes. I don't have convenient facilities like this, though.' The thought of a quick dip on a hot day like this appealed to her, until she remembered the implications. Donning her bathers would expose her to even more intense scrutiny from this far-too-masculine man beside her. He reeked of testosterone. She hastily pushed that thought aside. Highly sexed men preferred women who gave them the come-on, didn't they? Plunging necklines and short skirts and strappy heels had never been her style. She was shy about drawing attention to her attributes as a female. She couldn't see how Philip would rate her high on sex-appeal, with her penchant for covering every inch of her body with clothing.

Unwelcome thoughts. Why was she even thinking about Philip this way? And why was she under-rating herself? She didn't need more negativity. With Alex relegated to her past, the future beckoned more brightly than it had for a while.

She consigned any remaining gloomy thoughts about all the things she *wasn't* to a distant corner of her brain and looked around her with renewed interest. Apart from researching and writing about different aspects of history, gardens were her "thing". She surveyed the layout of this corner of the house paddock and considered its complement of greenery. Tall grevilleas bordered the far side of the pool. They provided welcome shade from the western sun on hot afternoons. Beyond the pool, a separate building had a small citrus grove beside it. Off to the left of this orchard, at the top of the slope, two large sheds loomed above a well clipped photinia hedge defining the boundary of the shed paddock.

Several large eucalypts framed the vista. Everything looked picture-perfect.

Hannah frowned. 'Your advertisement mentioned light caretaking duties. Would I be expected to keep everything as well maintained as this?'

He looked her way for clarification, and she continued, 'I didn't expect that pool cleaning, hedge clipping and general manicuring duties would be required.'

'Snippy little thing, aren't you.'

Little she was not, except by comparison with him. She frowned again.

'The answer to your question is *no*. A gardener comes each month to mow and keep the grounds in order. When I'm here, I like to get outdoors myself. It's good exercise.'

At least he earned Brownie points for noticing her displeasure and reassuring her. 'And I don't have to look after your huge house?' She eyed off the house, which so far hadn't formed part of her tour.

'That's right. I keep the house locked up when I'm away. A contract cleaner comes when needed.'

She breathed a sigh of relief before he said, 'I had in mind some different duties for your proposed role.'

Hannah's sleaze-detection antenna flicked upwards to vertical, listening acutely for the sound of sinister intentions, but no unwanted innuendo infected the tone of his delivery. She relaxed a little. He may be a chauvinist, a very handsome one at that, but he wasn't a predatory type as far as she could tell. She waited for his explanation, her face kept deliberately devoid of all expression. What did he have in mind?

'I'm here most weekends but in the coming months, I

have a few business trips to make, and one will take me over-seas for many weeks. So, for a start, I need someone onsite who will feed the cat.'

What cat? So far there'd been no sign of a cat. It raised an obvious question from Hannah. 'Who feeds the cat now, then?'

'I've been imposing on a neighbour who drives past my gate each day. It's not too hard for her … she only has to open a can of cat food. I feed her dog if she's away on the weekend.'

'Oh.' Hannah was surprised by all this neighbourliness. 'Is that all … feed the cat?' Hannah couldn't see how that justified free accommodation.

'No, I also need someone who'll notice if the house secu-rity alarm sounds, or a water pump breaks, or the cattle get out onto the road. I'll give you a list of numbers to call. I want a set of eyes and ears, with enough initiative to take some action if a problem occurs. Especially with water. Water is a precious commodity in the country. I don't want to come back after a month and find that my tanks have been drained by a malfunctioning pump or a break in a plastic hose-line.'

Hannah had ignored all his words but one. 'Cattle? I don't know anything about cattle.' Her anxiety returned. She could just manage to feed a cat, but cattle! That was too much. Animals did not form part of her world. They made too much mess and she'd always left the whole business of caring for animals to others. His advertisement had made no mention of a working farm. She'd been expecting that "light caretaking duties" meant cleaning and dusting and watering the garden, and generally being a deterrent to unwanted visitors trespassing around an otherwise empty country house.

'You don't need to know much. My neighbour knows what to do. Just call her.'

'Her? Do you mean the same neighbour that feeds the cat?' Hannah could barely suppress her surprise. A woman who knew all about running a farm? It astonished her that this hunk of masculinity relied on a woman for such a non-traditional role.

'Yes. Pat. She grew up on the farm next door. In fact, my property used to be part of hers. Or rather, her father's, before he died.'

'Oh, I see.'

Hannah didn't really see, but she guessed she might eventually cotton on to Pat's role in the scheme of things. Judging by her name, popular in Hannah's mother's day and earlier, Pat was bound to be one of those grizzly old-timers populating the Australian countryside.

'This discussion of the duties is all a bit premature. You haven't seen your accommodation yet. The bungalow. Come on, I'll show you.'

They skirted the pool fence to a pathway at the end and headed along that path towards a standard-sized Colorbond shed ... but no longer your standard shed. Cut into the side were windows, protected from sun and rain by attractive awnings. As Hannah climbed a couple of steps onto a wide concrete verandah, she noticed an easy chair and a garden table, perfectly positioned to enjoy the outlook across the pool towards the panoramic expanse of the valley below the farm. She turned to delight in the view as Philip unlocked the sliding glass door to this shed-cum-residence.

He motioned her to join him inside. Another world greeted her, a sweet little cottage, its simple furnishings selected and placed with amazingly good taste. Stunning views from the side windows directed her gaze across a broad gulley towards an imposing ridgeline, crowned with old eucalypts.

Hannah fell in love with the place immediately. How could she be so lucky? Resolutely she maintained her silence, exhorting herself to remember the old real estate adage of "silence is golden". Let him think she was undecided, still not too keen.

'The bungalow is self-contained, with every convenience … kitchen, bathroom, even an internet connection. We've entered via the back door. The main entrance is at the other end, where you can park your car. Your own private access is via the gateway into the shed paddock. You won't need to use the main driveway.'

Hannah didn't care about her implied underling status and couldn't resist her next admission. 'The internet's the key point for me. You advertised an internet connection.'

'You use the internet a lot, do you? Facebook and such?' Philip's bored tone suggested he had instantly stereotyped her as a timewaster on social media.

Hannah squashed his potential misconception straight away. 'Yes, I use the internet on a daily basis, because I write books.'

His storm-grey eyes flickered with interest. 'What kind of books?'

'Non-fiction. Histories, usually. Right now, family histories. That's why I need the internet. For research purposes, and to connect with people around the world.'

He nodded but frowned slightly and she noticed his body stiffen. Strange. She could have sworn he looked edgy.

She was well used to glazed-over eyes. Everyone regarded the subject as totally boring, except when it involved their own family. Ergo, the writers must be boring too. She wished she could have described herself as a world-famous novelist, seeking anonymity and a place to restore her writer's muse. That might have impressed him. Not that she wanted to impress him, of course. She'd need to impress herself first.

At the back of her mind, becoming a successful writer remained her goal. If only she could rewrite one of her non-fiction books as a gripping international best seller. That objective involved tampering with the facts. To achieve it, she'd have to step out into unknown literary territory. So far, she'd been unwilling to take that step. She was a prisoner to the concept of the literal truth, so far as the concept of literal truth applied to any historical writing. She found it impossible just to make things up and rearrange events for dramatic effect.

Her limited income as an author explained her old car, her out-of-date clothes and her attraction to a job with free accommodation. Alex was out of her life now, and without his contribution to her rent, she would enter Struggle Street if she stayed in Melbourne.

Philip Boulton waited impatiently through Hannah's long silence. Her interest in family history research had temporarily floored him, but he'd quickly recovered. He hoped she hadn't noticed him tense up. *His* recently-discovered family history was no business of hers. He'd be firmly resisting any attempt by her to stick her pretty little nose into it. He still needed time to digest it himself.

He put that thought aside. He needed a caretaker and he wanted Hannah to stick around. Why hadn't she shown more enthusiasm for the charming little bungalow? Although his advertisement legally couldn't discriminate, he'd hoped to employ a woman for the job, given the light duties. A woman would look after this bungalow better than the rough and tumble men on the dole, the usual candidates for jobs like these. A few men had applied, but he'd turned them down. He couldn't believe his luck when Hannah's letter of application arrived.

Sure, he'd expected the worst as her old car had approached along the drive. His eyes had boggled when he opened his front door. The woman was sensational to look at. Quite tall, slim, dressed stylishly in trim designer jeans and a very feminine high-necked, long-sleeved shirt. Her outfit might be well worn, but her good taste stood out. Even better, unlike so many Australian women, her luminescent pale skin proved that she'd tried to stay out of the damaging rays of a fierce sun. She exhibited what he thought of as "Irish" colouring ... dark auburn hair, navy-blue eyes and fair skin, the type that burned, peeled and freckled.

She was bound to turn him down, although he'd tried to make the bungalow cosy and appealing. She seemed a bit wary of him. Interesting. Normally he had the opposite effect on women.

He pressed on with the preliminary tour, even though

she looked like she'd never picked up a hammer or a screwdriver in her life. She hadn't said *No* … yet.

'You've seen your living quarters … the bungalow … but I'd like to show you the other dimensions to the role. All quite simple, really.' He dangled more bait, encouraging her to say *Yes*.

'Simple?'

'Yes. You need to see the location of the pump house, the watering system, the electrical power board on the house, the main water tap for the house, the hose connection points, that type of thing. All the places you need to know where to turn off the tap or the switch.' The scenic walk to these various maintenance points offered another selling point in the farm's favour. How could she resist?

Hannah bit her lip and said nothing.

Philip noticed her reaction and drew the obvious conclusion. 'You do have some familiarity with these systems, don't you? People responding to an ad for a country caretaker are expected to have the right background experience.'

'Yes, of course, I know about household maintenance issues. As a kid I was my Dad's shadow, and he was a professional handyman. It's just, er … on a larger scale here. I'd get the hang of it very quickly. Apart from the cattle, that is.'

'As I told you, my neighbour can help there. Good old Pat. All you'll have to do is a circuit in the ute every few days, keeping your eyes peeled, trying to spot any cows and calves in trouble. The ute's an old model, but it's easy to drive. I see you already drive a manual car, so you shouldn't have any problems. If you see an animal in a strange position, or out on the road, call Pat. Otherwise, I'll be attending to the cattle. I don't go away at times of high dependence, such as calving time, or during the autumn when the grass has shrivelled up to nothing and the cattle need hand-feeding.'

Hannah nodded her acceptance of these conditions and trailed round after him as he led the way to the various switches and water taps. They walked around a small ornamental dam, almost empty. Hardy prunus trees fringed the dam wall, with a large clump of flowering agapanthus creating a solid patch of dark green and blue on the uphill side of the dam.

'Lake Louise,' said Philip.

Hannah had never been to Canada, but she'd seen plenty of pictures of an extensive lake fringed by snow-capped mountains, and she had yet to see anything less like Lake Louise. She quirked an eyebrow at him but made no comment. Was he suppressing another slight grin?

A footbridge led from here to a small island—an island which would be in the middle of this dam, given plentiful water. In mid-summer, like today, the bridge was superfluous. One could scramble down the slope on the uphill side of the dam and cross the ditch without getting wet feet. The island itself was only big enough to host one small tree.

Philip casually flicked his hand in the direction of that struggling tree. 'Hamilton Island.'

Together they surveyed a scene as different from the real Hamilton Island on Queensland's Great Barrier Reef as it could possibly be. 'Named in honour of the bulldozer operator who dug out this dam for me,' he added. A flash of amusement sounded in his voice.

Hannah grinned in appreciation. This wryness was her type of humour too.

They crossed the gravel drive and he led her along a shady avenue planted with wattles and underplanted with correa, with a huge old eucalypt towering above. 'Acacia Walk, I presume,' said Hannah.

'You've got it in one.'

Hannah overflowed with the sense of *all's right with the world.* This garden was sensational, its design not reliant on fussy flower beds but vista … everywhere. The whole place should have featured in the Australian House and Garden or Australian Country Style magazines. 'Have you ever considered entering this place in the various gardening competitions?'

'No, but I toy with the idea of opening it to help raise money for local charities.'

How unexpected. He had a social conscience. Or was he just looking for praise for his possessions? She erred on the side of neutrality. 'Very commendable.'

'The garden looks stunning in the spring, but showing it to best advantage to the public would mean a lot of preparation work.' He shrugged. 'I don't have the time for that. I'm away a lot. That's why you're here, remember, applying for the job of caretaker.'

'For six months, as advertised. I'll be gone by the spring.'

'True.' He turned to her with renewed interest. 'Are *you* a gardener?'

'I enjoy gardening, but not on this scale.' Hannah resisted a crazy urge to apologise to him. The idea of holding a charity event in this garden was his half-baked dream, not hers. It wasn't her responsibility. She was tired of picking up the pieces for men. Correction … one man, Alex. She needed to follow her own dream.

They walked past the garage complex, back towards the main house. Philip turned to Hannah. 'That's it. You've seen everything now. Do you think you could manage that list of duties?'

A straightforward question. His actual words could have been interpreted as patronising, but his tone conveyed a hint of pleading as he sought her answer. Hannah took heart. There might be a vulnerable human being lurking beneath his confident manner.

'I'm sure of it.' How could she refuse? This was her dream job, in her current circumstances. Before she jumped in, boots and all, to grab the job she needed final clarification of the terms of employment. 'Let me get it straight. The arrangement is free accommodation for the next six months in return for the caretaking duties you've just outlined?'

'There will be no rental payment, true, but you pay for your own electricity and telephone/internet service. The water is free. Yours comes by gravity feed from those tanks up the hill there.' He pointed towards the sheds beyond the hedge above the house. Hannah looked in that direction and nodded that she understood.

'It goes without saying that you'll have to be economical with water use,' he said. 'You have only what falls out of the sky and lands on the shed roof. It's a very big roof, with lots of catchment area, but even so, it's limited. You need to take short showers, only run the dishwasher when it's full, that sort of thing. You should be used to that, after the long years of drought and water restrictions in Melbourne.'

'Don't worry, I'm well trained not to waste water. What about water supply to the house? Do you share those meagre tanks of mine too?'

'No. My restrictions are minimal. My water comes off the house roof, which is much bigger, and it flows into the main tank, with a much greater storage capacity than the shed tanks.'

'I don't see any other tank anywhere.'

'That's because it's disguised, under that gazebo.' He indicated across the garden to a decorative hexagonal structure built on top of a raised concrete platform. It reminded her of a band pavilion in a public park. With the right festoons of lighting, it could be the romantic setting for a play or a concert.

Hannah looked closely and realised the round concrete slab formed the top of a large concrete water tank partially submerged into the hillside. 'How ingenious. I've never seen that done before. Which clever architect designed that?'

'Actually, it was my idea.'

'Are you an architect?'

'No.'

Hannah waited for him to expand on his curt answer, but he said no more. He clearly didn't want her to know too much about himself. His house had proved to be off limits, the interior not shown to her. Likewise, his job was not for discussion.

What do I care? It's none of my business anyhow.

She turned again towards the house and narrowed her eyes. 'Did you design the house?'

'Pretty much. I drove round the countryside looking for structural designs that caught my attention. I liked this style and adapted it to suit the site here. An architect friend drew up the plans for me.'

Hannah liked his unpretentious explanation, which highlighted something else. Not once had he said "we". It didn't sound as if a wife or girlfriend had been part of the project. This must be the innate and genuine Philip on show, not Philip acting on the instructions of a partner he was trying to please.

She decided that her first impressions of the man might have been a bit prejudiced. An hour or so ago her Alex-trained instincts had warned that this man might be another chauvinist and very possibly a control freak, but maybe he wasn't so bad after all. It wouldn't hurt to act in a more friendly fashion and dispense a little praise. 'The house suits the landscape perfectly.'

A gleam of pleasure flitted across his face, momentarily revealing personal warmth she hadn't detected until now. Maybe she *could* like him. His expression disappeared as quickly as it came. He ignored her compliment and stuck to the business at hand.

'We've now finished the tour. What do you think? Are you interested in the caretaking role?'

CHAPTER TWO

Six days later, Hannah looked around the apartment and gave herself top marks for effort. The next tenant could move in tomorrow without any cause for complaint. Philip Boulton expected her today at *Wallumatta Farm*.

She'd spent all morning packing her remaining belongings into various suitcases, bags and removalist cartons, all now neatly stashed by the front door. The air smelled lemony fresh and clean after several hours of scrubbing, vacuuming and polishing. She'd defrosted the old fridge and wiped it out with special vanilla cleaner. The oven remained clean because she never used it. Bathroom and kitchen surfaces sparkled.

She didn't. She wilted in the heat like a lettuce leaf, and couldn't wait to discard her old jeans, a sweat-soaked T-shirt and some canvas espadrilles with the toes wearing through. She looked forward to the shower she'd have later, once she'd deposited her belongings in the bungalow. Bungalow ... she liked that word. It flowed off the tongue and had a cosy ring to it.

Already the thought of her new abode generated a positive vibe. Hmm … apart from the cattle. And Philip, that force to be reckoned with. A magnetic force that both attracted and repelled her.

Moving from a furnished apartment to a fully equipped cottage protected her budget and minimised the stress of moving. She'd decided several years ago that the minimalist approach suited her current lifestyle. Other people's furniture didn't bother her. It meant she only needed to take her clothes and other bare necessities.

Hannah lifted her assorted possessions into the foyer and locked the door on her previous life. 'Goodbye Alex,' she whispered. 'Next time you come knocking on my door, begging me to take you back, you'll get a big surprise. I'll be gone.'

She'd never appreciated Alex's constant and aggressive instructions as to how she should live her life. Whenever he'd tried to control her life, she'd resisted, strenuously. He acted, she reacted. Never before like this, with a disappearing act.

She felt like a rainbow was spreading across her sweaty face. It was so good to be free, unfettered, to discard that sense of living inside someone else's washing machine. Let him churn around all by himself. Let him work out his own problems without spinning her around and sucking her down his drain hole with him. Her clean break promised a brand new chapter in her life, with unpolluted mental space to work in and fresh air to breathe.

She grabbed some of the items stashed beside her front door and carried them to the car. Her new home lay ahead.

The image of Philip Boulton again filled her senses. A blast of internal heat matched the wall of heat that hit her as she stepped outside onto the pavement. She suppressed her involuntary bodily response, generated by the *idea* of a man. Granted, a man in the specific form of Philip, not an imaginary man, but right now she didn't need the complications and turmoil of a man in her life. Any man. She wanted peace.

Her neighbour Martin walked by with his dog Ralph and stopped at the scene of activity. 'Moving out, Hannah? I didn't know. What a bummer. Where are you off to?'

'My new life, that's where.' Her jauntiness must have said it all. Relief. Hope. Happiness.

A look of understanding flitted across his face. He knew all about Alex and his shortcomings. Everyone knew. It had been in the papers.

'Are you going to tell me where?'

She shook her head. 'Not right now. Best if you don't know.' Martin knew her story. He'd know why. 'I'll send you a card at Christmas and fill you in.' Her six-month commitment would end before then, but she saw no need to telegraph her intentions. She wanted Alex to think she'd gone for good.

'Oh, right. Yeah. Of course. Christmas! Got it.' His long face and flat tone of voice indicated his glumness at the prospect of her departure from the neighbourhood. 'We'll miss you round here.'

'I'll drop by and say hello sometimes, if I can.' Conscious of time moving on, and the journey ahead, she continued the process of gathering up her stuff, swiping her hand across her forehead to wipe off the sweat of her exertions.

He switched to practical mode. 'Would you like a hand with those boxes, then?'

'Yep, I sure would. Thank you.' She beamed at him.

He looped Ralph's lead around a fence post and loaded himself up with the assorted containers, three to every one of hers. What was it about men that gave them all that muscle power? Ah, how could she forget testosterone, that dreaded ingredient in Alex that he couldn't control and had made him so volatile. By contrast, Martin used his strength productively. Within minutes he'd filled the boot and helped her stack the car's interior to the rooftop.

'Thanks, you've been a huge help.' She high-fived him.

His forehead creased with doubt as he surveyed the loaded car. 'Can you see to drive?'

'Think so. There's a gap through to the rear vision mirror and I'll be able to see the wing mirrors. I'll be careful, don't worry.'

'Are you going far?'

'Far enough, I hope.' She shrugged.

'So do I. You deserve better.'

'I agree. That's why I'm going. But I'll miss you. Thanks for being such a good neighbour these past few months.'

'No worries. Don't forget that card at Christmas. Don't forget Gracie either. She'll be sorry she missed your disappearing act.'

Hannah guiltily remembered that she'd forgotten to farewell their other simpatico neighbour. She'd been too focussed on making her getaway. 'Please, tell Gracie it's not goodbye, just au revoir.'

He nodded. 'You do need to disappear for a while. I understand. Gracie will too.'

'I hope so. I think it's best if I just melt away. I'll resurrect myself, one day.'

'That you will.'

They exchanged a quick hug before she opened the driver's door and collapsed into position at the wheel, grateful for a seat after her cleaning frenzy.

Beside her car window, Martin's hangdog expression matched Ralph's. 'Good luck.'

'Thanks.' She gave him the thumbs-up sign before keying the ignition. As she zoomed up the driver's window, she called out, 'I might have found some good luck already.'

His dropped jaw was her last memory of her old life as she pulled out from the kerb.

She drove slowly through Melbourne's congested Friday afternoon traffic. Her car's air conditioner barely competed with the heat radiating off the road surface. Her clammy back and thighs stuck to her seat. As the air temperature crept towards the forecast 41 degrees, the radio host on *Drive* chattered about a cold front approaching from the west, with thunderstorms. Tomorrow Melbourne would be twenty degrees cooler than today. Where she was heading, on the other side of the ranges, there'd be no cool change for her tomorrow.

Arriving at *Wallumatta Farm* for the second time, Hannah braked at the open gate leading into the shed paddock. She bit her lip and thought for a second. She recalled the interview …

as the hired help, she had to use the equivalent of the tradesman's entrance. She turned and drove slowly through the gate and up the slope, around the back of the sheds, down the opposite slope to the bungalow and parked on the grass outside its front door. Her chest tightened and her stomach turned queasy as the realisation of her drastic change of lifestyle hit her. *It's too late to back away now.* Someone else would be living at her old address tomorrow. She needed to come to grips with this rather scary transformation from city-dweller to country girl. And she had to learn to deal with the intimidating force represented by Philip. *Relax, girl. He's not like Alex. He couldn't be.*

Her resolve firmed and she slid out of the car. Stepping onto the verandah, a twin to the verandah overlooking the pool, she retrieved from her handbag the key that Philip had given to her at the interview session. As she fumbled to insert it into the lock, she heard footsteps sounding on the pathway leading from the main house and along the side of the bungalow.

Philip appeared. *Damn, did he have to catch her like this, sweaty and dishevelled?* His face wasn't flushed. His clothes weren't grubby and rumpled. No, he looked cool and well groomed. Casual today. No jacket this time. His buff-coloured trousers and black polo shirt emphasised the impressive musculature which had been covered by his jacket last Saturday. Flustered, she tried not to stare.

'I heard you arrive. Thought you could do with some help unloading your belongings.'

This was unexpected. Another obliging man. Two in one day. She noticed that he didn't recoil from her faded jeans, bedraggled top and worn-out shoes. It surprised her. She'd had him stereotyped as a man who liked everything to be perfect, including the women in his life. 'Thanks, I'd love some help. The boxes are awkward, and some are a bit heavy.'

'If there's one thing my sister taught me it's that men are good for one thing … the heavy lifting. It's too hot to manage that task yourself on a day like today.'

Hannah wiped the beads of sweat from her forehead and shot a look of gratitude in his direction. 'I should have trained my brother better. One of my old neighbours helped me lift my stuff into the car.'

'Old, or former?'

She grinned at the incongruous thought of an elderly retiree slaving in this heat. 'What do you think?'

His eyes twinkled slightly. 'Right. Then I'll dump your belongings inside for you. You'll be able to slide the boxes around on the carpet quite easily, finding the right home for them without the need for any lifting.'

He made short work of emptying her car. 'We have a recycling system here, so when you've finished unpacking, stack the empty cartons inside somewhere, until morning.'

'Inside? I assumed you liked everything tidy.'

'I do but yes, inside. I'll show you the rubbish disposal system on Sunday afternoon. Don't leave anything on the verandah … it's going to be warm overnight; the sun gets up early and if you leave that cardboard on the concrete verandah, you might find that a tiger snake has made himself at home there by the time you go to move it.'

Hannah's heart began to pound. 'Tiger snake?' The words caught in her throat.

'That's the kind we get around here. They're deadly. Be careful.'

She sucked in extra breath, then bit her lip. *This country retreat idea of mine? Bad idea.*

She noticed Philip grin broadly.

Damn him for enjoying her discomfort. Just because he was used to it didn't stop her worrying.

He blithely continued his "welcome" spiel. 'About half an hour ago I turned the fridge on for you and left a small carton of milk for your breakfast.'

'How kind of you.' She hoped he noticed her irony. Fresh milk didn't cancel out dangerous snakes as a form of welcome.

'I'm sure you're not equipped to get yourself a meal tonight, so we'll go into town and have a meal together at the pub. They serve good food there.'

She stared at him. Was he another Alex, trying to boss her around? Or simply kind and thinking of her welfare? Being tired and hungry, she decided to give him the benefit of the doubt and this time her response contained genuine appreciation. 'Thank you. I'd like that.'

'Can you be ready within the hour? After all this work in the heat, you may want to take a shower.'

Was that a gentle hint? Did she stink of stale perspiration? 'An hour? It doesn't give me much time to deal with my stuff and get changed.'

'Don't worry about too much unpacking tonight. I'd like to get to the pub in time to avoid the tail end of the queue for meals. The kitchen closes at eight, and the chef gets grumpy if late customers stop him leaving on time. He'll cook us better food if we give him the opportunity to do so.'

'Then I'll freshen up a bit … a lot … and come straight over to the house.'

Philip nodded and left.

Seconds later, fear gripped Hannah and she screamed.

He came rushing back, concern showing on his face.

She stood frozen to the spot just inside her front door, staring across the tiles towards her fridge. 'I saw something moving over there. In the gap between the fridge and the wall. Something that looked suspiciously like a … s-snake.'

'Are you sure? My warning didn't just set your active writer's imagination to work?'

'Absolutely sure.'

'Damn. Must have left the screen door fractionally ajar last weekend, after I aired the place before you arrived for the interview. Very careless of me. Snakes slither inside every now and then.'

'What? Oh no!' Hannah's heart pounded even harder with fear. Country life be damned. She'd better rethink this crazy idea. She hadn't signed a contract. She could still run back to the city.

'This one must have found himself a comfortable hiding place on the coils behind the fridge. When I turned it on earlier, the motor's vibration must have disturbed him. It's great that you spotted him.'

'Sure. Great.' She hoped her sarcasm was evident. 'But now what?'

'I'm going to close those two doors leading into the rest of the bungalow, to keep the snake confined in this space.' Almost tiptoeing, he traversed the room and closed the doors. As the adjoining rooms were carpeted, the doors fitted snugly, with no gaps underneath.

Philip shepherded her into a position by the exterior door. 'Stay here. Don't take your eyes off the floor surrounding that fridge. I want to make sure the snake doesn't move. I'll be back in a minute.'

Hannah waited anxiously, ready to make a run for it if the snake slithered straight for her from across the room as it headed for the exit.

It seemed like hours before Philip returned wearing knee-high gumboots, carrying what looked like bird netting, plus a broom and a flat-bladed spade, both with long handles.

'Have you seen any movement?'

'No. The snake's still behind the fridge.'

'Good, so we know for sure where it is. Here, sit up on the kitchen bench and hold these for me.' He handed her the broom and the spade. 'And keep your legs up.'

'What are you going to do? We're always advised to stay away from snakes. They're more likely to bite when they're provoked.'

'I'll be keeping my distance, I can assure you. Tigers are aggressive by nature but we can't afford to leave him there overnight. Can't afford to lose sight of him at all. He could go anywhere next.' He eyeballed her. 'Do you fancy treading on him in the dark? Let me tell you, you don't want to be bitten on the ankle by a tiger snake. Especially in the middle of the night.'

She felt the blood drain out of her face. 'Now you're really scaring me.'

'Believe me, you *need* to be scared.'

Suitably wary and warned, she shifted tack. 'So how will you catch it?'

'First I'm going to slide that fridge out on its rollers. Then I'm going to throw this netting over the snake. If he tries to move, he'll most likely get tangled in the mesh.'

'And then?'

'You're going to pass me the broom and I'm going to attempt a hoist-and-flick manoeuvre to send that snake and netting flying straight out the front door, in one go.'

Terrified that the snake might accidentally be flicked straight at her, her instinct was to protest, but his confidence bluffed her into a too-feeble response. 'Think your aim is that good?'

'Of course.' He oozed infuriating male bravado. 'Or, taking your point, you could hold the snake in position by pressing down on him with the long-handled broom, while I chop him up with the spade.' He tapped his foot as he waited for her to choose.

'Eeek! I couldn't. And what a bloody mess on my floor.'

'My thoughts exactly. I'll be going for option one, especially as it's illegal to kill snakes. If Pat were here, she would have grabbed for her shotgun. That's what most farmers would do.'

Hannah had to think for a moment. Pat? Ah yes, the old girl down the road, Philip's obliging neighbour. Then she thought again. Guns? Hannah was anti-guns. Everything on the news broadcasts had convinced her that keeping a gun invited trouble. Was there no end to these country-life shocks to her system?

'As it happens, *I* don't keep a gun. Luckily, I found this leftover bird netting in that cupboard where I keep the cat food. The netting might work.'

Hannah's heart raced as she watched Philip slide the

fridge away from the wall. Slowly. Carefully. Quietly. Confidently. He grabbed the mesh and tossed it towards the animal writhing near the skirting board. It did the trick. The snake became immobilised in the netting.

Within seconds Philip deftly flicked the unwelcome intruder onto the front verandah. He charged through the doorway, shouting, 'Quick, Hannah. Slide the screen door closed after me.'

Hannah leant across from her perch on the bench and slammed the door shut, then watched proceedings anxiously from the safety of the bungalow. Philip sprang up onto the seat of a sturdy outdoor chair, reversed his hold on the broom to hold it by the bristles and used its handle to hook the netting off the snake, which quickly slithered away towards the paddock.

She opened the door a little and called out, 'Aren't you going to kill it? Legal or not? It might come back.'

'No point. There'll be lots of snakes over in that paddock, beyond the fence line.'

She followed the direction of his finger, pointing across to the fence. Her heart almost stopped when she registered her close proximity to a large paddock … containing cattle. She hadn't noticed them before now.

That fence looked old, rusty and very flimsy. What would she do if the cows got through the fence?

'Some of your cattle?' She tried to keep the nervousness out of her voice.

'Not mine. They're Pat's. That's her land across that boundary line.'

That sounded promising. Female company. Nearby. Pat,

a motherly type, able to help her settle in. 'Where's her house, I can't see it?'

'Actually, it's way down the hill, closer to the river flats, where she mostly keeps her stock. Lush feed down there.'

'You mean she owns land on either side of you?'

'Yep, it's a bit odd, I know. Years ago, her father subdivided his large holding in this way to protect the family's grazing options. This top paddock of hers contains a lot of high ground which is great in winter … she doesn't have to worry about boggy conditions and floods and it's warmer for the cattle.'

That made sense to her. *Cold air sinks. Warm air rises.* Hannah absorbed her first lesson about cattle … they must notice the cold. 'I can see I've a lot to learn about country life.'

'You don't have to learn it all in a day.'

'But I'd better learn quick-smart about snakes, eh?'

'Yep. The trick is to keep your eyes open and your doors shut.'

'That's reassuring … I think.' Hannah was unconvinced.

'Panic's over now. Let's go and eat. You'll feel much better. Dealing with the wildlife took time and it's nearly seven already, so come as you are. We're both hot and sweaty now, but the air-con in the car will help counteract that problem. Your attire won't be out of place. No-one dresses up for the pub.'

'If you say so. No way can I wear this T-shirt, though. It's a wet rag after today. Just a minute.'

Hannah rushed to a bag of clothing, rummaged for a few seconds and retreated into her bathroom to change her top and splash some water on her face. As she re-joined him on the verandah, she made sure that she firmly closed her sliding door. The snake episode had radically shifted her priorities. A safe house seemed infinitely more important than being untidy and decidedly sweaty for this unexpected outing with Philip. In any case, she was his employee, not his date.

That rationalisation didn't last long. Getting into his Merc, its exterior still as dusty as a week ago, gave her a thrill. He was so purposeful and in command of his situation, so different from Alex. Sitting next to him in the car gave her a thrill too. He had such physical presence, radiating a compelling pulse of energy. Her pulse beat a little faster, just being near him.

Hannah followed in Philip's footsteps as he claimed a table in the pub bistro, crowded with locals, and they sat down. There was no waiter in sight, but periodically a harassed-looking woman wearing an apron emerged through a swing door carrying plates of food.

'What would you like to drink?' he asked.

'A glass of chilled white wine would hit the spot, help to calm my nerves.'

'I agree. We can share a bottle. It's Friday night. We can let our hair down a little tonight. Sleep in tomorrow.'

Hannah started. Was he that kind of man, planning a move on her already? She sneaked a look at him, but he could have been making a business presentation, he was so darn matter-of-fact. It was a bit deflating, but then again, being hot, tired, sweaty and needy ... that scary snake incident … wasn't exactly *femme fatale* territory.

He continued blithely, 'We'll need to choose our food now too, to save me having to queue up again.' He pointed to a window in the side wall, which opened into the main bar. A small queue lined up at the window to place their orders for drinks, select their meal from the limited menu choices and pay up-front. 'There's no menu as such. What's available is chalked on that blackboard in the corner.'

Hannah hadn't seen such an offering in years. 'This is very different from Melbourne restaurants.'

'It's a country pub, Hannah. Here, they like their meat and they know how to cook steak. If you're not a vegetarian, I can recommend the porterhouse steak. The T-bones are too big. They take up half the plate. For vegetarians they have basic pasta dishes too.'

'I'm not a huge meat eater, but I like it every now and then. Okay, I'll go with your suggestion.' She added a little ironically, 'No doubt hot chips come with it.'

'You got it. Also a huge serve of fresh salad. You don't have to eat all the chips, but I'll guarantee you will. Here they're perfectly cooked. Just right.'

'In that case, I'll indulge myself. I *am* hungry. It's been a long day.'

While he stood in the queue, Hannah surveyed the room. And Philip's back view. Even with that damp patch of perspiration on his black shirt, he cut a fine figure. As well as being tall, he stood tall. No slouching. His dark hair fit snugly against his well-shaped head.

When he returned to the table, carrying the wine bottle in one hand and two glasses in the other, she said, 'It's got a good ambience, this pub. Basic, but friendly.' She noticed the attention directed their way from the other diners. 'And you're a somebody in this town.'

'That wouldn't be hard to achieve.' His eyes flicked around, surveying their fellow diners. 'Most of the people in this room were born here, went to school here and work locally. They don't mix much with the likes of me.'

'Which is?' She didn't want him to know she'd stalked him on the internet over the past week.

'Oh, you said you're into research so I thought you must know all about my so-called "big job".'

She raised her eyebrows a little but otherwise didn't react.

'No need to go into details right now. It's my night off. But roles are often exaggerated in the media, and that's how the man in the street sees me. Like these people.' He flicked his eyes around the room again.

She let it slide. He clearly preferred that his job be ignored as a discussion topic. 'How about your family, then? They must be proud of you.'

As if someone had flicked a switch to the off position, he shut down. Just picked up his glass, took a sip, and said nothing, with his eyes focussed on her, his jaw set and his lips pressed hard together.

Surprised at his reaction, she swallowed hard. This man sure was touchy about the word *family*. 'You mentioned a sister this afternoon,' she reminded him.

He simply stared at her and for a few moments he didn't answer. Eventually he neatly parried. 'How does your family see you?'

She pondered. 'Come to think of it, I'm not exactly sure.'

The arrival of their meal broke the tension. She picked up her cutlery as she changed the subject to a topic that would ease their conversation over dinner. 'I couldn't believe how you handled that snake. Well done.'

He laughed. 'It was a salutary lesson in a few of the realities round here. You nearly paid the price of my moment of carelessness.'

She grimaced. 'You won't need to tell me again to keep my screen doors closed.' She stabbed her fork into the stack of food on her plate, raised it to her mouth and swallowed her mouthful of delicious, salty, deep-fried potato. 'These chips *are* good.'

'Told you so.'

'Told me so? How come you made no mention of snakes at our interview?'

'How come you didn't know?' He grinned. 'They go with the territory, my dear Miss Stockton. Countryside. Snakes. I thought everyone knew that. They generally avoid you. They sense the vibrations through the ground as you approach and they slither away. Most of the time you don't know they're there.'

'So they say. I've yet to be convinced.' She shook her head.

They were silent for a few minutes as they tucked into their steaks. A few mouthfuls later, she spoke. 'This food hits the spot, Philip. Well cooked. Just what I needed tonight. It's been a stressful day. Thank you.'

'It's my pleasure.'

Simple words. Nice words. She savoured them as she sipped her wine.

He raised his glass and clinked it against hers in a gentlemanly fashion. His eyes met hers, his expression in no way flirtatious. 'Welcome to country life.'

He was being polite, keeping his distance. Hannah took his cue, relieved. Practicalities were safe topics for discussion. 'So tell me quick, I'm all ears, what other hazards are in store for me?'

He laughed. 'The odd spider. Nothing too serious. Don't forget to always wear shoes outside, proper shoes. No bare feet. Wear gloves if you like to do a spot of gardening. And keep an eye out for spiders in the pool. A fat black type likes to hide in the pool filter. It swims.' He incy-wincy-spidered his hands across the table.

She recoiled instinctively. 'Pleeeease, don't scare me like that. Swimming spiders. Ugh. It's not what I need to hear on a hot day like this.' She grabbed her table napkin and fanned herself.

'It's okay. They're easy to see. And easy to deal with.'

'What's easy to deal with?' A woman's voice intruded.

Hannah looked up to see a walking advertisement for a top fashion house. A pair of frosty eyes glared down at her. They warmed when they turned to her dinner companion. 'Didn't expect to see you here tonight, Philip.'

'G'day, Pat.'

Hannah nearly choked on her wine. This was Pat? Young. Gorgeous. And making eyes at her handsome neighbour.

Pat said, 'I thought you were heading off overseas. I was

just beginning to wonder what to do about the cat.' She stood so close, she loomed over him.

He rubbed his neck, twisted at an angle to see her, and pushed back in his chair. 'You know I wouldn't have gone without contacting you. And in any case, my trip's been deferred for a week or two.' His face creased into a smile. 'I've actually got some good news for you. No need for you to feed the cat now. Meet my new caretaker, Hannah Stockton.' He turned towards Hannah. 'Hannah, this is Pat Drysdale.'

Pat nodded curtly at Hannah. 'Saw an old car pull into Philip's place a while back. Is that yours?'

"Fraid so.'

Philip interjected. 'Pat, you never miss a trick, do you?' He turned to Hannah. 'See, told you that Pat's a good neighbour. Old habits die hard. She's always kept a good eye on my place for me.'

'And I'll continue to do so. After all, I *live* here.' Her tone implied that she didn't expect to see Hannah lasting the distance as a resident caretaker.

Hannah's dominant intuition kicked in. Pat had clearly set her sights on Philip and wasn't going to help her, an interloper and city girl, with the cattle. In her effort to escape Alex, now she had four new things to fear … snakes, swimming spiders, the cattle *and* Pat's animosity. Philip should have known this Pat arrangement would never work.

Hannah tried to defuse the tension with a friendly gesture. 'Next week, when you're driving past, why don't you call in for a coffee? If my car's there, it means I'll be in the bungalow, writing away.'

'Writing?'

'That's what I do.'

'A writer? You?' Pat turned to Philip, her eyes wide with astonishment. 'I thought you'd be getting a retired handyman as caretaker. You know, an old codger.'

'So did I. Until last weekend, when Hannah turned up on my doorstep.'

Pat turned back to Hannah. 'You a country girl, then?'

'No.' That one-word answer sounded a bit abrupt to Hannah, even if her inquisitor wasn't exactly socially adept. 'I'm here to learn,' she purred sweetly.

'I bet you are.' Pat sneered, as she turned to Philip. 'And, Philip, you want me to teach her while you're down in Melbourne?'

'Not at all. I'll do the teaching. On weekends.'

Pat turned back to Hannah. 'So what do you write, then? Bodice rippers?'

Hannah groaned inwardly. The public image of a female writer was so limited, the stereotype so predictable. Proud of her work, she raised her chin and replied, 'No, actually I write history. At present, I'm researching a family history.'

Pat nearly choked at the words. '*Family* history! Family! I don't believe it.'

Hannah agreed with her. Families and relationships seemed to be a very touchy subject with these two. 'Well, as I said, you're most welcome to call in next week. Seeing is believing.'

'I might just do that. For now, I'd best be off. It'll be dark soon. I want to see how one of my cows is doing. She's been a bit lame.'

Hannah watched Philip's eyes follow Pat as she stormed off. It was clear from his pensive expression that Pat's comments had set him thinking but the direction of his thoughts did not show on his face.

Philip set down his knife and fork and checked out Hannah's empty plate. 'Looks like we're finished here. It's time to be on our way.' Making no comment about Pat, he drained his glass and stood up to leave. Mr Bossy was back. Puzzled by the undercurrents, Hannah scrambled to her feet. What was going on here?

CHAPTER THREE

Hannah had a sleepless night, stressing about her impulsive decision to change her life so radically. Periodic sharp cracking noises had kept her scared and awake. It sounded like someone intermittently wielding a sledgehammer against her new place of shelter. Eventually she realised that no-one was trying to break in. The sound stemmed from the Colorbond metal of the bungalow walls and roof contracting with the overnight drop in air temperature.

She got up with the sun, as the metal began to expand again, and took stock of her surroundings. Reassurance might come from establishing the rhythm of her former life. That included keeping up with current affairs via the early morning news broadcasts. Her dad had warned her about lack of mobile reception here. She rummaged in one of the boxes, extricated his old portable radio, the one he'd used in his shed and had given her "just in case", and twiddled the dial. Only one radio station had satisfactory reception, the ABC, and even that reliable institution crackled with intrusive static at key moments. Her sense of isolation grew. Belatedly she remembered her new goal, to think positive. *Looks like I have what I wanted … the simple life.*

Needing a mild injection of caffeine, she made a cup of tea. Her friends back in Melbourne, all coffee-drinkers, often laughed at her old-fashioned ways. The melodious warbling of the magpies enticed her outside, to listen to their glorious welcome to the new day. She sat at the corner of her balcony, cradling her cup, still in her nightshirt and flip-flops, still a bit forlorn despite the magical sound of the birds. Beyond the pool and the valley below, little wisps of mist defined the course of the river in the distance.

It was all so different. Should I unpack, or should I get out of here? What was I thinking? She recalled last night. Instead of feeding a friendly cat, I'm suddenly dealing with a spitting cat … Pat. She scanned her surrounds. How will I cope with country life? Snakes in the house. Spiders in that pool. Those big cows of Pat's mooing over there. From her corner position she could see them, and she glared in their direction as she took a sip of her tea, as if glaring would make them vanish from her sight.

The hot liquid sliding down her throat and the early morning light bathing the serene landscape gradually soothed her. She remembered why she'd come to *Wallumatta Farm*. She'd managed to deal with Alex, to dispatch him from her life. She could deal with Pat. Good old Pat. Of course she could. Philip? Perhaps not. He was far more attractive than any man should be.

She stamped on the pendulum of her errant thoughts, swinging high and low from the moment she'd met this baffling man, so hard to read, so unlike any other man of her acquaintance.

She swallowed her last mouthful of tea and went inside, being very careful to slide the screen door to the fully closed position. It was time to shower, dress and unpack her boxes.

Her furnished cottage speeded up her task of settling in. In no time she'd stacked the books on the shelves, filed her papers, set up her desk and plugged in her computer to the power point and landline connection to the internet. Having a defined workspace all to herself cheered her spirits. She easily tackled and completed the rest of the homemaking effort by 9am. Excellent. She'd always been an early riser and country living encouraged this habit.

The bungalow proved not to be air-conditioned and already the day was very warm. She located her oscillating fan, set its rotation on 'slow' and sat at her desk. Cool and comfortable in shorts, sandals and her favourite loose cotton top, she began to write. She could indulge her writing passion freely now. Alex had hated her inner world and her focus on writing. In his self-obsessed view, she was supposed to focus only on him.

***

Over at the main house, Philip spreadeagled himself on the bench seat on his front verandah and surveyed much the same view as Hannah would see, but on a wider angle. Alley, his cat, abandoned his favourite dozing spot in the sun on the front door mat and slunk around his ankles before springing into his lap and settling down with a contented purr.

The house faced north, minimising the impact of the summer sun, but at this early hour of day the angled rays from the east evaded the verandah's shield and caused him to squint a little. As he stroked the cat, his thoughts strayed to Hannah. Only a hundred metres away and yet so untouchable. What would it be like to stroke her hair, so bouncy and springy, not soft, smooth and shiny like Alley's? Her skin looked soft. Stroked in the right way, would she purr with cat-like contentment? The thought enticed him, until he remembered that her occupation automatically made her overly inquisitive and not part of his agenda. Besides, her standoffish ways had made it abundantly clear he played no part in *her* agenda.

What she was running away from? Something, that's for sure. He had a nose for things that weren't quite right … that sixth sense explained his successful career in the finance world.

He watched his resident eagle circling overhead, hunting for breakfast. Its eyrie on a rocky outcrop at the highest point of *Wallumatta Farm* provided a panoramic 360-degree view of the surrounding district. He admired that eagle, soaring over the vast Australian landscape, melting into the dazzling glare of the sun and disappearing into the blue heights of the stratosphere. He had wanted to soar like an eagle and he'd achieved his professional goals. Sitting here, at one with the cat and soaking up the morning sun, it meant little. Here he'd created a place that felt like home, without a soulmate to share it with. His newly discovered family background troubled him.

His thoughts returned to Hannah. What was she doing right now? He resisted the urge to invade her space. Despite the pub dinner last night, their caretaking deal did not imply that they should socialise.

During the weekend, she'd heard his car on the drive a few times, and his phone ring once or twice. No sign of the man himself. Hannah was relieved, in a way. She needed a break from the world of men, even an attractive one like her benefactor. Alex was too fresh in her mind.

When a light tap on her door disturbed her concentration, she looked up from her desk to see Philip standing there, dressed to impress, in tailored pants, a blue and white fine-checked business-style shirt open at the neck, and a navy blazer. Alex had never looked this good.

'Don't want to disturb you, but I did promise to show you the rubbish disposal system and I'm heading back to Melbourne in a few minutes.'

'Oh, is it that time already? Past lunchtime?' She often lost track of time when writing.

'Yes. Hours ago.' He looked at her curiously. 'Did you eat?' he asked, in a tone indicating concern for her welfare.

'Well no, I didn't. I was a million miles away, engrossed in my story.'

'It must be a good one, for you to forget time. You'll have to tell me about it one of these days. For now, the rubbish calls.' He was polite, but firm, as he looked around for her rubbish.

She stood up and said, 'This rubbish process sounds complicated.'

'Not complicated. Just unusual. Where are your cartons and so on, from your move?'

'There's a pile just inside the door here. All the recyclables, anyway. After Friday night, I wasn't game to put them outside. There's a bag of general rubbish in the kitchen.'

'Okay. You get the rubbish bag, and I'll pick up this pile of cardboard. Meet me at my car.'

'Your car?'

'Yes, the bins are three kilometres down the road.'

'What?' She widened her eyes. 'Why?'

As he disappeared with her load of cardboard, he called back to her, 'Because the council's rubbish collectors don't come down this dirt road. Everyone who lives along here keeps their rubbish bins down on the bitumen road.'

She tied up her bag of kitchen rubbish, located her sunglasses and scurried over to the car. He lounged in the driver's seat with the engine idling, air-con on max, his jacket now hanging neatly over the back of his seat. She settled beside him, placing the garbage bag carefully at her feet so it wouldn't spill. It seemed totally wrong to be loading up a Merc with this stuff.

It seemed disturbingly right to be sitting next to its driver. He smelled fresh and clean, as if recently showered, and a hint of aftershave lingered. Despite the air-con, he radiated that special heat that men generate at close quarters. At the wheel of a powerful car, he also radiated an air of confidence and calm control. Resisting an unexpected urge to make eye contact and then lean into him, she jiggled her position and fiddled with her sunglasses to distract herself.

Philip noted her obvious signs of discomfort. She looked perfect sitting there, just as she had on Friday evening. Long slender legs. A pert little nose propping up her sunnies. Hair he still longed to touch. The slight sheen of moisture on her skin. On a hot day like this, and in the right environment like this farm, he didn't mind a bit of wholesome sweat on a woman. It made him think along lines that he shouldn't. She was so different from Pat.

They set off down the road. Hannah heard Philip exhale softly as they approached a vehicle coming in the opposite direction, leaving a swirl of dust in its wake. Philip stopped to say hello and let down his window. The other driver did the same. It was Pat, looking like the Cheshire Cat. Her expression tightened when she saw Hannah in the passenger seat.

'Just showing Hannah the intricacies of our rubbish collection system,' Philip remarked.

Hannah leaned forward in her seat to engage in the conversation with Pat. 'My new life is full of surprises.' Hannah was careful to speak in a neutral tone. Already she'd picked up the vibe that she should empathise with, rather than criticise, the inconveniences of rural life.

Pat ignored Hannah's remark and her presence, and simply changed the subject. 'Will you be here next weekend Philip? I've got a favour to ask of you.'

He nodded. 'I'll be here.' More cautiously, he asked 'What's the favour?'

'Some friends are coming to stay for the weekend and I've just heard that one of them is in a spot of bother with his business. Could you come for dinner with us on Saturday and have a quiet chat with him, in a corner somewhere? I know he'd appreciate having the benefit of your expertise.'

*So, Philip's business advice is valued. He must be respected by others.*

'Sure. I don't see why not. I may be able to steer your mate in the right direction. What time?'

'Around 6:30? We'll have drinks before dinner and it's always pleasant in that late afternoon summer light, no matter how hot the day has been. That sweeping view of the river always appeals to my friends.'

'Me too. Will you be making any of your specials?'

Hannah picked up on their obvious camaraderie. This was a regular thing, then, Philip's sampling of Pat's good cooking. She gloomily reflected on her own culinary efforts, tasty and healthy, but irrefutably basic.

'I definitely will. Some of your particular favourites.'

'Fantastic. See you then.' He raised his arm in farewell, pressed the button to close the window and they continued on their way.

He made no comment, but Hannah had plenty of food for thought. *Pat ignored me and Philip seems to think that's normal. Well, I guess I know my place.*

They arrived at a collection of rubbish bins, lined up like sentinels in a small clearing beside the road. Philip pulled up alongside the bins. 'Hannah, each bin has the owner's name.

Two for each property. The recyclables go into the bins with the yellow lids and the rest into the bins with red lids. Much like the Melbourne system. The actual collection day is Tuesday, but I usually leave my rubbish in the bins as I drive away each weekend.'

'That's something I can do from now on, isn't it? It seems wrong to mess up your car with smelly rubbish.'

'It's no trouble, because I drive past anyway. But you need to know this routine, for the disposal of your own rubbish, and for when I'm not here. Sometimes you'll have to take my rubbish too.'

'I agree, I did need to know. I would have struggled in vain to find the bins back at the farm.'

'Some farmers bury their perishable rubbish and make regular trips to the local Council tip, but we don't have to do that. It's civilised here, by country standards.'

He collected their rubbish from the car, disposed of it, and they drove back. Along the way she noticed a couple of roadside mailboxes. 'What about your mail?'

'I have a box at the post office. No need to do anything where the mail's concerned, as I collect it myself.'

'Me too. I mean, I have a postal box too, down in Melbourne. It makes life much easier when you move around. And it keeps your mail safe, and private.' She thought of Alex.

Philip looked sideways at her. 'You need to keep things private?'

'Sometimes.'

The car rolled to a stop beside his house. 'Just one more thing before I head off.' He jumped out of the car. 'Round here.' Philip walked ahead to his back verandah while

Hannah followed. He opened the built-in storage cupboard. It contained tins of cat food and packets of dry food, plus assorted gumboots and Driza-bone coats, a broom and an electric leaf blower.

Hannah surveyed the vast expanse of verandah surrounding the house on all sides. So that's how he kept it clear of grit and debris. 'Do you want me to clean the verandahs with that thing?'

'If you like. If there's a windstorm in particular. Hadn't thought of that as part of your duties, until you mentioned it. Having piles of leaves blown up against your front door sure does advertise your absence. So far I've had no problems.' As he spoke, he pulled out a can of cat food and a knife. He pulled on the ring top.

'Alley only needs feeding once a day, at dinner time. He's usually prowling around, looking for the food but, if not, you just clang on the can with the knife, like this, and he appears out of nowhere.'

'Alley's the cat?'

'Yes, Alley for alley cat. No longer a stray kitten. Out running in Melbourne one morning I heard him in a rubbish bin, miaowing piteously inside the bag he'd been tied up in.'

'How awful.' Her stomach churned in disgust. 'How can people be so cruel? He's lucky that you rescued him.'

A medium-sized black and grey cat catapulted down the hill from the direction of the sheds and began pacing impatiently around Philip's ankles. 'I agree, he's got a better life now.'

She reached down to pat the cat as Alley explored her ankles too. 'Do you lock him up at night?'

'No, I'm not here to do that and anyhow, he earns his keep at night, keeping the mice under control in the hay shed. He sleeps there, where it's dry and warm, and it's easy for him to come and go via the gaps under the sliding doors. Fewer mice in the hay shed mean fewer snakes. They like to eat mice. Alley must hunt at night, acting as some kind of deterrent, as I don't see many mice. Anything that scuttles is soon despatched.'

'I've only been associated with life on a farm for a week, and already I've learned about a whole new world.'

'I hope it's not too fazing. I don't want to scare you away. I need someone here.'

Need. That powerful word. How long was it since anyone had needed her? In a positive way, especially. Hannah ignored his last remark and addressed the first. 'So far, so good.' She thought about the scary animal life but decided to stick to a matter that currently worried her more. 'I don't know about Pat though.'

'What do you mean?' he mumbled, as he bent to scrape the cat food into the bowl.

'She doesn't seem very friendly.'

'Not friendly? Pat?' He stood up and gave her a puzzled look. 'Oh, that's just her way. Country people can be a little wary of newcomers.'

'I'm a bit concerned, as I have no idea what I'm supposed to do about the cattle.'

'I've spoken to her about the cattle. Rang her this morning. She's a trooper. She'll keep an eye on everything this week, as usual, to give you time to settle in.' As he turned to dispose of the empty can into a sealed bin and close the cupboard door he said airily, 'Next weekend we'll do the cattle run together. After that, you should be able to handle the observation task with no worries.'

'You sound more confident than I feel right now.'

'Trying to talk yourself out of this job, then?' Facing her again, he raised an eyebrow at her.

'Not at all. It's just a very different world.'

'With a new challenge, I've always found it's best to jump into the deep end sooner, rather than later.'

She sighed. Men. Always so gung-ho, so keen to rush into action. 'Even a big challenge like this?'

'Once you get to know Pat and a few of the locals, you'll be fine. Now, it's time to fly. I'm getting away a little earlier than usual as I'm attending a special function in Melbourne tonight.'

She eyed off his attire. 'A business function on a Sunday night?'

'No. A birthday.'

She squizzed at him. 'Yours?'

He shook his head. 'Not mine.' A long pause. 'My sister's.'

'Oh, great. I'm all in favour of family celebrations. I'd like to hear about your sister one of these days.'

His face shuttered. 'Hannah, let's get one thing straight. You might be crazy about family stuff. Most women seem to be, without going to the extra trouble of writing about it, like you. I'm not. Please leave it alone.' He turned his back on her. 'See you next weekend,' he growled.

With that token concession to good manners, he marched inside his house, still out of bounds to her, locking the back door from the inside. Hannah stood nonplussed on the verandah beside the storage cupboard. She heard his footsteps as he exited through his front door. His car door slammed and the wheelspin on gravel indicated his take off for the city.

She returned slowly to her quarters. What family demons are driving that man?

The farm seemed very quiet and lonely now. The thought of facing her first night on the property without the comforting thought of Philip at hand, over in the main house, overwhelmed her. The prospect scared her, if truth be told. Turning to face the spectacular view one more time before she locked herself in the bungalow for the night, she remembered another female down the hill, also living alone. 'If Pat can do it, so can I.'

## CHAPTER FOUR

Making their distinctive *chet* calls, a huge flock of galahs glided in to forage in the paddock below the bungalow, carpeting the ground in a seething mass of pink and grey. Such sociable birds. Something spooked one of them, he screeched a warning and they took off with a chorus of loud squawking.

From her lookout on her verandah, Hannah was buoyed by their gregarious hyperactivity as she sipped her early morning cup of tea. With five solitary days stretching ahead of her before Philip returned, she contemplated the possibilities of her new routine. *I can't sit at my computer all day long, as I did for most of the weekend. What can I build into my day as a bit of exercise, now that I'm in charge of a farm?*

The unattended patch of dirt a few feet in front of where she sat grabbed her attention. Brightening up the space between her favourite vantage spot and the pool would keep her busy. During her initial interview with Philip, trekking around his garden, she hadn't admitted to having the green thumb and landscape artist's eye her friends told her they envied. They regularly sought her help. *Pat's cooking may taste better than mine, but I'll bet my garden will look better. I need to get some supplies from the supermarket, so I'll go into town early. There must be a nursery … and I'd better get some sturdier footwear too.*

Easier planned than done in a small town. Country shopping held many surprises. She eventually hunted down elastic-sided boots and several bales of pea straw at the local stock and station agent. Who would have guessed?

Enquiries revealed the nearest nursery to be 30km away. Fortunately, she spotted some punnets of rather tired-looking seedlings at a fund-raising stall in the town's main street and purchased them all for bargain-basement prices.

'Good luck luv, the heat's knocked 'em for six,' said the stallholder as she counted out the change.

'Thanks, I hope they'll respond to some TLC.' Hannah had faith in her gardening skills. She loaded the pink echinacea, marine blue salvia and dwarf white cosmos into the boot of her car. All hardy plants, she hoped they'd soon create a colourful wildflower carpet to brighten her outlook from the balcony.

Back at the bungalow, she evaluated her priorities—writing, or gardening? *Today's word target can wait. I'd better get these seedlings into the ground before they dry out completely.*

She donned her old jeans and her new boots and retrieved her well-worn gardening gloves from the side-pocket on her car door. That's where she stored them, being so often called upon to help her friends with their gardening problems. Locating the mattock, the spade and the metal rake in the main sheds, she got to work. The effort of swinging the mattock got her blood flowing. Because of the low humidity, the action invigorated her, despite the heat. She broke up the clods with the sharp edge of the spade, picked out all the clumps of grass that had dominated the patch and finally raked everything into a smooth garden bed.

While the soil was still freshly turned, she planted the seedlings that had been soaking in their trays in the kitchen sink. Already they looked fresher. Uncoiling the hose by the pool, she then gave everything a good watering. She filled the watering can she'd spotted near the house, tipped in a generous capful of Seasol and applied the liquid fertiliser to each plant before spreading the pea straw. The straw would protect the seedling roots from too much sun and help retain a little of the moisture. To further minimise the shock of transplanting, she rigged up some shade using the umbrellas beside the pool. She planned to add a further layer of mulch once the seedlings grew a bit taller, to help them out-compete the weeds that would surely sprout from the disturbed soil.

Job done. Her morning's work would surely impress the hardest taskmaster. She sank into her chair on the balcony, enjoying a late sandwich lunch, several large glasses of water and a well-earned rest.

The sounds of a visitor arriving in the main driveway disturbed her peace. Conscious of the need to earn her keep as caretaker, she set off to investigate. Pat came round the house into view. All fresh, neat and clean.

Hannah's heart sank. Sure, she'd invited Pat but what normal person made social calls at 2pm on a Monday? Pat's timing could not have been better calculated to catch

Hannah unawares and at a disadvantage. *I won't let her see that she's caught me off guard.* 'I'm glad you called in, Pat.'

'Hello, Hannah. Since it's too hot to be out in the paddocks at this time of day, I thought I'd take you up on that coffee offer.' She surveyed Hannah's sweaty face, dirty damp clothes and dusty boots at the same time as she sniffed the air. Her eyes swivelled towards the freshly turned earth and pointed to the new garden. 'Been busy, I see. Philip will be impressed.'

'Just beautifying that particular patch for my own pleasure and enjoyment.' Hannah had no wish to enter a game of competition over Philip. 'I'll put the kettle on. Coffee, or would you prefer tea?'

'Tea, thanks.'

'Tea bag okay?' Pat nodded. 'Wait here on the verandah, in the shade. I won't be long.'

A few minutes later Hannah returned bearing the tray with two bone china mugs of tea, milk in a jug, sugar in a bowl, a box of tissues for wiping sticky fingers and a small plate of sweet temptations. Indulging her own sweet tooth, she'd purchased a few assorted slices at the bakery while in town. Cut into quarters, they made tempting bite-sized offerings. Her mother had taught her something about style as a hostess, even if her cooking skills were a bit rusty.

Pat stared at the tray resting on the table. 'You like to play ladies, I see.'

Hannah decided to let that sharp comment go through to the keeper. They took their cups and settled into an awkward silence. Hannah felt obliged to ease the tension. 'This is quite a place, isn't it? Philip's created something special here.'

'It's the talk of the district,' Pat said.

'Really?' That would do as a response. She had no wish to indulge Pat's "glory by association" tendencies.

'Really. It was just a paddock when he arrived. One of Dad's old paddocks, which he'd subdivided, and I eventually put up for sale.'

'Bet you were surprised when your dashing new neighbour turned up for the first time.'

'Oh yes.' A day-dreamy look crept over her face. 'Philip and I go back a few years now, you know. He started off very green at first. I've taught him just about all he knows about the farming game.'

'So I've gathered. He seems to appreciate your help too.' It never hurt to pay small compliments.

'I've noticed him spending a lot of time with you. Friday evening. Sunday afternoon,' her guest replied somewhat churlishly.

'Not that much,' Hannah protested. 'A few hours at most. I think he's keen to hand over some of his responsibilities and he's simply making an effort to help this newbie to country life understand what's required.'

'As long as that's all you're trying to understand.' The message could not have been clearer—*keep off my territory*.

It had to be challenged, politely but pointedly. 'Now that's a remark laced with innuendo.'

Pat backed off a little. 'What I mean is, he's not interested in sticky-beaks. He keeps his private life very private.'

Hannah giggled to herself. This visit was turning out to be entertaining. 'So, you think I'm too curious for my own good?'

'That's your job, isn't it? Delving into other people's

secrets?' Pat crammed half her chocolate brownie into her mouth, as if to shut her own mouth.

'If you think dead people have secrets, perhaps you're right. Philip, however, is very much alive. Are you telling me he has secrets?' *It sure is fun to tease.*

Pat swallowed her mouthful and rocked back on her chair, folding her arms across her chest. 'He always clams up whenever family matters are mentioned.'

'So, I've noticed.' She offered the plate of goodies to her guest. 'Would you like another slice?'

Pat again selected a brownie. 'He never mentions his family, except he did let drop that his mother died about a month ago.'

'Ah! If his mother died recently, that explains a lot.' "Mothers play a key role in our lives." No wonder he's a bit touchy at present.

'I doubt they were close.' *That demolishes my theory.* 'I've never seen her, or any other family member, visiting him here. Plenty of corporate events, over the years, but never family.'

Hannah couldn't resist an urge for one-upmanship. 'He mentioned a sister on the weekend.'

'A sister?' Pat almost choked on her mouthful of slice. 'Are you sure?'

'You okay?' Hannah waited for the spluttering to stop before pressing ahead. 'Sounds like she lives in Melbourne.' It pleased her to be better informed than Pat about *something.*

Her visitor gaped. 'He's never mentioned a sister to me.'

Hannah paid no attention to Pat's obvious disbelief. It

might pay to explore this minor mystery with her visitor. 'You've got me intrigued now.'

'About what?'

'Right from the start I noticed certain wariness on Philip's part about my research activities, but I never paid much attention. Just thought it was a guy thing. It seems he's very touchy about the word *family*.'

'Touchy? Of course he isn't. Just private.' Pat shook her head. 'What about you, Hannah? Your family, I mean.'

'My parents have retired down the coast. My brother works in Sydney.'

'So, you're all alone.' Pat stared at her. 'No boyfriend?'

*Pat sees me as potential competition for Philip's affections?* 'No boyfriend. At present.' Let Pat make what she liked of that. 'I guess your relatives live in the district. Philip told me your family has been here forever.'

'Yes, five generations of us.' After a few seconds she added, 'Philip said that, did he? He mentioned me?'

'Yes. He mentions your name quite a lot. And I've already told you, he appreciates your help.'

Pat slid her glossy hair through her fingers and twisted the ends with a flourish.

Hannah hid a smile. Pat's eagerness to catch her man amused her. Philip oozed sex appeal, but she'd never throw herself at a man, like Pat. She did have to admit to a certain curiosity about him, though. Her Googling efforts had yielded surprisingly little about Philip's private life, although he appeared to live a bachelor lifestyle. She pressed on, never one to waste an opportunity for research. 'I've heard that some wives won't be seen dead in the country, and let their husbands off the leash to do their "country boy" thing without them. Does Philip have a wife down in Melbourne somewhere?'

'Definitely no wife. I know that much.' Pat gave her hair a final confident flick before a shadow flitted across her face. 'Not short of girlfriends though.'

'All of them featured on the internet, you mean?' Hannah asked. If so, she hadn't seen much trace of them.

Pat snorted. 'I don't have much interest in computers. Friends down in Melbourne have told me. They've heard talk. He's something big in banking. Must earn a packet.'

'That puts him way out of my league.' Hannah's circle of friends and acquaintances was far more modest in their means.

'You said it.' Pat smirked at her.

She retaliated. 'What about you? Any hunky males in your life?'

Pat heaved a sigh. 'Other than Philip you mean? Yeah, there's Horace, I guess.'

'Horace?' Her mouth fell open. 'What a name!'

'His legal name is Richard, but everyone calls him Horace. Don't know why. It's a country thing. Like people with red hair get called Blue. One of the men round here lost his legs in a tractor rollover. We all call him Legs now.'

Hannah raised her eyebrows. 'Sounds a bit cruel.'

Pat shook her head. 'No, it's our way of showing affection, that we understand.'

'I'll take your word for it. Is Horace a farmer too, like you?'

'Nah, he's a fencer. Big and strong. Lives in the town.' Pat thumbed her hand in that direction.

'A fencer?' Hannah thought about that for a moment. 'Is

there much call for that round here? This is such an old, well established district. Aren't all the fences already built?'

'A lot of city-slickers are moving in. Putting in cattle races, planting grapes. Changing the district.' Pat's gloomy tone suggested she lacked enthusiasm for so much change.

'Like those hobby farmers down the road. Did Horace build their fences?'

'Yeah. Horace keeps busy.' Her tone didn't suggest much enthusiasm for Horace either.

'Has he worked for Philip too?' Hannah was on a roll with these questions and answers.

'Sure has, he put in Philip's internal fences, breaking up Dad's big old paddock into smaller areas. We'd have done that too, while Dad was alive, but we've never been able to splash all that cash around.'

*Maybe envy explains why Pat appears disgruntled.*

'Will I meet Horace?' With a name like that, he might be as entertaining as Pat.

'Maybe. He doesn't come to *Wallumatta Farm* anymore, unless Philip has a specific odd job for him. And all the fencing work is finished along our road, until the next place is sold off and subdivided, that is.' She checked her watch. 'Speaking of finished, I've gotta go.' She replaced her mug on the table. 'Thanks for the tea. And the brownie. Our chat's been enlightening.'

'I hope you'll continue watching over the cattle this week, while Philip's down in town. I haven't been shown the ropes yet.' Hannah didn't want to admit to Pat that the prospect of dealing with the cattle scared her.

'Sure, I'll do that. Anything for Philip.'

The week dragged after Pat's visit on Monday. No-one else came to the farm. City-girl Hannah had never felt so isolated in her life, but her work kept her busy. That work included more surfing on the internet, the key words being "Philip Boulton".

Frustrated, she wondered how anyone could be almost invisible in today's world. He had no personal social media profiles. She'd earlier found mention of his name in connection with some large financial deals reported in the media. She'd found pictures of him at various business functions, suited up and chatting to men and women with household names. His professional life made her feel inadequate and unimportant by comparison. Several pictures showed him standing very close to a female who could have stepped out of the pages of a glossy magazine, wine glass in hand, sharing a moment. Was this woman someone special? She continued to hit a privacy brick wall when it came to his family.

She wouldn't give him the satisfaction of knowing about her "research". Yet she could hardly wait for the sound of his Merc returning on Friday night.

CHAPTER FIVE

Hannah abandoned her keyboard at the sound of purposeful footsteps crossing the courtyard behind the main house. It must be Philip. Anticipating his call to action on this second Saturday morning of her new life, she plonked on her sunhat, hastily swapped her bare feet for socks and boots, grabbed her sunnies and emerged to greet him at her back door.

No longer was he the man-about-town. His attire shouted "country-dweller" … old jeans, shirt with the sleeves rolled back to his elbows, well-scuffed boots and a battered Akubra tilted at a careless angle across his forehead. A tiny shiver vibrated through her. What a hunk.

She also looked the part, on the outside. Her bare feet had been a concession to staying cool as long as possible in the heat before pulling on her boots, but she'd earlier applied sunscreen and donned jeans and a shirt with a collar and long sleeves in preparation for her introductory tour of the paddocks. Her nerves, already on edge at the thought of a face-to-face interaction with cattle, jangled even more at the thought of interacting with Philip all morning.

She watched him flicking his eyes from her head to her toes. Would her attire win his approval for the task ahead?

'Good morning, Hannah. Glad to see you're ready.'

No pleasantries on the conversational menu today, then. She may be skittish but he seemed fully in calm, practical mode.

'How was your first week, then?' he asked as they walked towards the garage complex housing the Merc and its still-hidden companion. 'I see you've been busy creating a flower garden in front of the verandah. Good job.'

'Other than that bit of hard work, it's all been very quiet,' she replied, pleased that he'd noticed her garden. 'No dramas with anything. Only one visitor. Pat.'

'She came to see you? See, I told you she's a good neighbour.'

'You did.' No need to tell him that he'd been a major topic of conversation between the two women.

They reached the ute, parked in its usual spot in the covered bay adjoining the garage.

'We'll go round the circuit twice this weekend. Today I'll drive. Tomorrow it'll be your turn. After that I'll leave the spare key with you. Hop in.'

He fumbled in his shirt pocket for his sunglasses, jammed them into position, swung up into the driver's seat and revved up the engine. Hannah scurried round the vehicle and scrambled up into the passenger seat. It was a new sensation to have such a high vantage point. And thrilling to be sharing this new experience with Philip. Her heart beat a fraction faster in anticipation.

They drove first to the hay shed, where he sprang out to stack bales of feed onto the back of the truck. The smell of sweet hay filled the shed and she pinched her nose to curb an urge to sneeze. Any idea of helping him dissolved when she discovered the weight of a hay bale. She could barely lift one off the ground and no way could she hoist a bale up onto the truck. Puny Alex would have had the same problem. Philip tossed the bales as if they were no heavier than a small bag of supermarket shopping. His strength astonished her. She stood and watched.

He must have read her mind as she gazed at him, mouth half-open, because he said, 'You get stronger with practice. One day you'll be lifting these as well as Pat does.'

There was that dratted name again … Pat. His paragon of country virtues. It riled her that he seemed oblivious to Pat making eyes at him, but she nodded sagely.

The loading complete, they climbed back inside the vehicle and set off. 'I keep the ute in four-wheel drive mode for use around the farm as I don't take it out on the roads much,' he explained. 'You won't need to bother about that yourself as you'll just be driving around my paddocks. This button controls the driving mechanism.' He pointed to a button near the gearbox.

'Good to know.' If that sounded a bit abrupt, it was because she was so scared of her imminent meeting with the cattle that she'd zoned-out. She should concentrate. Vaguely recalling his words, she added, 'I've never driven a four-wheel drive vehicle.'

He turned his attention from the road to challenge her with a direct look. 'You said at our interview session that you were the little shadow for your handyman Dad. Didn't he introduce you to four-wheel driving?'

Did he think she was a fraud? 'Nope. Sorry. Look, things on my mind. You can show me how that button-thingy works when we get back from our tour.'

They were approaching the first farm gate. After her lapse in focus, Hannah needed to earn some Brownie points. 'I'll get it.' From her lifelong love of reading, at least Hannah had learned that much about country etiquette … any passenger aboard a vehicle was the one who opened and closed the gates.

She looked around nervously for any signs of cattle and relaxed a little at the sight of clear territory. It was safe to leave the truck and she jumped out, a woman on a mission. Nevertheless, her jittery state caused her to fumble with an unfamiliar locking mechanism, as she juggled the ring and chain off the hook on the gatepost. The gate swung both ways, so she walked it away from the ute, into the paddock, wrinkling her nose as she concentrated on dodging the cowpats. It amazed her that they didn't smell too bad. Uneasily scanning her surrounds as the ute drove by, an irrational fear as no animals roamed this paddock, she yet managed to catch a glimpse of Philip's amusement at her anxiety and distaste. She relocked the gate and tiptoed her way back to the ute.

He grinned at her. 'Thanks. Glad you wore your boots now?'

'Ugh. Messy.'

'Just you wait. I moved the cattle out of here a week ago. There'll be heaps of new sloppy cow pats where we're going.' He grinned again.

Uneasily, she slid back into her seat. Did he have to *enjoy* her new-chum status? She switched his focus back to him. 'You moved them last weekend?'

'Yep.'

'I was here then. I didn't hear you.'

'Didn't have to do much. I just walked down to a gate near Pat's, opened it and went back two hours later and closed it, after scanning the original paddock to make sure there were no stragglers.'

'I don't get it.'

'Cattle love a fresh pasture. Once they realise the route to it lies open, they quickly follow the leader and leave the old paddock. No need for much fuss. Pat taught me that trick.'

'Good old Pat.'

If he noticed her sarcastic tone, he ignored it. 'She's taught me everything.'

Damn the man, he liked to rub it in. And leave her deflated and doubtful. What else had Paragon Pat taught Philip?

The ute ground slowly up the same hill that Hannah surveyed every morning from her kitchen window. A proper dirt road had been carved out by a bulldozer, to keep vehicles from tilting sideways on the slope. She reverted to practicalities to take her mind off Pat's never-ending list of attributes. 'This gradient is steeper than it looks from the bungalow.'

'The terrain is why I decided to run cattle. My block doesn't suit sheep, as they'll wear tracks which will become watercourses when it rains and lead to unwanted erosion.'

The extent of his wide-ranging knowledge impressed her,

but she kept that thought to herself. Instead she asked, 'Where *are* the dreaded cattle since you moved them? I can't see any.' It both mystified her and relieved her anxiety.

'Congregated on the other side of this hill. There are a few more gates to deal with.'

She tried to sound well-informed. 'Some of Horace's handiwork, I suppose.'

He looked at her sharply. 'How do you know Horace? Has he been here too?'

'No. He hasn't. Pat mentioned him last Monday.' Cheekily, she added, 'Horace seems to be the man in her life.'

'Is he now?' Philip replied noncommittally.

It fuelled Hannah's curiosity. What was going on? Was there a love triangle?

As they breasted the hill and reached the highest point of the farm, a magnificent panorama unfolded before them, with tier upon tier of hills fading in the far distance into mauveness and a hazy sky. She gasped. 'It's breathtaking.'

'Pretty special, all right. We're in the foothills of the Great Divide.' He braked and pulled up for a moment, calm and still as he drank in the view.

'I'm surprised you didn't site your house up here,' she said, 'given your obvious enjoyment of the scenery.'

'I realised the constant wind would blow me away. To compensate, I make a point of coming up here whenever I can. It brings home the vastness of our country. I like that feeling.' He gave her a sheepish grin and took his foot off the brake to resume their journey.

They bumped along a level but rocky track winding between the old grey box trees that formed her horizon when she stood at her kitchen sink. He extended his left arm, pointing, and almost dislodged her sunnies. 'Sorry. My enthusiasm got the better of me.'

Her glance in his direction caught him looking at her, and for a moment she almost hoped that his enthusiasm was for being so close with her. Sadly, no. His expression remained impassive, hard to read. Perversely, given her experience with Alex and her plan to avoid men for a while, she longed for a clue that she had an impact on him, female upon male.

He continued in his relentlessly practical, tour-guide mode. 'Look to your left, down there. You can see the cattle now. They stand out clearly because they're Angus.'

She peered out. 'Those black cattle, you mean? Is that your land too?'

'Yep. It's easy to spot them against the pasture, which is a lush green in winter, straw-coloured in summer, like now. I used to run poll Herefords, but they tended to develop cancerous growths from too much sun so I switched over to Angus.'

'You're kidding me.'

'I speak the truth. Their eyes and noses were especially vulnerable. It's funny that cattle are the same as us … people with dark pigmentation, like the Aborigines, can cope with our fierce sun, but people like you, with your Irish skin, have to be careful.' He turned his gaze towards her. 'I'm pleased to see that you're covered up and wearing a hat.'

His comments aroused Hannah's curiosity. 'Why did you say Irish skin?'

'That's what yours is, from what I can see of it.'

At last, another tiny clue about him. Two, in fact. First,

he watched her more than she realised, and he'd actually noticed something about her. Second, most men wouldn't make such a connection. 'Is that a problem in your family too?'

Her innocent question snapped a change in him. 'My family? Could be.' His expression hardened and he changed the subject. 'Here's the next gate. Would you mind doing the honours again?'

Before hopping out, she looked for cattle. Relieved to see that the coast remained clear, she performed her task more quickly this time. She studied his sternly clenched jaw as he drove past, a few feet from where she held the gate. Some family issue definitely lurked here, a secret maybe. It continued to pique her detective instincts.

He'd recovered his equilibrium when she scrambled back into the cabin after hooking the chain through the gate mesh and over the knob on the gatepost. They drove in silence down another dirt road on a tricky slope, then turned left towards the last gate. There was no graded roadway here. The ute tilted sideways on the slope. Alarmed, she clutched the handhold above the door and braced her feet on the floor to push her back hard up against her seat.

He noticed. 'Don't worry. This is nothing. You just have to take it slow.'

The cattle had heard them coming along the ridgeline and began heading towards the gate leading into their paddock, some of them running, some straggling. Their hooves kicked up the dust in the parched paddock.

The scene ahead petrified Hannah. 'Do I have to open that next gate as well?' She tried to keep the panic out of her voice.

'Yes, we're going into that paddock.'

'Oh.' Her voice shook. Her stomach churned.

'Do you have a problem with that?'

'Umm … I feel much safer in here, inside the cabin.'

'What? What are you scared of?' He took his eyes off the track ahead and turned to scrutinise her.

She bit her lip. 'Those cattle. They're so huge. There are so many, all pushing and jostling.'

'Not that many. And there are some easy ways of dealing with them.' He spoke reassuringly.

'How?'

Philip stopped the ute before they reached the gate and turned to her again. 'Cattle are big, but just like children. Remember those bales of hay on the back of the ute? Come on. Relax. We'll get the truck through the gate and I'll show you what comes next.'

By now all the cattle had arrived at the gate. It clanged as they shouldered against it, trying to reach the truck.

'I don't want those animals to come into this paddock yet. So, this is what's going to happen. You're going to open the gate and I'm going to drive straight through, very slowly, and park some distance from the gate. They'll turn their heads to follow the progress of the ute because they'll get a whiff of the hay as I drive past. It's your job to close that gate quick-smart the minute I get through.'

'Won't they trample me?'

'No. This gate swings both ways too. All the gates do. Drag it towards you and walk backwards briskly, keeping between the gate and the fence. Don't dawdle. I'll be just clear of the swing, beeping the horn madly and ready to drive the truck through the opening. The cows are used to the truck. They'll back off as I come through the gate. Swing it shut immediately and latch it. They won't charge you. They'll follow me and the truck. If a few hang around the gate, trying to stick their noses through the wire mesh, don't panic. Stand quietly in position. They'll come back to the mob and the hay after a few minutes.'

Hannah's stomach continued to churn with nerves as she approached the gate, on the other side of which was a mass of cattle, all pushing and shoving and snorting. They looked even more terrifying at close quarters.

Hannah tried to apply the rule she'd learned years ago when confronting strange dogs. *Never let them know you're fearful. They can sense it.* The truck was right behind her, its horn blaring. Steeling herself, she hastened to do as she'd been told, as much to impress Philip as for any other reason. It astonished her that it worked.

She watched as he parked the truck a reasonable distance from the gate. The cattle milled round but he shooed them back from his door by waving his hat out the window at them and yelling, 'Back, back.' The animals near him retreated for a moment, clearing a space sufficient for him to jump out and clamber up on the tray. He used his Stanley knife to cut the binding on the bales. All the while, big heads with soft eyes and long tongues leaned over the sides of the ute, grabbing at the loosened hay as he tied the twine onto the rollbar above the cabin. He returned to the task of shooing the cows with his arms to create space enough to distribute the contents of several bales onto the ground around the back of the truck. Once he'd sufficiently distracted the animals, he jumped back in the cabin, drove forward a few truck lengths and heaved out the bulk of the hay so the jostling cattle could spread out more as they chomped their way through their food bonanza.

He looked across to where Hannah was still standing nervously behind the locked gate. He called out to her, 'Don't be scared. They've been well treated by humans, so they're calm, gentle animals.'

'They look extremely boisterous to me,' she shouted back.

He shook his head. 'They're okay. It's all relative. I need you over here now.'

'You mean I have to walk *past* those cows?' Her voice screeched.

He made no concessions to her being "a girl" about this task. 'Yep. They're focussed on their food, Hannah, not you. Walk quietly but purposefully round the back of the cattle— well clear of them—to the front of the truck and climb up here beside me. We're going to count the cattle. I usually count them to make sure they're all here.'

'Philip, I'm terrified of those animals.' Her shouty voice cracked.

'Show no fear and they won't bother you. Come on.'

Show no fear, he says. Easier said than done.

She steeled herself. Gingerly, she opened the gate. The cattle took no notice. A good start. Ugh, it was hard to avoid all the steaming deposits of sloppy cowpats. The ground near the gate, where the cattle had congregated, glistened with the evidence of their recent presence. She focussed on not stepping in any. It was disgusting but it took her mind off the fear of being chased by a cow.

When she reached the safe haven of the vehicle, he leaned down to show her the footholds and grabbed her hands to hoist her up beside him. Her sunnies slipped off as she stumbled against him and tried to regain her balance. His hands grasped her upper arms to steady her. He bent to retrieve her glasses lying among the remnants of hay on the floor, gave them a quick brush off and handed them back to her. Her eyes met his storm-grey eyes, which flickered with an expression she yearned for … connection, seeing into her. Her heart beat a little faster. She hastily averted her gaze. No, despite today's earlier moment in the truck, she had no intention of vying with Pat for Philip's attentions. Her role on this farm was to *work*.

She turned her attention to the stock jockeying for position around the piles of hay. 'Now that I'm standing up here on the tray, there don't seem to be so many animals.'

'I sold most of my herd last December. It stressed me too much to be greeted by hungry cattle mooing for food every time I stepped outside the front door, which the cattle can see from the paddocks. Useful rain might not fall for months. I had insufficient hay to hand feed so many cattle for so long. Besides, who was going to do it? Feed them, I mean.'

His eyes engaged with hers as he answered his own question. 'Not me—I was down in Melbourne. You weren't here then, and I couldn't ask Pat. She had her hands full with her own stock. I've never asked her to do my farm work for me. She's only ever acted as my adviser and friend.'

Hannah blinked with surprise. Was this true and, if so, had he enlightened her by accident or by design? She wasn't sure.

'Sure, she used to feed my cat, but I helped her with her dog and occasionally with financial matters relating to Pat and her friends.' His casual tone made this surprising neigh-bourliness sound normal. 'Feeding cattle is another matter altogether. Quite time-consuming.'

'Very considerate of you.'

He frowned. 'I had little choice.' His face cleared. 'As my breeders were still in good condition, they went into the store cattle sales, not the slaughter yards. A farmer in another district, with a better feed supply, became the bene-ficiary of my predicament.'

'So they're still happy little Vegemites, chomping their way around greener pastures.'

'For the time being, yes. Of course, they'll enter the food chain eventually.'

'Don't remind me. No wonder some people become vegetarians.' She turned to survey the herd and changed the subject. 'How do you count them when they're all milling round like this?'

'They're usually fairly static while they're eating, although there's a bit of pushing and shoving and they do change positions in a random fashion. Especially the calves.'

She peered at the animals. 'I don't see any calves.'

'Calves don't have to be frisky newborns. See those smaller animals, not as tall and bulky as the others.' He pointed to a group at the back.

She scanned the herd again. 'Yes.'

'They're some of the calves. I'll count them, because they run around more. You focus on their mothers. Usually I have to count several times, to be sure. Just start at one end of the pack and count quickly. It'll make a change having you here. We'll compare numbers at the end.'

He said 'Great' when she came up with the right

number. 'You mightn't think so, but you're a natural, Hannah. I've had a few women here and they've all been terrified of the cattle. Scared stiff to be in the paddock with them, just like you, but unlike you, totally unwilling to try to overcome their fear.'

*A few women?* 'Not the usual way for men to entertain women.'

He glanced sideways at her, a puzzled look creasing his face, before he responded, 'Oh, I see what you mean.' He laughed. 'Not dates. Corporate functions. Corporate wives. One turned up in her stilettos. Of course, she couldn't come around with us on the back of the truck. Some have worn more suitable attire and have joined their husbands for the ride. They screamed, literally, when I got them to walk a short distance in the paddock, because the cows followed them, and the women thought they were about to charge.'

'I sympathise, one hundred per cent. I only appear to be coping because I'm taking my lead from you.'

'We dominate the cows, I can tell you. Never stand in front of cattle on the run, you could be trampled underfoot, but in most grazing situations all you need do is face them and wave your hat at them purposefully and they'll back off.' He swiped sideways at a few pesky flies. 'Except when they have newborn calves. Then they're fiercely protective and they might charge you and do serious damage. These calves of mine are half-grown, so there's no need to worry as much.'

'I wasn't worrying specifically, until you suggested that I should be.' She surveyed the peaceful scene of placid mothers and their offspring, and then thought about the implications. Human mothers and babies needed a lot of time and attention. 'Cows and calves seem like a lot of trouble for an absentee owner.'

'In some ways. I take extra care at calving time, but cows and calves are calmer and easier to manage than a bunch of wild steers.'

'Pardon my ignorance, but what's a steer?' He must think I'm stupid, not knowing this stuff.

'A castrated bull. Here, and on most properties, new male calves are castrated and once they're weaned, they're described as steers.'

He's so patient with his explanations, I really like that about him. 'So what's the management problem with steers, then?'

He caught her eye, theatrically bounced up and down on the spot and said, 'This. Energy. It's like having a pack of teenage boys on the rampage. They gallop around the paddocks for fun, charge through fences, get out on the road, that sort of thing. And since this isn't good fattening country, they're generally sold around the age of two years and you have to start again with the next class of rowdy teenagers.'

Hannah nodded. 'I can see it's a problem if you're not here.'

'Pat helped me to see that it's much better to keep a group of older grazing animals, familiar with you and the ways of your property. With cows and calves, the experienced mothers who've been here longer set a good example and are a calming influence on the friskier newbie mothers. If any of my cows have delinquent temperaments, they're soon loaded on the back of a truck and sent to the sale yards.'

'Sounds harsh. So, it's survival of the fittest?'

"Fraid so. Look around you. Do you notice something about these cows?'

Hannah glanced around the herd. 'No. Should I?'

'You should. They're in calf again.' He sounded mildly amused at her ignorance.

Hannah inspected the cattle anew and noticed their rounded bellies for the first time. Slowly she made the connection between the birds and the bees. 'So which one's the bull, then?' Worried, she scrutinised the animals pushing and shoving each other as they competed for the choicest bits of hay.

Philip laughed. 'We'd have been much more careful if he'd been here. You wouldn't have been walking around among the herd, that's for sure. Never trust a bull. When he's not earning his keep, he's in a separate paddock with an electric fence and a couple of steers from last year's calving. When his buddies eventually go to market, the process will be repeated, using a few of the steers milling around us right now.'

'Why do you do that?'

'So the bull has company. Mates. The steers keep him calmer. He doesn't challenge them. They're not his rivals for the ladies.'

She surveyed all the calves and the pregnant cows. 'One bull is responsible for all of this?'

'He is. The calves are due in the autumn, so he's very happily occupied towards the end of winter.'

She chose to ignore the suggestive tone and the way Philip waggled his eyebrows. It didn't bear thinking about.

'For my herd size, I only need one bull and he's quite

enough for me to handle. They can be feisty, and when they sense the presence of another bull they often charge through a fence.'

'Hence the electric fence you mentioned.'

'Correct. And since they can't engage in biffo, the rival bulls just make a lot of noise. You'll soon find out why most of those country sayings exist. Eating like a horse? That's because horses eat twice as much as cattle. Not within a bull's roar … wait till you hear Taffy in action against Pat's bull.'

'Taffy?'

'My current bull. Bought him from a bull breeder who happens to be Welsh.' Philip grinned.

She couldn't help her giggle as she recalled an old nursery rhyme. "Taffy was a Welshman, Taffy was a thief" it began … and his thievery involved beef, lamb and meat. 'You have an ingenious way of naming things.' She thought for a moment. 'Why do you say *current?*'

'You can't keep a bull for too long, or you get too much in-breeding in your herd. I sell most of my calves but also progressively sell off the older cows, replacing them with their daughters. Called heifers in the trade, just so you know.'

'Thanks, teach.' She wrinkled her forehead as she thought about what he'd said. 'You mean Taffy breeds with his own progeny?'

'In a very limited way. That's why you replace the bull about every three to four years.'

'I see.' She watched the gentle faces of the cows. She had to admit, today she'd discovered something very appealing in the trusting expression of their big, soulful eyes. 'Do the cows have names too?'

'Nope, even though I don't have many cattle by farming standards. Just numbers … see those ear tags … no names, even though some of my cows have distinct personalities.'

'You mean you don't feel emotionally attached to them?'

'As a herd, yes. To individual animals, no. I might, if I was here more often and spent more time among them.' He shrugged his shoulders.

She turned to face him, her feet planted wide apart. *Everything had a name, didn't it?* 'Earlier, you said your herd is smaller than normal. You could name the cows too, if you wanted to.'

'Now you're being a girl. Show me a farmer with a herd of cattle individually named. You can't let yourself become too attached. They're not pets, like dogs and cats. Even the cows in a small herd like this have to be sold off, at some point. It'd be too gut-wrenching.'

The flat monotone of his voice warned Hannah that this was a sensitive topic. She nodded her acceptance of his explanation. Time to move on. 'You say this is a small herd. *Could* you maintain more cows, beyond what you had before?'

'If I really had to. My strategy is partly dictated by these hills. Carrying a small herd means the farm isn't over-grazed and I avoid unnecessary erosion and the need for a lot of hand-feeding at the leaner times of year.' He extended his arm towards the crest of the ridgeline. 'See that slope. These hills also enforce regular exercise on the stock. Having enough tucker and exercise, the animals stay in good condition without much intervention from me. They calve easily and I hardly ever need the vet.'

She liked that he thought of his land and animals in such a holistic way. 'Your approach sounds very enlightened. I thought farmers liked to extract the max out of their properties.'

'I'm lucky. I don't need to earn my living from this farm. It's an interest, a kind of hobby farm, but purposeful. Running the place teaches me a lot that's useful at work. And having originally bought the place as one massive paddock, I inherited certain responsibilities. I run the cattle mainly to keep the grass under control, because the neighbours are all petrified of fire.'

She scanned the environment, puzzled. This was his second reference to fire in the short time she'd known him. She recalled the fire-fighting precautions near his house. The pool's water supply. 'I can't see any actual bush round here. Just dusty paddocks dotted with occasional trees, with some heavier timber growth along the river over there.' Hannah waved her arm in the general direction of the river, across the parched river flats.

'Grass fires do a lot of damage too. One came through here some years ago and burnt out a number of homesteads plus kilometres and kilometres of fencing, not to mention the stock casualties. Miraculously, no people died.'

Hannah tried to imagine this tranquil scene engulfed by fierce winds, dense smoke, leaping flames, fear and destruction. It proved impossible to conjure up this image when standing alongside a man who exuded such a strong sense of calm control. A strange happiness crept over her, as if this "tree change" was meant to be. This man, so different from

Alex, was meant to come into her life. *When the pupil is ready, the teacher arrives.*

Philip stood quietly beside her, drinking in the beauty of the landscape and of his companion, thinking his own thoughts. This stranger he'd hired as his caretaker was such a quick learner. Now that he appreciated how much the cattle scared her, he admired her guts too, as she faced her fears. She'd only been here for a week but already a bond had flickered into life. He treasured that moment in the truck when he'd steadied her and gazed into her navy-blue eyes. He'd better be careful about continuing to keep her at arm's length. She held rare appeal for him, but she wasn't one to trifle with, like all his previous girlfriends. She deserved better than his confused self could offer right now.

CHAPTER SIX

The morning had brought an unexpected sense of togetherness, but at sundown that mournful time of day, Hannah's sense of apartness, of not belonging, overcame her. She drooped listlessly on her back verandah, quenching her summer thirst with a Gunner. Her overseas trip last year had converted her to Hong Kong's specialty drink: equal parts of ginger beer and ginger ale over ice, with a dash of bitters. So refreshing. Its little touch of exotica cheered her flagging spirits. The rays of the setting sun illuminated the cloud of tiny insects dancing above the pool and her nose detected the faint trace of chlorine fumes evaporating from the water. The camaraderie she'd shared that morning with Philip had buoyed her but now her mood had flattened out, like the thinnest crepe.

This Saturday night, and those to come, promised too much solitude. She'd been alone last Saturday, her first on the farm, but had been occupied with settling in and comforted by Philip's unseen presence over in the main house. Tonight he enjoyed himself at Pat's, while she felt left out of life, slightly sorry for herself. If not for Alex, she wouldn't need to be here, away from her friends.

Another car drove down the road towards Pat's, marking its passage with billows of red dust. Her thoughts reflected her sense of disappointment: *Country people. Friendly? Huh!* She stirred her swizzle stick vehemently, crashing the ice cubes against the sides of the glass.

By the time she'd crunched on the cooling remnants of the ice cubes, half-a-dozen cars had passed. At this time of day, the air was still and sound travelled easily up the valley. She heard car doors slamming and general camaraderie as Pat's guests arrived. The refrain of the old song "Oh Lonesome Me" rang in her head. It hit her for the first time that the countryside could be a lonely place at close of day.

Down on the river flats where the eucalypts grew tall, the kookaburras bid her goodnight, their unmistakeable peals of laughter echoing up the valley. A flock of swallows, swooping and twittering as it headed towards its choice of bedroom, reinforced her awareness that nightfall was imminent. As she cleared up to move inside, she had a new thought. It wasn't so much that she wanted to be among Pat's guests ... unlikely to be her soulmates if they were anything like Pat. But were *they* his preferred type of company? Had he spoken the truth about his neighbourly relationship? What was the story with him and Pat?

She retreated indoors to face her evening of solitude and after a quick snack, she opted for an early night, anxious not to be awake when his car scrunched home along the gravel. She'd rather not know the answer to her question ... would he return at midnight, or with the dawn?

Sunday dawned hot, bright and blue, just like most summer days on the inland side of the Great Divide. Hannah contemplated her imminent test-drive of the ute, retracing yesterday's route. She prepared herself mentally for a second round of emotional deflation, half-expecting Philip to entertain her with talk of his evening at Pat's.

When he surfaced from inside his house around nine, dressed similarly to yesterday, he didn't say a word. He seemed subdued. Had something happened at Pat's?

Their test-drive began with a lesson in manoeuvring the old-fashioned gear stick. From the passenger seat, he leaned over, placed his warm hand over hers on the gear knob and guided her hand expertly through the various tricky gearshifts. She thrilled to the intimacy of his firm touch and suffered a small pang of regret when he withdrew to his side of the cabin. As she drove along and quickly got the hang of the vehicle, he pointed out a few tricky places on the internal roadways where she needed to be cautious. Being the passenger, he handled all the gates and as Hannah sat with the engine idling at these stops, she noticed something very odd. Both windows were open, yet she wasn't under siege from annoying insects. When he returned to the cabin she asked, 'Where are all the flies? I've hardly seen any.'

'It's the miracle of the dung beetle. It eats the cattle manure and thereby minimises fly numbers. There's another bit of trivia for you.' He grinned as one errant fly looked for the best landing spot on her face.

She swatted it away. 'It's worse than this down in

Melbourne in the summer.' She engaged the gears, took her foot off the brake and the ute bumped forwards.

He sprawled in his seat, unconcerned by the bumps. 'Plenty of breeding grounds for flies down there. And no dung beetles on city pavements.'

She sniffed the air. 'The smell's not too bad either, even with the windows open. I expected worse. It's earthy, but not unpleasant.'

He twisted in his seat to look directly at her. 'So you give farming life your seal of approval?'

She took her eyes off the track for a second and levelled her gaze on him. 'Let's just say "so far, so good".' The engine mimicked her own hesitation by spluttering a little.

He laughed. 'Drive on, Miss Undecided.'

It pleased her to see his mood had lightened.

They reached the last gate into the paddock containing the cattle. 'Stop here,' he said. 'I want to teach you something else about cattle.'

'Okay.' She braked, disengaged the gears and located the handbrake.

'Watch. They have a pecking order. There's always a lead cow.' He pointed across the paddock. 'See that cow heading the charge towards our gate?'

'Yes.'

'The lead cow is the key to managing cattle. Once the lead cow starts to move, the others generally follow. The trick is to get the lead cow moving. Pat taught me some of the tricks.' His voice rang with the enthusiasm of an evangelist.

'What would you do without Pat?' She tried to modify the derisory tone in her question, to turn it into a gentle leg-pull about women in general rather than Pat in particular.

'Exactly. Women understand these things better than us blokes. We get impatient, wanting everything to happen yesterday. Go on the rampage with our cattle dogs and motor bikes and stock whips and electric prodders, shouting and yelling.'

Once again he hadn't taken the bait. Deliberately? He always dealt with her references to Pat so matter-of-factly, with a straight bat. He never gave her a clue about his feelings for Pat. What an infuriating man he could be. He needed to see that she too could wield a straight bat. 'I've seen it all in the movies.' She hoped she sounded bored with the ways of men.

He hesitated, looked her way, frowned slightly and pulled his hat down more firmly on his head. 'Maybe cowboy behaviour is okay sometimes, especially in the outback, where there are huge paddocks the size of a small country or no fences at all, and they use helicopters to move cattle. Here it's different. The cattle are small in number and well contained in relatively small areas.' His confident voice brooked no disagreement.

'It's not cowboy country, I can see that.' *Does he think I can't? Surely not.*

'Pat's proved to me that a little bit of patience pays dividends.' There was the hint of a cheeky grin.

Is this "guru Pat" thing a game with him? Is he secretly teasing me about Pat?

Deadpan, he continued. 'She's taught me that it's quicker in the end to stand at the gate with a bale of hay. Sometimes you have to call them, especially in spring when they're in a paddock with lots of lush green feed but you need to move them, for some reason.'

Okay, so she'd better ignore his possible game of Pat provocation and get back to pupil mode. 'Call them? How?'

'"C'mon girls" yelled out in a friendly tone works well. Cattle are incredibly curious. Eventually the lead cow will succumb. If you always have a bale of hay with you, they quickly equate your presence with a bit of variety, a welcome change in that day's diet.'

'Like the Pavlov's dog principle? Makes sense.' She had to give Pat credit for convincing a male to adopt her female ways.

'Exactly. And it works. See?' He gestured towards the gate in front of them. 'They've all trotted up here, following that lead cow, because they suspect I have hay bales with me.'

'Which you have.' She craned her neck to check the tray behind the driver's cabin. 'I see you've loaded more since yesterday.'

'Good observation. You'll make a farmer yet.' He gave her the thumbs up.

She remained in need of convincing about the hay trick. 'It must help that they're hungrier at present.'

'It does,' he said, 'but it always works, eventually.'

She looked at the mass of cattle pushing and shoving at the gate, anxious for their fix of hay. 'Is it time for me to drive through that gate?'

'Not today.' He shook his head.

She turned back towards him in surprise. 'Won't the cattle be disappointed?'

He reached over and patted her forearm. 'No, I intend

to reward them for coming to the gate. You'll see in a minute.'

She welcomed his reassurance … and his unexpected touch. Time spent with Philip filled her with that comforting sense of "all's right with the world", unlike Alex's company. That line of thinking must be abandoned. She snapped back into pupil mode. 'So when will I practise what you did at this gate yesterday?'

'Next time we do this tour together, we'll take the lessons a step further. In any case, it's not something you'll have to do when I'm not here. I'll never ask you to drive through a gate into a paddock full of cattle by yourself. I never intended that as part of your duties.'

She breathed a silent sigh of relief and her white knuckles relaxed on the steering wheel.

'Right, now I'm going to instruct you on how to turn the vehicle safely from this sideways tilt on this slope, so we can retrace our tracks. In the process, I'll feed some tidbits to our friends over there.'

Stopping her halfway through her backing and filling training, he hopped out of the cabin and, using the hand-holds and footholds, swung himself up onto the tray. Same as yesterday, he cut off the nylon twine on a couple of hay bales and tied the twine to the rollbar behind the cabin. This time, though, he chucked the broken-up bales over the fence, close to and parallel to the truck.

In the rear vision mirror, the strands of coloured twine flapped in the breeze. When he got back into the cabin, she said, 'I saw you tie that twine up yesterday too. I assume you don't want that twine down on the ground, where the cattle might eat it by mistake.'

'Correct. I make a big effort to keep these paddocks very clean. Always pick up anything you see that shouldn't be there. That's definitely one of your duties.'

'Aye aye, sir.' She saluted. 'Come to think of it, what am I likely to see?'

'Stuff blown in by the wind, like plastic. Sometimes you find short bits of rusty wire along the original fence lines, dropped years ago by a careless fencer.'

'Oh, okay.' She couldn't resist the fencer reference. 'Is Horace careless?' she asked.

'Not at all. He's reliable and competent. I wouldn't employ him otherwise.' He looked and sounded annoyed at her reference to Horace.

Being caught in the middle of a potential love triangle had its drawbacks. She smiled sweetly at him. 'Of course. That's why you employed me.'

He seemed to studiously ignore her flippancy. 'We're finished here now. Let's go.'

Fuming inwardly at the way he'd closed down their conversation, she drove off. She remained silent on the return journey. Clearly, something bugged him.

He kept quiet too.

She parked the ute back in its bay and they retreated to their respective homes with barely a grunt of farewell. Being in his company was proving to be very disconcerting. Always his intelligence and sense of humour shone through, but one minute his kind, caring and courteous nature showed, the next his touchy and withdrawn self. Maybe he had as many hidden depths and problems as Alex, but of a different kind.

For the rest of the day all remained quiet. From her kitchen, as she prepared her dinner, Hannah heard a knock at her back door. At this time of day, it could only be Philip. Wondering what he wanted, she walked through the bungalow. Outside the glass door she could see him lounging against the verandah post. She slid the door open to him.

He quickly stood to attention, as if a bit nervous. 'I'm just about to head off.'

'Oh. Okay. Is this your regular going-home time?'

'Yep. Six o'clock.' He cleared his throat a little. 'Should have told you that you did well this morning. You're a natural with that ute. You didn't thrash it, as some drivers would have.'

She hadn't realised he'd been putting her through an off-road driving test. She took a deep satisfied breath. 'Thanks. I was trying to be careful.'

'You're used to nursing along your old car.'

'Do you have to remind me of that fact?' She pursed her lips. In a consumer society, her car made her a loser, not a winner.

He grimaced. 'Sorry. I meant it as a compliment to your awareness of machinery.'

That was better. Praise from him meant something. Warmth flooded through her and she held her head high. 'I might be scared of animals, but cars don't bother me. I'm a city girl, don't forget.'

'I haven't.' He shifted on his feet. 'That's why, last night, at Pat's, I realised that you need to meet some of the locals. It'll be too lonely for you here otherwise.'

'My exclusion from the gathering didn't go unnoticed?' She kept her tone deliberately wry.

'It was rather unfriendly, I agree. Here's my chance to make amends. I've been invited to the opening of the annual Rotary Art Show in town next Friday. Would you like to come with me? Everyone who's anyone will be there.'

Hannah's heart skipped a beat. The neutral way he'd extended the invitation meant it wasn't a real date, but it sounded like the next best thing. She'd love the chance to get to know this enigmatic man a little better and join the life of the town's community as well.

'Meeting the locals appeals to me, so yes, thanks, I'd really like to accompany you.'

A hint of relief flashed across his face. His stance relaxed. She wondered, had he been nervous about asking her?

'Is it a dressy affair?' Thankfully, she remembered to ask that important question.

'The invitation says smart casual. I'll be wearing a jacket and tie. The ladies usually go to some trouble to look their best.' His eyes twinkled.

'Aha! They like to make the most of a rare opportunity for a night on the town?'

'Guess so. Nothing glittery, mind you,' he added. 'That would be a bit over the top for here. Since it's an art show, creative spirits sometimes fly in for the evening.'

'Then thanks for giving me enough warning to dream up a suitable outfit.' She frantically considered the options available within her limited wardrobe.

He gave her an ironic grin. 'I'm sure you'll be the star attraction, whatever you wear.'

'Meaning what?' Was he actually going to pay her a personal compliment on her appearance?

'In small towns, people love to talk. They know I've

hired a caretaker. They'll all want to take a squiz at you and compare notes afterwards.' Not a compliment after all. Just another statement of fact from him.

She groaned. 'Sounds daunting.'

'Don't worry. They're mostly good-natured people. Their gossip's not usually malicious. A happy, open face will get you a long way with them.'

His nonchalance chased away Hannah's worries. 'I appreciate your reassurance and advice. Smiles come easily.'

Philip raised an eyebrow. 'From you? Not that I've noticed.'

She gave him a quizzical look.

He said, 'You haven't directed too many smiles my way.'

'And vice-versa,' she retorted.

CHAPTER SEVEN

They entered the small hall looking just like any other couple would at a city function, except for the attention they attracted at this country event.

Philip's height, broad shoulders and confident, upright bearing marked him out as different from this crowd. As did his perfectly cut, dark navy business suit, city office attire, "jacket and tie" taken to an extreme. Who was he trying to impress tonight? Pat? Hannah would be on the lookout.

She'd gone to some trouble with her outfit. She knew who she wanted to impress. She wanted to look like his companion … a date … and not an employee.

She wore one of her few dresses—a graceful tea-length item fashioned last summer by an up-and-coming Melbourne designer. Hannah had spotted the dress on one of her window-shopping excursions last year. A bargain then, she'd pay double now, as the designer had become a darling of the fashion world. Her high-heeled sandals, gold but not gaudy, brought her eyes level with Philip's collar-line. She'd paid extra attention to her hair, nails and makeup. She'd sprayed a mist of Chanel No 19, one of her few personal extravagances, behind her ears and on her wrists, to get herself into the mood for whatever adventures might come her way this evening. Not that Philip had hinted at anything.

Why was he so hard to read? The longer she spent with him, the more she became aware of his physical presence, his potent masculine aura. Well spoken, confident and competent, he oozed the sex appeal so often attributed to tall, dark and handsome men. If she didn't watch out, she'd start simpering at him, just like the other younger women gathering to enter the hall. On his part, he seemed impervious to the ploys of females.

People purchasing entry tickets caused a crush at the door, allowing little time for anything but the briefest of greetings. The organiser of the night's raffle beamed at Philip as he shelled out for tickets. 'Glad you could make it Philip,' she said. Introductions didn't get much past "this is Hannah Stockton" before the next person crowded in on them to say hello.

Obviously a big wheel in this small town, someone with whom everyone liked to claim acquaintanceship, he never actually explained to anyone who Hannah was.

They shuffled with the crowd into the small hall. A table arrayed with glasses of champagne, beer, wine, orange juice and mineral water stood just inside the entrance. He stopped and turned to her. 'What would you like?'

She surveyed the choice on display. 'A glass of bubbly would be perfect.'

'Right. Coming up. Regardless of the quality, it seems

well chilled, so it should hit the spot.' He passed her the glass, moist with droplets of condensation.

'I'm having a beer myself.' He took a swig, like all the other men were doing.

Hannah glanced around her. 'I see beer's the preferred choice for the men.'

'You won't find many country blokes who drink anything else.'

They made slow progress through the crush of bodies inspecting the art works. The whole town seemed to be intent on seeing the show. With little space to form a group, stand and chat, Hannah did not enter into much conversation. She sipped her champagne and stood quietly by Philip's side as some of the strangers mumbled "G'day mate" while others simply raised their drink in silent greeting. It was as if the presence of a big man in the city reassured them of their town's importance. Curious glances came her way, but he made no effort to satisfy the townsfolk's obvious wish to know where she fitted in the scheme of things.

They discussed their preferences for the art on display. 'Most of these paintings make me think I'm in a time warp,' Hannah confided in a whisper.

He nodded. 'I know what you mean. Traditional landscapes à la 1950s. Chocolate box flowers.' He scanned the display panels further away. 'Don't despair. A couple of locals are good artists. Come over here. I'll show you.' He pointed towards a scene of the local stockyards, full of colour and movement.

Hannah looked that way. 'Now you're talking.'

They'd almost reached the exhibit, excusing themselves as they pressed through the crowd, when Hannah tripped over the metal legs supporting one of the portable stands on which the paintings hung.

She stumbled and almost lost her balance, lurching sideways into Philip while trying not to smash her slippery glass into the stand. His right arm whipped round her back to steady her, while his other hand shot sideways to support her. A little shiver sent a slight tremble through her, a tremble nothing to do with the cold beer pressing against her left upper arm and everything to do with his arm wrapped around her body.

'Careful. You okay?' His breath so close to her ear sent another little shiver down her spine.

She gathered her wits. 'Yes. Sorry. You know I haven't had too much.' To prove it, she waved her half-full glass at him, but let out a slight bubbly-style giggle anyway. 'I tripped on that protrusion there.'

He looked down, still with his arms around her.

Pat chose that moment to approach them. Her expression combined a comical mixture of bright pleasure at seeing Philip, alternating with scowling displeasure at seeing Hannah in his arms.

He lingered over letting her go. Slowly he withdrew his left arm and slid his right hand down her back, but it hovered in place behind her, as if he might have to grab her again if she remained unsteady on her feet.

'Hi there, Philip. Wish I'd known you'd be in town tonight. We would have asked you to be one of the judges.' Grudgingly she added, 'And, er ... hello Hannah.'

Hannah simply nodded an acknowledgment as her companion responded to Pat. 'A judge? No way. I'd have been out of synch with what the judging panel chose. You'd have hated my choice.'

'Our choice,' offered Hannah provocatively.

Pat glared at Hannah, then turned her focus to Philip. 'Oh, why?'

'You picked all the traditional landscapes, those that look like a camera shot.' He waved his beer hand at the "First Prize" label attached to a painting opposite them. 'I prefer some of those more ethereal, imaginative, dreamy versions of this fantastic countryside.' He looked around him, seeking a work of this type. 'There. See that one?'

Pat glanced across the room at his chosen example. 'Hmph!'

Philip ignored her and pressed on. 'And I really love this picture of the local sale yard.' His genuine enthusiasm shone through. 'All those restless cattle and shouting buyers and that swirling, over-the-top bright red background. It's full of energy and the imagery of red dust. It's what a sale yard is all about.'

'Really?' Pat's tone was slightly sarcastic, as if he wouldn't know anything about cattle sales.

Philip obviously picked up her vibe. 'Okay, okay, so I've never attended an auction. The stock and station agent handles that for me. It's how I imagine the event, Pat.'

'It's my favourite, too,' said Hannah. 'I thought that painting should win.'

'So, are you our resident art critic too, as well as our resident writer?' Pat's question could scarcely have sounded more patronising.

'No. Just a writer. Even so, we're all entitled to our preferences.' She kept her expression bland, her tone neutral. No need to fuel the fire of Pat's defensiveness.

Philip nodded. 'Well said, Hannah. Couldn't agree more. In fact, I've just decided to buy that painting. Excuse me Pat, I'd better find whoever's in charge of the red stickers, before someone beats me to it.'

He angled his way through the congregated viewers towards the front desk where the committee members were handling sales.

Hannah watched Pat gazing after him. Hannah inwardly groaned. A little diplomacy seemed necessary, especially given her likely dependence on Pat for possible help with Philip's cattle. 'It's very good of all you committee members to organise this art sale for charity,' she said. 'It clearly involves a lot of work.'

'It does. A lot. Every year.' Pat sighed.

'You must like art yourself, to be involved.' Hannah gave herself a mental pat on the back for persevering with her tact mission.

Pat's face brightened a little in response. 'Yes, I dabble a bit. Learned a bit of art at school. It's hard not to be sucked in by the appeal of the local landscape.' Her shoulders slumped. 'My efforts look like those camera shots Philip mentioned.' She spoke in a monotone, her bubble pricked by her failure to impress him.

Hannah saw the need to try a little kindness. 'Art is all in the eye of the beholder. Plenty of people like traditional landscapes.'

'Not Philip, it seems.' Pat still sounded glum.

'Maybe not, but I see there are red stickers on quite a few of those. Did you enter something?'

Pat shook her head. 'Mine aren't up to standard, and I was a judge anyhow. Conflict of interest.'

'There's a way to get around that. Yours, if entered, could have been excluded from the judging.' Hannah noticed a flash of interest spark in Pat's face, so she continued with her diplomacy mission. 'Someone might have liked to buy your work. You might have a secret admirer in the district.'

'Fat chance.' Pat snorted. 'There aren't too many eligible bachelors on offer.' Her tone was bitter. 'Except for Philip, of course.' Her blend of "secret admirer" with "eligible bachelor" said it all.

Just then, the man himself reappeared alongside them, jubilant. 'Got it. Trouble is, it can't be picked up until the exhibition closes. I won't be here then. I've nominated you to pick it up for me, Hannah. Told them you're my new caretaker.'

'I bet that caused a stir,' Pat said with palpable irony.

'Let's just say that quite a few people now seem keen to make the acquaintance of my new assistant.'

With that remark, the first inquisitive local sidled up.

Hannah found it overwhelming to be introduced to so many people at once. None appeared to have much in common with her and her city-based interests, apart from the artist who'd painted the stockyards picture. In demand as a local celebrity, that artist only had time to exchange a few words.

Then Bill Brownlow, the president of the local history society, was introduced. His head tilted at her name. 'I've heard that name before.'

Philip's eyebrows rose a notch.

Her nerves jangled. Don't tell me I can't even hide here.

'You're that historian, aren't you? You wrote that book.'
Bill's keen eyes betrayed eager anticipation of her answer.

She nodded and immediately relaxed her guard. She
wasn't known for all the wrong, Alex-related reasons.

Philip looked at her, intrigued. 'What book?'

'Just a book about some of the earliest settlers of
Melbourne.' She *should* accentuate the positive and boost up
her image in his enquiring eyes, but somehow, she couldn't.
After the Alex fiasco, the new people in her life had to take
her as they found her, not as they imagined her from the
newspaper version of her life.

'Does it have a name?' If nothing else, he was persistent.

'*Batman's Battlers*, after their leader John Batman.'

That topic seemed to impress him because his eyes
widened. 'Where can I get hold of a copy? I'd like to read it.'

Surprise siphoned through her. He liked history? 'I'll
gladly lend you a copy.'

Bill Brownlow had hung around during their exchange.
'We could do with someone like you in our group, Hannah,'
he interjected eagerly. 'Will you come along to the next
meeting of the historical society?'

This first "welcome to the town gesture", from the
unlikeliest of sources, cheered her. She had no idea that she'd
find history lovers in a town this small. 'I'd like to. Your
group sounds like it might be right up my alley.'

Delighted, he shook her hand to seal the deal. 'Not quite
in your league, but we're reasonably active, for a bunch of
bushies.'

'Does that mean you have some local publications to
your credit?' She'd be interested to read them.

Bill's chest swelled with pride. 'One. A history of the

town. It needs updating, though.' He hesitated, as if he'd just realised the implications of his statement. 'It'll take a lot of work. It's an overwhelming prospect.'

Hannah could empathise with him. She said, 'Trove makes it much easier.'

Bill nodded in agreement.

'Trove?' Philip sounded puzzled.

'Trove, as in Treasure Trove,' she explained. 'It's a project by the National Library which includes the digitalisation of Australia's newspapers, from the start of European settlement.'

'You don't say.' Philip cocked his head to the side and nodded slightly, as if this interested him.

*Is his thing technology, not history?* 'We researchers love it. Papers and stories we never knew existed are so easy to find now.' She enjoyed being able to demonstrate to him that she possessed professional skills, extending beyond family history.

'Trove is great, I agree,' Bill added. We'll definitely make great use of it to help us flesh out our current town history. A resident here might have been written up in the Sydney and Melbourne papers but you could never hope to search all those papers on the off chance of finding something. Court cases in particular provide a goldmine of local gossip.'

A dark shadow flitted across Philip's face.

Without pausing to digest his reaction, Hannah said, 'I can read and search those papers from the bungalow, via the internet.'

Philip rubbed the back of his neck and shifted his weight from one foot to the other. 'You can search the newspapers by individual key words?'

'Yes. And it's very easy to find information.'

Philip's jaw tightened. She noticed. Was he worried about something she might find on Trove, something about his family?

'Of course, the most recent papers aren't part of the process,' Hannah said. 'We're talking history here—starting forty to fifty years ago.'

Philip's tense jaw relaxed a little. She took note. Old history didn't bother him. Newer history did.

Bill seemed oblivious of the undercurrents. 'Aside from delving into Trove, we're not sure that we've identified and given due recognition to everyone who founded this town,' he said.

Hannah liked Bill's enthusiasm for balancing the often lopsided versions of history. 'Have you used the online birth, death and marriage indices much, Bill? They'd allow you to develop a comprehensive list of all the people who ever lived in this district in its first hundred years.'

Bill rubbed his chin. 'Not yet. Good idea!'

Hannah said to Philip, 'Until recently, most local histories have had to rely on the usually self-serving stories passed down by the long-established families of the district.'

Philip said, 'Meaning that the important contributions made by many others were overlooked?' His mental gears seemed to click into action.

'Exactly.' She beamed at him, pleased that he was quick to take her point. 'History is pretty much always written from the perspective of the dominant players. Now we have better tools for building up a fuller profile of the communities of bygone eras.'

'Who cares anyway?' He swigged the last of his beer.

Philip disappointed her with that comment and she frowned at him. His abrupt manner proved he'd obviously not fully recovered from his grumpiness.

'Lots of people care.' Bill seemed to take personal affront and turned away from Philip, an apparent Philistine. 'So, you'll help us?' he asked Hannah.

'To update the local history? Yes, I'd like to. There's nothing I like better than uncovering the past, especially where people are concerned.'

This was a deliberate taunt to Philip and his mysterious sensibilities. His behaviour of the last few minutes infuriated her. She reached into her bag, extracted a card and her pen, wrote her new phone number on the reverse and handed it to Bill. 'Here's my card.'

'Wonderful. Someone will contact you with the details of our next meeting.'

'Time to go, Hannah.' Philip's gruff voice interrupted them. 'See you, Bill.' With his hand resting lightly in the area of her left shoulder blade, Philip began shepherding her towards the door.

She fumed inwardly. For the second time in as many weeks, he was acting in a dictatorial fashion. It couldn't be jealousy, like Alex, because Bill was an old retired guy and the first time had been with Pat, at the conclusion of that impromptu dinner at the pub. Hannah made a mental note. *There won't be a third time. This man is not going to boss me around.* Then she remembered the practicalities of her current situation. Best not to challenge him on this tonight … I'm his guest, a stranger in town, and I need the lift home.

They drove home with minimal conversation. He kept

his eyes glued to the road ahead, his hands gripped to the steering wheel. Her fanciful dreams at the start of the evening flew out the window.

He stopped at his front door, bounded out of the car and switched on the external floodlights to light her way across to the bungalow. She exited her side of the car, determined to act with nonchalance, and plastered a movie-poster smile on her face. 'Goodnight Philip. I enjoyed the evening very much.' She hoped her gentle irony showed. 'It was interesting to meet some of the locals.' That part was genuine.

'They're good-hearted people,' he finally said.

'Especially that artist. And Bill.' She stirred him some more, hoping for a reaction.

He reacted as she'd expected, by frowning. 'I'll turn off the outside lights once you get to your door. Sleep well. We'll do the cattle run on Sunday.' He turned on his heel and went back to drive his car into the garage.

Her earlier "will he, won't he" anticipation of what might happen when they reached *Wallumatta Farm* had fizzled like a spent sparkler.

CHAPTER EIGHT

Philip lazed on his front verandah, soaking up the early morning sun as he tried to set his mind free. Whenever he could, he enjoyed his Saturdays as his day of rest and recovery. Today he felt out of sorts. He hadn't handled things well last night.

He was annoyed with himself, just as he'd been for his over-reaction last Sunday to Hannah's mention of Horace. He liked Horace, who was uncomplicated as a man, a good worker and a good bloke. By comparison, his own life at present troubled him. He'd like to be more laid back and carefree, like Horace, more comfortable with the past, like that bloke Bill last night.

He trailed his eye after his resident eagle, hovering high above him, waiting for the chance to swoop in for the kill. His eagle held potent symbolism for him. In its dual role of tender nurturer of its young and instrument of death to its prey, the eagle epitomised the world of banking, where Philip did battle every day.

Last night rotated back into his mind's view. Hannah.

That girl had burrowed under his skin, becoming an irritant to him, filling him with sexual agitation and emotional discomfort. He had to struggle to keep from touching her whenever a social opportunity provided an excuse to do so … yet he recoiled from her enthusiasm for researching the lives of other people, and the realisation it was so easy for her to do so from *his* bungalow.

She tempted him with her reserve, her hidden depths. He'd like to unzip her, set her free, confident and soaring like his eagle, but at present he couldn't spot an easily accessible tag to her zipper.

So far, she'd given no clue that she knew how he spent his weekdays. Would she share the view of the general public, seeing his world as a morally desolate occupational landscape, plundered by the evil forces currently bringing many individuals, businesses and countries to the point of ruin? Historians, like that dratted Bill fellow she seemed to like so much, might think along such lines. In the past he himself hadn't cared much about the opinions of other women, so why did it seem increasingly important to him that *she* should think well of him. Darn it, he wanted her to like him, despite his job … and his father. Why couldn't he accept his recent discoveries about his father and be more mature about it?

He refocussed on his eagle. From his own perch in the higher branches of the banking tree, Philip reflected that he enjoyed a bird's eye view of the world, just like his eagle. His perspective today differed hugely from his days as a fledgling in the banking nest. He'd wanted to soar like an eagle, and he'd achieved that goal, but modern bankers could only grip their branch with vice-like claws and hang on tight. The winds of change buffeted them all, shaking the less tenacious from their branches. At his level, he needed to be on his guard at all times. Fortunately, he'd made his own way before he found out about his father. That discovery would certainly have dented his confidence.

His tough working environment, dog-eat-dog, ruled on the principle of survival of the fittest. Banks tried to give economic life to targets selected as strong and, like eagles obeying the inexorable laws of nature, were forced by the rules of banking to snuff out the life of weaker players. One major international bank even used the eagle as its corporate symbol.

By contrast, the country's largest bank had once used the elephant in its advertising campaign ... *Get with the Strength*, the billboards had proclaimed. Long gone were those days, when kids saved their coins in an elephant moneybox. Gone too was the elephant logo, a victim of concerted sneering. People who didn't understand the essence of banking had twisted the "gentle giant" image into "slow and lumbering", not realising that the gentle giant approach perfectly signified how a bank should operate. He knew one thing, for sure. There'd be a lot less trouble in the world with less rush-rush and more thinking.

Banks now rejected the natural world of eagles and elephants as the source of their corporate image, preferring the clinical approach of an acronym and a stylish logo. His soul-destroying weekday world was fast-paced and slick, a creation of numbers, sustainable only by maintaining public confidence in *the system*. He revelled in his weekend retreat, supplying his chance to keep his feet firmly on the ground.

Philip watched the eagle up high in the sky and transported himself mentally to that high point of the farm where, last weekend, Hannah had been so impressed with the view. Damn it all. She'd crept into his thoughts again, burrowing far too deeply under his skin. He loved how her mouth turned up at the corners, just like one of those smiley-face, no-teeth emojis. Strangely, his every mention of Pat disabled Hannah's ability to generate these reactions. Interesting!

He planned to keep to himself today. Maybe he'd cool off in the pool later. Meanwhile, plenty of business stuff needed his attention.

On second thoughts, he'd leave work aside for a while and relax here in the early sunshine, enjoying his favourite zoning-out place. He'd once heard of a senior banker over-seas who deliberately removed himself from the fray to gain management perspective by living part of every week at his farm. He agreed with that bloke … rebalancing was the right approach. The here and now made him happy. Apart from those niggles created by Hannah.

---

Saturday quickly turned far too hot for outdoor work. With all her windows and doors closed in a vain attempt to insulate the bungalow against the heat, Hannah laboured at her computer, the rotating fan unable to ward off the sweat that dripped to her elbows, leaving little patches of dampness whenever she leaned on her desk. Her thoughts strayed to Philip, that infuriating but far-too-attractive new "boss" of hers. *What does he do to amuse himself inside the house?* She could hear the condenser humming on his roof. His air-conditioned house. Lucky man. She supposed his day job kept him busy on the phone and the internet for a good deal of his time.

At 4pm she heard the pool gate clang shut and then the sound of a splash. She opened her door to investigate and stepped into the furnace outside, sliding her door shut with a bang.

The noise prompted a response from the pool. At the centre of a swirl rippling outwards in concentric circles, a dark head turned her way, directing a pair of storm-grey eyes straight at her.

'Oh. It's you Philip. Just checking. Doing my job.'

As his feet found the bottom of the shallow end of the pool, he stood up, now only half-submerged in the water. She couldn't take her eyes off his water-slicked shoulders and the muscles flexing in his chest and arms as he squished the water off his face and hair. She watched him, watching her watching him.

Humour danced in his eyes. 'Good to know. Are you going to join me? There's plenty of room for two.' His wicked grin conveyed every possible suggestive innuendo.

'Well, um,' She was very tempted, but somewhat puzzled at his flirting, after his cold-shoulder treatment last night.

She walked down towards the pool fence. Philip teasingly flicked a few drops of water in her direction. They landed on her sandals and bare toes.

'See Hannah. Very refreshing. Come in and cool off.'

In this heat she couldn't see how she could refuse without seeming bonkers. 'Thanks, I will. I'll get changed.'

As she withdrew to change into her swimsuit, her breath

quickened, her heart raced and her muscles tensed. She was naturally modest, not an exhibitionist. With him already immersed in the pool, it meant that when she returned, traversing the distance between her door, the entrance gate to the pool and the water, she'd have to parade before him with next to nothing on. She'd have nowhere to hide from his scrutiny. All guys ogled women, especially those like Philip, surely able to attract the most stunning of the female population. She didn't measure up to that high standard.

Nor did her swimmers. Once a stylish, slinky and figure-hugging one-piece from the days when her finances were in better shape, it suffered from too many years of wear in salty and chlorinated water. The Lycra had faded and sagged a bit in places.

Why should she care? She shouldn't, feminists would reproach her. Feminists be damned. Somehow she wanted to spark his sexual admiration of her. As she admired him.

On the positive side … at least her costume still fitted. Her breasts, hips and thighs hadn't expanded in the five years since she chose it. That single irrefutable fact about her body image cheered her … she wasn't bulging out of her clothes. She'd hold on to that thought as she faced his scrutiny. And she'd be mad to turn down the chance to cool off on a day like today. She hoped like crazy that he'd be absorbed in a few laps when she reappeared.

No luck. No laps. He floated lazily in the pool, facing in her direction, waiting for the show, with her as the star attraction. She baulked a little at her doorway. Then with a *What the heck*, she proceeded, just as a model would on a catwalk with a hundred pairs of eyes on her. She had good posture … all those years of ballet lessons had been good for something … but try as she might, she couldn't convey that air of haughtiness perfected by models.

At the gate she fumbled with the safety knob, overly anxious to reach the safe haven of the water. Rather than risking a dive, with its spluttering after-effects and bedraggled wet-hair look, she chose the daintier option of the steps at the shallow end, quickly dunking herself to the shoulders.

He watched every minute of her nervous entry to the pool. A wicked glint danced in his eyes.

She glared at him, as if to say You bastard, you didn't have to stare at me.

As if he could read her thoughts, he said, 'You checked me out. I was reciprocating. Did you think I wouldn't?'

'I hoped you'd be a gentleman and look the other way. I hate to be the centre of attention.'

'Nothing wrong with what I saw.' His teeth gleamed white in his cheeky grin.

'No need to pull my leg.' She pushed off from the wall and took a few breaststrokes towards the centre of the pool.

'What?' he called out. 'Do you doubt yourself? Have you looked in the mirror lately?'

Shocked, Hannah almost forgot to swim. It sounded like a genuine compliment. Her heart kicked over. He'd noticed her, as a woman. She tossed her head and replied cheekily. 'I haven't noticed a full-length mirror in the bungalow.'

'Touché.'

She joined in his infectious laugh. It relaxed her. She took a few more gentle pulls of breaststroke down the pool, keeping her head above water to keep her curly hair dry.

He followed her and met her at the end. They rested their backs against the pool wall.

Without looking at her, he said, 'Sorry I was unsociable last night.'

She half-turned towards him, hoping for an explanation. 'I couldn't work out what got into you.'

He still didn't glance her way and he didn't elaborate. Instead he changed tack to uncomplicated small talk, and this time he looked sideways to catch her eye. 'You been working over there all day?' He tilted his head towards her office.

'I have. You too?' She tilted her head towards his house.

'Just relaxing. Reading a bit. Thinking. Dreaming. That kind of thing. A lazy day, for a change.' He cupped some water in his hands and let it run out through his fingers.

'You must need a rest on weekends. I hear you're a big wheel in town.'

'Been doing a bit of detective work? Your specialty.'

He could have sounded accusatory, but she detected no annoyance in him today, just fact checking. A half-truth would suffice as her answer. 'Pat told me you're something big in high finance.'

'I guess Pat would say that.' Now he did sound slightly annoyed and he changed the subject. 'Tell me something more about yourself. You're far too young to be embroiled in family history. I thought that was for old guys, with too much time on their hands, like that Bill fella last night.'

She checked to make sure that an angry facial expression did not contradict his polite questioning. Alex had taught her to be cautious whenever other men were mentioned. It seemed safe to assume that Philip was focussed on her work, not her past or potential love life. 'Time does help, but plenty of younger people are interested in their family tree.

These days many schools are using genealogy as a tool for teaching history.'

His jaw dropped. 'You're kidding me.'

'Nope. And it's not all deadly serious and boring, you know. There's the occasional glimmer of a sense of humour.'

'Yeah?' His scepticism showed.

'You want an example?'

'If you've got one.' The gruff, downward inflection of his voice indicated his doubt.

'I have. There are fantastic shipping records and incoming passenger lists for Australia from the start of European settlement—'

'And?'

She detected an unstated but impatient, "so what?"

'Our ancestors known to be living in Australia but not showing up on these records are categorised as *Swimmers*.' She hoped that would prove her point.

He chuckled. 'I have to admit, that ridiculous idea of anyone swimming to Australia *is* funny.'

She found herself ticking a little checkbox inside her head—a checkbox she hadn't known existed—at the discovery that they shared the same sense of humour. The mirror thing, and now the swimmers.

'Wait, there's more.' She grinned at him. 'I've had a few private laughs too. On one of my research days, a woman sitting nearby discovered an unpalatable truth. She jumped up out of her seat and shouted, "Oh! Another lie exposed! If he was alive, I'd kill him".'

Her anecdote didn't prompt the laugh she'd expected. Hannah could have sworn she heard him mutter under his breath "That's how I feel about my mother."

'What was that?'

Philip started, but replied, 'Nothing.' He slid his body down the wall, submerged himself for a moment and then stood tall, sluicing the water off his hair and face. Staring towards the pool fence and not at her he asked, 'Have you discovered any unpalatable truths, about your family I mean?'

'Plenty, but it's important to accept what you find.' Curious at his response, she added, 'You can't change it. It's already happened.' She shrugged. '*C'est la vie*. That's life.'

'What if you don't like it?' He slumped lower in the water, crossing his arms over his chest.

She watched his continuing display of unease. This was sensitive ground for him. 'Well, you could try looking further into the story. You might find another angle, some mitigating circumstances which help you to accept the events.'

'And what if you don't find a silver lining to that black cloud sullying the reputation of your forebears?' This time he turned to face her squarely, a troubled look on his face.

At last he'd provided her with a clue to his odd behaviour … an unpleasant family secret. 'Then you have to find a way of digesting it,' she replied firmly.

'Is that what you do all day? Digest facts, discern their meaning?'

'I guess you could look at it that way. I always try to flesh out a full understanding of the life I'm researching.'

'Where do you start?'

'You genuinely want to know? Really?' This conversation has taken a serious turn.

'Yep. I'm interested.'

'Here goes, then'. She splashed a handful of water at him to lighten the mood and grinned. 'The obvious places — family stories, computerised records, archives offices, library books, old photos.'

'These are your normal tools of trade, Madame Professor?' He cheekily splashed his own handful of water in her direction.

She wiped the drips off her face. 'Yep. As well, I try to walk in the shoes of my ancestors. I find myself picking my way around cemeteries I never knew existed.'

'Some might think that spooky.' He let out a ghostly "woo hoo".

She laughed. 'They're peaceful places.' She added, 'I also try to align old maps with modern streetscapes to work out where they lived. I've even knocked on a stranger's door asking permission to take photos.'

'An amazing array of activities. I had no idea.' He sank down in the water, pushed himself off from the wall with his powerful legs and cruised to the other end of the pool. From there he called across to her, 'How do you know where to look in the first place?'

'You mean once you have a name and some rough dates for when they lived?' *Some kind of family secret is definitely on his mind.*

'Yes.'

'You need to think creatively, morph into a detective, create possible scenarios, follow the trail, go looking for evidence, that kind of thing.' She tried to restrain herself. He'd think she was a crazy woman, in love with dead people.

'It's a refreshing change to see a woman passionate for her work.'

She didn't expect that reaction from him. It gave her more confidence with him.

He swam back to her end of the pool and said, 'Last night I found out that you're actually a historian. That's a different kind of thinking. All about storytelling.'

Relieved, she snapped her fingers at him. 'Exactly. You've got it. My academic background helps me to integrate my family history clues into a coherent "narrative" and write it up as a story.'

'So why are you hiding away here?'

*The killer question. How will I answer?* She gulped. 'What makes you think I'm hiding?' She gazed at him, daring him to elaborate. The word "hiding" had such a negative ring to it. He'd spoilt the moment.

He returned her gaze, steadily. 'Maybe I'm rather good at seeing through people. Or is it just that I can't figure out why you're not still down in Melbourne, where all the academic resources are located.' He playfully flicked a bit more water at her.

It eased her sudden tension. 'I'll have you know, Mr Grand Inquisitor, that I've done all the research. I'm at the writing-up stage. Haven't you ever heard of writer's retreats?' She flicked some water back.

'Of course. But they're for real writers.'

Her confidence evaporated with the moisture rising off the pool into the hot, blue sky overhead. She let out a heavy breath and felt her shoulders slump.

'Sorry, I didn't mean how that sounded. What I mean is, I picture a writer as someone like, er … Agatha Christie for example … writing her detective novels. Not people writing about their great-grandmother.'

'Then you've got a lot to learn about writers.' She turned her back on him and cruised to the other end of the pool.

He followed her. 'Please help me understand,' he said quietly. 'I've never met another writer.' He seemed contrite. 'You're clearly a good one, or Bill wouldn't have been so excited to meet you. I "get" history. I just don't understand the appeal of family history.'

He stood close enough for her to poke him angrily in his wet chest with her index finger. 'Let me explain, Philip. When you were a kid, did you find that puzzles were very addictive?'

'Maybe. Come to think of it, I *do* enjoy my Sudoku fix on Saturday mornings.'

'There you go. You understand how you can't leave something alone until you've solved the problem.' She gave him another jab in the chest, softer this time. 'I rest my case.'

'I like it when you do that. But feel free to run your wet, slippery hands *across* my chest as well,' he said, teasing her, as if trying to make up for hurting her feelings.

She hastily moved away. Damn the man, he was too cheeky for her own good. Being this close to his chest did funny things to her insides.

'I still don't get it. What problems do you solve with family history?'

Good, he'd returned the conversation to safer ground. Even so, she fumed. 'Isn't it obvious? The biggest one of all. Who are you? Where did you come from?' She thought about his behaviour, his likely family secret. 'Family history research can be a great personal development tool. You gain insights into yourself.' Insights he needed badly. 'You should try it,' she said defiantly.

'Thanks, but I know as much as I want to know.' He edged closer to her and said, 'So *you* find family history as addictive as Sudoku?'

She nodded. 'Very. Once you've experienced the exhilaration of finding that something or someone from long ago impacts on your current life, you'll want more. If you're lucky, you'll be able to control the urge to keep looking for the next clue.'

Her antagonism towards him was abating, now that he showed awareness of his lack of tact.

'The clue to help you go back another generation? I'm beginning to be interested in the whole process.'

He sounded contrite. Good. She needn't allow her hurt feelings to continue spoiling their pool time. 'Yes. I didn't expect to become hooked. It's changed my life.' She couldn't suppress a wry grin. 'People being treated for gambling addictions should be introduced to family history research … that way, they'd have more to show for their money and their time.'

'Not my idea of fun. Isn't it boring, doing that all day long?' A puzzled frown creased his forehead.

'No, without a boss telling you what to do, you can drop one line of enquiry when you tire of it or reach a dead end, and head off down another enticing avenue.'

'How come you don't have a boss? Not many people your age can afford to retire. I have to confess, I've been curious about this since the day we met.'

'I've taken all my leave, and then some, because … er … I need a solid bank of time to finish writing my book.' She glanced sideways as she spoke, unable to look him in the eye as her voice faded away.

'Right.' He gave her the "and pigs might fly" look.

She hadn't fooled him. So now they were equal, she thought, with each suspecting the other of hiding a secret.

He glanced at his watch. 'Damn. Much as I'd like to continue this fascinating conversation, I have a conference call booked in a few minutes. Gotta go!' He climbed out and grabbed his towel. 'You're welcome to stay here, cooling off.'

She squinted up at him. 'Thanks. I'll do a few laps. Need to relax the tension in my shoulders … the disadvantage of too much computer work.' No need to add that the impressive specimen of humanity standing above her generated his own form of tension. She quickly rotated her shoulders to release some of it.

'Why didn't you tell me? I could have given you a massage,' he teased.

She shivered at the thought. She'd like nothing better than him massaging her neck and shoulders, her fingers and toes … and a few other much more private places on her hungry body.

As he clanged the pool gate shut, he called, 'Don't forget our cattle round tomorrow. Nine am.'

CHAPTER NINE

Ready and eager, Hannah stood by the ute, waiting for her instructor to emerge from the house.

Philip sauntered out. 'Morning Hannah.' He greeted her as if he'd just bumped into her in the street and hadn't seen her barely clothed in his pool yesterday. 'This time you're driving, remember, so hop in.'

This was normal instructor-pupil interaction, not a man trying to control her. She smiled back demurely and did as she was told.

He swung himself into the passenger seat and they set off. Neither acknowledged yesterday's disclosures in the pool. Men might be able to compartmentalise their lives, but Hannah couldn't. Now she'd seen him practically naked, she found it difficult to think of him in any way other than as a *hunk*. The effort of tempering her reckless fantasies caused her to stamp down on the accelerator by mistake. Naughty girl! Keep your mind on your driving. The engine raced but the upward slope minimised their forward surge. 'Oops, sorry.'

Whatever he thought, he took it in his stride. 'No worries. This old truck takes a little bit of getting used to.'

After that, she concentrated hard and all went well until she parked at the final gate. The cattle pushed and shoved on the other side, scuffing clouds of dust into the air. It petrified her … they looked very stirred up. Her courage failed. She had zero desire to drive through this gate. Above all, she feared hitting one of the animals.

Trying to find an excuse to avoid the task, she stalled by saying, 'There's a lot of dust. I can hardly see.'

If he picked up on her anxiety, he ignored it. He stared ahead and seemed preoccupied by the dust itself. He mused aloud, 'I'll have to be careful with these animals once the rains come again.'

That startled her. 'What do you mean? Won't the rain be good?'

His attention seemed to be elsewhere, yet he managed to answer, 'Yes, but it won't come before the autumn break.'

She sighed heavily. 'There you go again … another unfamiliar term.'

'What?' His head swivelled her way as he must have tried to recall what he'd just said. 'Oh, you mean autumn break?'

'Yes.' She sat with the engine idling and tried to forget about the cattle. Any excuse would do to delay her having to drive into that mob. She didn't care if Philip took all day to explain autumn breaks to her.

He turned his shoulders sideways in his seat to face her. 'Okay, here's your lesson for the day. Other than thunderstorms, we generally don't get much summer rain in this part of Australia. The pasture grasses have adapted accordingly.

When the high-pressure zones move northwards as winter approaches, they start to bring westerly winds and cold fronts and regular rain. We call that first rain the autumn break.'

'And it's precious, eh? Even though I'm a city girl, I do know the traditional rainfall pattern hasn't happened the way it should for some years. Even in Melbourne.'

'Yep, the autumn break's been a total fizzer for almost a decade. Pat says she used to slosh round in the gullies, up to her ankles in mud. You could see surface water running into the dams. Since I came here, my gumboots have scarcely got wet. These past few winters we've had the odd day of rain, but it's just settled the dust and produced a green drought.'

'Green drought? There you go *again*.' This was good. He was in teacher mode and he'd have to explain that term, giving her another excuse not to drive through that gate.

He shifted his gaze from her to the cattle and back again. 'I keep forgetting that it took me a while to learn the farming game.' He gave her a patient smile. 'The term describes paddocks that look green from a distance, but where the greenness is an illusion. The grass seeds have germinated and surfaced, but there's not enough moisture in the subsoil for the grass to grow any higher. The cattle can't feed on it as it's too short for them.'

She didn't answer straight away, needing to process his words. 'Maybe my presence will bring you luck and you'll have a good season this year.'

He turned further in his seat and rested his right arm along the shelf behind their seats.  'I think that's already happening.' He gave her a cheeky grin. 'It's already a good season, Miss Stockton. You're here to help me.'

Her heart skipped a beat. He sounded quite flirtatious. Not sure, she opted for safe ground. 'Trying to.' She returned him a smile more rueful than cheeky. 'I still don't understand. Why might the rain be bad news?'

He stared at her, his eyebrows raised. 'You love learning all this stuff, don't you! You have an enquiring mind.'

'Should I apologise for that?' She lifted her chin, challenging him to say *Yes*.

'Never. I'm impressed.' Another cheeky grin.

She breathed a deep, satisfying breath. Who doesn't like to hear that they impress someone? 'Thanks, but go on.'

'Here's why rain might be a problem. This long drought has dried out and cracked the hoof area of my cattle, leaving fissures. Water and infections can easily invade once the ground turns to mush. I think I told you I haven't needed the vet much, but Pat tells me that will probably change.' He turned back to watch the cows and calves, growing ever more frenzied at the gate, bellowing for the food drop.

Hannah flinched. Pat. That damn name. It kept on cropping up. Was there anything that guru Pat didn't know? And when did all of Pat's lessons take place? She hadn't seen much interaction between them in the three weeks that she'd been living here.

He gestured towards his animals and prepared to hop out of the ute. 'Come on. Feeding time. Remember, just take it carefully. I'm going to open the gate towards the cattle today, yelling at them and kind of pushing them back with the gate as I go. They'll back off a little and you must follow right behind me, bipping the horn. As soon as the truck clears the gate, I'll swing it back and fasten it. You keep driving, slowly and carefully, and stop over there.' He pointed at the spot.

'Won't the cattle crush you, if you're on the same side of the gate as them?'

'Nope. They'll scamper after you, kicking up their heels, chasing the hay on the back. Ready?'

She nodded. He jumped out and slammed his door. She engaged the gear as he swung open the gate and pressed the horn as she moved forward. Her part seemed straightforward enough, if nerve-racking. Once she'd stopped in the designated place, she baulked, uncertain what to do next. The truck rocked as the cattle jostled for position around her, craning their heads over the sides of the tray, trying to pull bits of hay off the bales. One curious cow shoved its head in through the open driver's window and gave the side of her face a big lick. *Ugh. Gross.* She reared back and wound the window up in a hurry as soon as the cow withdrew. No way would she get out and help Philip. He had it all on his own.

Without her noticing, he'd walked round the animals to approach the truck from the front. He strode firmly towards the heaving mass, waving his Akubra at them and shouting, 'Get back'. A few cows retreated enough for him to swing himself up onto the tray from the passenger side. She twisted in her seat to watch him cutting the strings and offering handfuls of hay to the hungriest open mouths.

He shouted out to her, 'It's a bit windy today. I don't want the loose hayseeds to blow into their eyes. Drive forward very slowly, so I can drop a trail of hay behind the truck. Stop where we stopped last week. The ground's level there and it's easy to turn around. No turning on this part of the slope. Keep it straight.'

She obeyed his instructions. Still, she wouldn't get out of the truck … that rasping tongue had unnerved her. Philip seemed perfectly capable of handling the task on his own and she supposed that he always had, before her arrival. Unless Pat had been his trucking mate.

The task completed, he clambered back in beside her. 'Scared, eh?'

'I'm still recovering from being slavered by a cow. Horrible. Ugh.' She shuddered at the memory.

He laughed. 'We'd better get back. You can wash it off in the pool later.'

'Oh my God. Another chance for you to check out the size of my behind?'

This time he roared with laughter. 'As I said yesterday, there's nothing wrong in that department. You amaze me, actually.'

'I do?'

'You show every sign of being an active person, but your chosen occupation is so sedentary. I gather you huddle for hours over your computer screen and you must do the same in libraries, peering at their screens and reading reference books. With that lifestyle, you should be as wide as you're tall.' He spread his arms wide and almost clipped her on the chin.

Instinctively she recoiled, then laughed. 'I watch what I eat. And I do a lot of walking.'

His jaw dropped. 'What? Here too? At the farm?'

'Not yet. I will, though.' She *should* be walking, walking away from him. He was far too attractive, and she risked falling for a man out of her league.

They relaxed in the pool, same as yesterday afternoon. Surreptitiously, she pinched herself. She'd somehow stumbled into a little corner of paradise.

The sound of a car door slamming alerted them to the arrival of a visitor, clearly someone familiar with the setup as footsteps pounded along the front verandah towards them. Pat appeared around the corner. Hannah's jaw tensed and her mouth turned down at the corners. Paradise lost.

The expression on Pat's flushed face hardened at the sight of Hannah lazing in the pool with Philip.

He called across to Pat. 'What've you been doing? Running a marathon in this heat?'

She reached the pool gate and glared at him. 'Been down in the paddock, rescuing a calf bogged in that dam that's drying up,' she replied crossly. She clicked open the gate, walked in and plonked herself on one of the poolside chairs. 'The mud's very thick. I must get that dam cleared out soon.'

'You should've asked me to help.' He oozed sympathy.

'Just as well I didn't. I can see that you're busy.' She couldn't be mollified. She stood up again, as if to leave.

'Now, now, Pat, no need for sarcasm. You look like you need a drink. The usual?'

Philip didn't wait for her answer. He hauled himself out of the pool, the water sluicing off his broad shoulders and chest and streaming down his strong thighs. Hannah found the sight as mesmerising as yesterday and tried not to stare. Pat had no such qualms. She ogled him.

He grabbed a towel and tied it round his waist. 'What

will you have, Hannah? Sorry, I should have asked you earlier.'

'A tonic water if you have it, thanks.' She turned and breaststroked lazily to the other end of the pool, away from Pat, now standing on the edge and glaring at her.

Within minutes, Philip emerged from the house bearing a tray with two cans of beer and a tall glass of tonic water over ice cubes. Hannah sat on the step at the shallow end of the pool and he handed down her drink.

He sat with Pat on the pool deck, under the shade of the large umbrella. They popped their cans and took a swig. He surveyed his sweating, cross companion. 'Pat, when you've had your beer, go home and get into your swimmers. You look like you desperately need to cool off.' It was a well-meant command.

'I do, and I will. Thanks, Philip.' She gulped down the last few mouthfuls. 'Back in a mo.' She almost skipped off to her car.

*Oh no ... now I'm going to be shown up against Pat's voluptuous figure.* Trying to take her mind off the scene to come, Hannah swizzled the ice blocks in her glass more vigorously than good manners allowed.

Philip glanced down at her. 'Something bothering you, Hannah?' he asked, his face the picture of childish innocence.

So he'd set up this parade of flesh on purpose. She wouldn't give him the satisfaction of admitting her discomfort. 'Just trying to make my ice melt faster.' She spoke deadpan and aimed to keep an innocent expression on her face.

Sure enough, Pat returned looking as if she'd just

stepped out of an advertisement for swimwear, happy to show off her wares. Almost gloating in her confidence that she outshone her competition, Pat took a graceful dive into the deep end of the pool, scarcely making a splash. Philip watched with undisguised interest. A nasty little green-eyed monster reared up at Hannah and she clenched her teeth.

Pat surfaced as sleekly as any Olympic swimmer would, her sun-bleached hair hanging like a curtain down past her shoulders, and peeked to ensure that Philip had been watching. Like the cat licking its cream, once she saw him paying full attention, she smoothed down her hair to remove the excess water, slowly and sensuously.

Hannah fumed. Pat was definitely performing for him. And he was enjoying the show.

Hannah gritted her teeth and acknowledged skills, not looks. 'We're miles from the sea, Pat. Where did you learn to be such a water baby?' She tried to sound friendly, chatty.

'Our place has a frontage to the river. We played there as kids, swinging from overhanging branches and diving off logs. We had great fun then. This is heaps better.' The broad sweep of Pat's hands encompassed the pool, and Philip too, as she playfully flicked droplets of water at him.

Hannah wanted to prick Pat's bubble by removing her from centre stage, so she reverted to her role as country ignoramus and turned to Philip. 'I suppose you have to be mindful about the water in this pool. No dive-bombing.'

He replied, 'You're right. We lose enough water from the pool as it is, through evaporation. Too much hot air.'

Did a flicker of humour light in his eyes, prompted by the game being played by the two women? Hannah wasn't sure.

'Speaking of hot air, I'm still parched. I'll get us another round of drinks. Same again, everyone?' No-one objected and he disappeared back inside the house.

Pat climbed out of the pool, collected a short pole and a round tray lying on the ground near the loungers, and carried both objects back to the pool. She pushed the pole into a slot on the floor of the pool at the shallow end, clipped the tray on top and, hey presto, a handy table resulted, somewhere to put their drinks while all three lazed in the refreshing water.

Pat may have been keen to show that she knew her way around Philip's lifestyle, but Hannah chose not to "ooh and aah" at the ingenious table set up. She preferred that Pat think she'd sampled this arrangement already. She decided to change the subject altogether, having pondered the matter of splashing, evaporation, no rain and her own limited stocks of water for cooking and showering. When the man of the house returned and deposited the drinks on the table, she splashed at the water in the pool and asked him, 'Where did all this water come from, anyway?'

'At the start, I used the fresh water from those tanks up there.' He pointed to the corrugated iron tanks catching the rainwater off the roof of the sheds. 'Now that you're in residence, I top up from my own supply. It's much bigger anyhow, and I don't want you to run out of water.'

'Do you remember the day those tanks went in, Philip?' Pat was ever-ready to mark out her territory and claim ownership of his past.

'How could I forget?' He heaved a great sigh.

'What happened?' Hannah's genuine curiosity overrode

her unwillingness to let Pat maintain control of their conversation.

Pat rushed to explain. 'The truck rolled up carrying the two four-thousand-gallon water tanks. The tanks were deposited on site, but not tied down. The plumbers were due next day but a violent windstorm came up overnight and recreated the tornado scene in the Wizard of Oz.'

'Uh oh!'

'Yep, the tanks had no water in them to weigh them down,' he added. 'Pat rang me in Melbourne to tell me that one of my tanks had rolled right down the hill and was flapping alarmingly against our shared boundary fence. The other was rolling on its side, backwards and forwards around the shed paddock, out of control.'

'No longer safely moored on those beautiful tank stands Philip built.' Pat batted her eyes at him. Her fawning was sickening.

'I had to rush up here in the middle of the night to anchor the tanks. It was winter, and bloody freezing.' He returned his neighbour's admiration. 'Couldn't have done without you that night. You were great. Go on. You tell the story.'

Pat tossed back her hair and gave a self-satisfied smirk, clearly loving this chance to stake further claim over Philip. 'I had a torch and ropes, but the tanks were too bulky, too heavy and too dangerous for me to manage on my own. Even with Philip's muscle-power, it turned out to be a big job.' She tilted her head back to gulp down some beer, and turned to Hannah. 'We ran ropes over the one that had finally impaled itself on my fence and anchored the ropes to star posts driven into the paddock. Like you would for a circus tent.' Pat's tone seemed patronising.

Hannah finger-impatiently tapped her glass. Did Pat regard her as stupid? 'What about the other tank?'

'Philip slid open the double doors to his big shed and somehow, between wind gusts, we rolled and manhandled that other tank inside, out of the wind.'

'Incredible. I suppose the tanks suffered a lot of damage.' She looked to Philip for her answer.

He nodded. 'They were holed and dented and had to be taken away and rebuilt. When they were delivered the second time, the tank builder tied them down, as he should have done to begin with.'

'I saw the second lot of tanks arrive and I came up here to lay down the law.' Pat leaned against him, as if she owned him.

'You did, Pat. I don't know what I'd do without you.' He gave Pat a brief hug around the shoulders before wriggling away a little to restore his personal space.

Totally excluded from their camaraderie, Hannah listened quietly.

'Not long afterwards, another disaster struck.' Philip chuckled, ruefully. 'All genuinely *Australian* farms, or so I thought, support their water tanks on wooden tank stands. I built some. My pride and joy.'

'I tried to warn him.' Pat smirked as she waved her can of beer at him.

'Of course, I didn't listen. I do now. Thanks Pat.' She looked gratified as he clinked his can against hers, in appreciation, before he continued. 'That tank man could have warned me too, but he chose not to. He was the type who liked to see city-slickers fail at country life. It gives them the big-man sense of superiority.'

That piqued Hannah's boundless curiosity. 'Fail? What do you mean?'

'Just that. Have things go wrong. Waste money. Give up.'

A mean spirit generated by an inferiority complex? She knew something about men like that! She wrinkled her forehead. 'So what happened?'

'Maybe I used the wrong timbers, or not enough timber, who knows, but as the tanks filled with each shower of rain, the weight on those stands increased and the supports sank further into the ground. Some struck rock and some kept sinking. Not my finest hour as a builder.' His eyes glimmered with humour as he gave a wry laugh.

*His self-derision appeals to me. I don't like men who brag.*

He tilted his head back and drained his can of beer. 'Eventually, the load spread unevenly, and one support cracked, triggering a chain reaction. In the end, both tanks tilted alarmingly and were very dangerous.'

She raised an eyebrow. 'Dangerous? I don't understand.'

'It's bad enough when empty tanks roll around. A tank containing water and snowballing down the hill would have been a deadly missile heading Pat's way.'

Philip and Pat exchanged looks which spoke volumes for his concern for her.

'That's when I emptied them, draining them with long hoses into this pool, which was new and had barely begun to fill. Then I called on a few mates from Melbourne and we carefully manoeuvred them back into the sheds ... the sheds are very large, as you know.'

Hannah nodded.

'I had the concrete slab built, re-sited the tanks on the slab and I've had no problems since.' Water cascaded from his thumbs up sign.

'So now I know the story of my water supply. Fas-cin-a-ting.' Hannah dragged out every syllable of the word to indicate that she might think the opposite. *Even my showering water is yet another way for Pat to Lord it over me.*

Pat seemed oblivious to the implied message. 'It's also the story of how Philip has well and truly succeeded as a farmer. He's had the last laugh.' She leaned across and patted him on the shoulder in her proprietorial fashion.

'They're the best kind.' Hannah decided the time had come to excuse herself and leave them to their mutual admiration society. She stood up and stepped out of the pool onto the deck. 'I've had enough sun for one day. Think I'll head indoors.' She wound her towel around her torso. 'Are you right with these things, Philip?' She pointed down to the empty cans and glasses on the pool table. Politeness dictated that she not leave without making the offer.

'I'll help him clear away.' Pat's quick volunteering made it obvious she couldn't wait for her rival to leave.

Hannah managed to arrange her face into her smarmiest expression of thanks for Pat's benefit. Addressing Philip, she said. 'Then I'll see you next weekend. Have a good week.' She did her best to sound offhand and cheery.

His face flushed. 'Oh! Forgot to mention. Got things on in town next weekend.'

Dismay overwhelmed her. Things on? Did they include Pat? That relationship puzzled her. If he lusted after Pat, as distinct from normal male ogling, he never gave any indication of it in public.

Casually he added, 'See you in a couple of weeks.'

As she fumbled with the knob on the pool gate he called out, 'I'll give you a ring before then.'

She hoped his promise to call meant he'd interpreted her dismay as anxiety about managing the farm alone for two weeks. Having no plans to fall for another man so soon after the Alex debacle, her own slightly jealous reactions today caught her by surprise. She hoped he hadn't noticed any giveaway signs on her part.

She retreated to her study and tried not to notice the bursts of laughter coming from the pool, or the unusual lateness of the hour when Philip eventually drove off to Melbourne and Pat headed down the road towards her house.

## CHAPTER TEN

The following week dragged. News of market festivities in the main street attracted Hannah into town on Saturday. Festivities included a programme of public entertainment. A few singer-songwriters sang their latest songs from a makeshift stage set up on the back of their ute. It surprised Hannah that the local residents seemed to have a tin ear and didn't congregate to listen. The most effective drawcard was a skipping performance by a team of primary school children. A demonstration of the skills they'd acquired in a school holiday camp guaranteed that their parents and siblings would come to watch. Hannah marvelled at a display of fitness second to none by these children. They were a miracle in action and so well drilled, their moves with the ropes were as spectacular as any magician's tricks.

These hidden dimensions to life in a small country town propelled Hannah into a pleasant daydream. She imagined living here permanently, having her own children, with them experiencing this same sense of security within their community. Her children would be full of *joie de vivre* like these kids. And she'd be standing here with their dad beside her, sharing a moment of parental pride. Reality forced its presence into her thoughts. Dad? Who'd be their dad? The obvious answer? Philip, of course.

She berated herself: Damn that man, he's arousing in me that renowned instinctive female desire to attract the best possible mate.

Pat appeared at her side. 'Not bad are they, those kids.'

Pat seemed incapable of "hello, how are you?" and Hannah wondered if she'd ever become used to it. Two could play at that game. 'I wish I was as aerobically fit as they are.'

'Too much sitting at that computer of yours? Makes for a very dull life. A very dull person.' Pat tossed her blonde hair defiantly.

*My God, this woman certainly calls a spade a shovel.* 'Each to her own, Pat. I like to travel the world in my imagination.'

Pat snorted. 'Travelling it for real is better.'

Hannah ignored the barb. She'd never been one for one-upmanship, so declined to elaborate on the extent of her own overseas travels. She remained silent.

'Has Philip rung you yet?' Pat asked.

Hannah wondered … did Pat genuinely want to know, or just test out the level of Hannah's connection with Philip? Was she about to gloat over having a superior connection with the man?

'No, but he said he'd ring, so I expect to hear from him

over this weekend.' She added the last bit on purpose, as Pat's proprietorial attitude annoyed her.

'He rang me last night.' Pat's triumphant tone reminded Hannah of the children she sometimes heard saying to each other "My dog's bigger than your dog".

'I hope you gave him a favourable report on my progress as caretaker.' Hannah's bland statement hid a stab of disappointment that he hadn't yet rung her.

'No, you weren't mentioned.' Pat definitely went for the jugular!

Right, so that put her in her place. It did hurt a little, to be forgotten.

'He did ask about the cattle. He's worried about whether they're getting enough to eat.'

She'd wondered about that herself. 'Are they?' she asked. They'd been so anxious to tuck into that hay last weekend.

'I told him they'll survive for a bit longer,' Pat said.

'So I don't have to do anything right now.' Relieved, she let out the breath she'd been holding.

'You? Of course not. What would you know about it?' The reply was full of disdain.

Even with Pat, she had to concede that point. 'Exactly.'

'I reminded him it's not a bad thing for the pregnant mothers to cut back on their food at this stage. They'll have less trouble when they calve.' She waved at one of the skipping team before adding, 'The main concern is their water supply. The dams are getting low and those cows are still feeding their existing calves, who turn more to their mothers' milk as the pasture diminishes.'

Hannah frowned. 'I can't do much about the water.'

'Don't worry. Philip will handle it. He always does. For a

Collins Street farmer, he's doing well, much to the surprise of the locals.'

A chunky man of average height, in his late thirties, wearing the local uniform of an Akubra, a chambray shirt with the sleeves rolled to his elbows, old blue jeans and dusty boots stopped beside them. 'G'day, Pat.' His strong, tanned arms, weather-beaten face and gravelly voice completed the rough and tough image of a man who worked outdoors for a living. He placed an arm around Pat's shoulders, as if he had every right to do so, and gave her a squeeze.

She looked less than thrilled to see him and wriggled out of his grasp. 'Horace! I didn't expect to see you here. Thought you were busy on that big vineyard job.'

'Got today off. Hoped I might catch you. You been avoiding me?'

'Don't be silly. Why would I do that?' She lowered her eyes and shuffled her feet, as if guiltily embarrassed at his question.

His slow grin widened. 'Now you're so palsy-walsy with your fancy neighbour, I suspect I don't quite measure up.' Her quick disgusted snort signalled her impatience with this comment and he changed tack. 'Who's your friend, anyhow?' Horace tilted his head towards Hannah.

'This is Philip's new caretaker, Hannah … er …'

'Stockton,' said Hannah helpfully.

'You don't say,' he drawled. His eyebrows rose slightly, as if in disbelief.

'She's that historian I mentioned, come to join us country bumpkins. Does a lot of family history.'

Horace chortled. 'A family historian! Working for Philip!

Unreal!' Pat saw whatever joke he intended, and she sniggered too. 'Come on Horace, since you're not on duty, let's have a drink at the pub and get something to eat. It's nearly lunch time.' They strode off together without a backward glance at Hannah.

Hannah sought solace at her favourite café, ordering a latte and burying her nose in a book. These country types were beyond her understanding.

A man's voice interrupted her at a crucial point in her story. 'Mind if I join you?'

Slightly irritated, she looked up, then relaxed when she recognised Bill Brownlow, the friendly grey-haired man from the art show. 'Not at all. It'll be good to have your company.'

He pulled out the chair opposite her and sat down.

'Coffee?' she asked.

'No thanks. I'm meeting my wife at a rival establishment in a few minutes. I prefer this café, but it's important to keep the wife happy.' His mouth curled and humour danced in his eyes. 'I happened to see you through the window and thought I'd say hello. I wanted to explain that I haven't called you because we aren't meeting until next month.'

'No need to apologise. I'm still finding my feet.' At least this man had some manners and thought of others.

'You seem to have landed *on* your feet, living at Philip Boulton's place,' he replied wryly.

She had to agree. 'It *is* pretty special.'

'Most of us have never been invited there, of course.'

Was he being wistful, or snaky? She hastened to defend the man who'd given her the chance to escape Alex. 'He doesn't seem to be there that much himself. I guess that's why he wanted a caretaker.'

'Don't get me wrong. Despite that exchange about history at the art show, most of us think he's a good bloke. He gives something back to the town. He supports the local economy … buys locally, uses local workers, supports the raffles and the art show, that kind of thing.' He looked around with interest. 'He's not here today?'

'No. Should he be?'

'We usually see him around town on Saturdays. He often has lunch in here, as it happens.'

'By himself?'

Bill gave her a speculative look.

*Does he think I'm being nosey? Or does he need a moment to review Philip's habits?*

Eventually he replied, 'Lately, yes, come to think of it.'

So, Philip isn't an item with Pat … or anyone else. She felt so much better.

Bill elaborated. 'Last year was different. People got to know him as a regular in this café. It became his local office. Just like I did with you, they often sat down and had a yarn with him. He helped where he could, with ideas or contacts. As a matter of fact, he did a lot to help get the Men's Shed set up. He helped that committee by writing the business plan that encouraged some corporate support.'

'So he's been a model citizen then, although I gathered at the art show that he hasn't had much to do with your group.'

Bill laughed. 'Probably we're too boring. And, we meet during the week when he's not here. If you're involved, he might take more interest.' His eyes twinkled as he stood to leave.

Hannah looked at him, amused at his comment. 'In your dreams, Bill,' she quipped. 'Family stuff's not his scene, I've discovered. See you soon.'

The strident screeching of the cockatoos drove her mad as the shadows lengthened at day's end. As pets in large cages down in Melbourne's suburbia, they may be intelligent and amusing and even learn to mimic their owners with simple words but, out here, they were completely over the top. Their penetrating calls, anything but melodious, pierced her ears.

Flocks of these brilliant white parrots had wheeled overhead and descended on the farm in the last few days, screeching, cawing and squealing. They'd selected an old dead gum in Pat's adjacent paddock as their favourite perch, where dozens of them jostled for the best position on each branch, making a hell of a racket as they did so. As she watched their antics from her front door, Hannah realised that these stocky birds, en masse, had probably been responsible in the past for killing that tree with their destructive beaks.

In general, she liked birds. She preferred creatures that soared freely, seeing everything, rather than creatures of the slithering or scuttling variety, but she made an exception of these raucous visitors.

Hannah hoped the unwelcome orchestra would soon move on to their overnight roost, as the cacophony added to her sense of being decidedly out-of-sorts and out of her element. Ten days had passed since Philip's last visit. To give him his due, he'd rung as promised, but he'd been busy and the conversation had been brief. He'd given her instructions to open the gates into the largest paddock so that the cattle had more grazing options and a fresh dam to drink from. Water would keep them alive even with grass in short supply. He didn't mention the "things on" keeping him in town.

With the realities of a solitary life on the farm beginning to take hold, the lure of the distant city strengthened. She needed to revisit her old life for a day. Tomorrow she'd spend some precious time in the State Library, following up on some research leads. The internet was invaluable, but only up to a point.

***

Her resident parking sticker remained valid, so she parked her car in her old street. Almost immediately, she bumped into Martin walking his dog.

'Well, well, well, what have we here?' he asked. 'You've only been gone three or four weeks, and you're back already. Good to see you.' He enveloped her in a bear hug.

'Martin! How are you?'

'All the better for seeing you.' He sounded very upbeat. Then a shadow fell across his face. 'I need to tell you something … Alex has been trying find out where you live. I'm glad I have no idea, except the state of your car tells me that you've been driving along some very dusty roads.'

'Yes, I have. Quick. Tell me more about Alex.'

'That bloke's an arse-hole. Whatever did you see in him, Hannah?'

A judicious silence should answer that particular question, so she asked one of her own. 'What's he been up to?'

'Let's go for a coffee up the road and I'll tell you all about it. Got time?'

'Sure. A few minutes. I'm heading off to the Library for the day.'

'Ah, your second home.' Martin touched her shoulder affectionately.

In the local café, as she sipped her latte and he toyed with his flat white, he took up where he'd left off. 'In effect, Alex doesn't believe that you've done a runner. He keeps turning up, knocking on my door, asking where you are, as if I've secreted you away in a safe-house somewhere. He won't take no for an answer.'

'I don't like the sound of that.'

'I reckon he's a nutcase. You shouldn't come back here again in a hurry. You might bump into him and he'd probably follow you. He always comes in his car.'

'Then I was right to keep my new address a secret, even from you.'

'Absolutely.' He gave her a cheeky little boy look. 'Of course, I could dampen his ardour by making out that you and me are an item now.'

Hannah leaned across the table to give him an affectionate pat. 'Oh Martin, we've been best friends forever. That wouldn't convince him.'

'Why not? Lots of best friends develop into ...' He trailed off at her obvious lack of enthusiasm.

Lovers? Hannah's thoughts zoomed straight to Philip.

Now that she knew a man like him existed in the world, her chances of becoming attracted to someone like Martin—always doubtful—had fallen to zero. Martin was a dear friend, sweet really, but a pussycat by comparison with Philip. And as for Alex? How could she have *ever* accepted him as a lover? Her skin crawled with repulsion as she recalled his selfish ways in the bedroom.

She refocussed her attention on her helpful neighbour. 'That's very gallant of you, Martin, but you know you'd be asking for trouble. A punch up at your front door, at the very least. I think my way is best. Alex'll get tired of a phantom girlfriend after a while and find himself a new victim. Meanwhile, I'll take your advice and park elsewhere from now on.'

She stood and bent over to give Martin a peck on the cheek. 'Thanks, but gotta go. I've a lot to do today.'

With Martin, she'd projected every appearance of being unperturbed at his news, but inside she'd been spooked at the thought of Alex after her. On her tram journey to the Library, she mulled over her situation.

What if Alex somehow found out where she lived? Doubtless they had some friend of a friend of a friend in common, maybe even one of the attendees at that art exhibition, where everyone had been mighty interested in her and her connection with Philip. What if Alex had reported her as a missing person? The police would find her in an instant. They had their ways.

She relaxed for a minute, remembering that all her mail

went to her long-term post box and she'd seen no need to fill in any change of address records. This was a sabbatical, in effect, and she fully intended returning to live in Melbourne by the end of the year. Meanwhile it would have to be pure coincidence for her to bump into Alex at her post office. He wouldn't waste time hanging around there all day, day after day, on the off-chance that she'd turn up to collect her mail.

The tram rattled along and she calmed down, until she realised that her phone records would be in her name at her new address. She must ask Philip about this a.s.a.p. Had he registered the change for billing purposes?

There wasn't much she could do about Alex right now, so when the tram delivered her to the Melbourne Central stop, she put her worries aside. She turned her mind to enjoying the ambience and resources of one of the world's great libraries.

Her day there turned into a marathon effort and she didn't return to her car until after seven thirty. Summer evenings were long, but today not long enough. She was only part way home, stressing about being late to feed Alley, when the growing dusk forced her to switch on her head-lights. *Damn.* The thought of finding her way round the farm in the darkness, with just her torch to light the way, scared her. The fear of a bogey man in her childhood had always been powerful. Now that fear resurfaced in the shape of Alex. It terrified her to think that she might confront him at the farm.

Distracted by these worries, she forgot to give her full attention to the road. Four kangaroos appeared in her field of vision, by the left-hand side of the road, probably grazing on the sweet grass growing luxuriantly in the moisture run-off from the bitumen tarmac. She bit her lip. With so much roadkill as evidence, how could she have forgotten this classic hour of the day for wildlife to be on the move, looking for dinner? She snatched her foot back off the accelerator and prayed that the animals wouldn't be so dazzled and startled by her headlights that they would jump into her path.

At the last moment, one did jump towards the road and she swerved to avoid the impact, fighting to keep control of the car, while giving silent thanks for the absence of traffic approaching from the opposite direction. She tipped the animal with her side-vision mirror but otherwise managed to avoid harming either it or her car. Her heart pounded as she released her withdrawn breath. *Phew. I'm getting the hang of this country driving business. Disaster averted. That kangaroo could have bounced off the front of the car and come straight at me through my windscreen.* She willed her heart to slow down and relaxed her vice-like grip on the steering wheel, remaining hyper-vigilant for the rest of her drive.

The skittishness of those kangaroos had nothing on her jumpy nerves when she reached her destination. Needing to feed Alley, she parked near the ute and looked anxiously about for signs of intruders before getting out of the car. Something flew at her out of the darkness and her heart rate picked up again until a fur ball rubbed her ankles. Thank God, it was Alley. His presence and needs calmed her, but she didn't feel safe until she'd made her way by torchlight past the pool to her door and into the sanctuary of her home.

Home. How true. She loved being in this space, with the spirit of Philip all around. She'd passed another milestone today. She'd faced up to her fears—Alex, being alone in the country at night, even the challenge of night driving. She'd survived. That country road had brought her home to a place where she felt she belonged.

CHAPTER ELEVEN

Hannah knew not to expect Philip today. He'd telephoned last Monday with news of his obligation to attend a weekend retreat for work, one of those "group hug" sessions for senior executives, being held at a luxury resort down on the Bay. He hoped to get away in time to make a flying visit to the farm on Sunday.

She anxiously wished he could be here right now. The weather made her uneasy. Something in the atmosphere didn't feel right. The beginnings of the extraordinary temperatures, the low humidity levels and the high winds forecast for today could already be sensed.

The whole state was on high alert for bushfires. Everyone had been warned to fear the day that lay ahead, to prepare themselves and their properties, to stay hydrated, to seek shelter from the sun and wind. The authorities had advised everyone living in a high-risk area to "leave early". That advice didn't apply to her, as *Wallumatta Farm* lay far from the huge forested area close to Melbourne.

She stood on her balcony and sniffed the air for the

distinctive smell of bushfire smoke. Anyone who'd grown up in Australia knew what a burning eucalypt smelled like. Better to be sure, not sorry. All clear. So far. She squinted through the glare towards the paddocks. Proof that animals needed shade was never more evident than today. Normally, this early in the morning, the cows would be scattered across the hillside, quietly grazing, their half-grown calves trailing in the rear. Today all lay hunkered down under any patch of shade they could find.

She stared at the pool, remembering Philip's words on the day he'd hired her. She'd had no fire training since and didn't know what she'd do if fire struck here, other than jumping into the in-ground pool to save herself. The pool had enough cleared space around it to suppose she could survive there while any passing fire front moved onwards.

She guessed today to be "situation normal" for Philip. The farm had always been exposed to fire risk in his absence. It would have to stay like that until he turned up tomorrow, when she would insist on a practice run operating the gener-ator and the fire pump. She retreated indoors into her hot box to drink more water.

***

The day got scarier and scarier. The temperature reached 46 degrees Celsius. The scorching wind blew at 100 kph from the outback deserts far to the northwest of Melbourne, sucking all humidity from the air. Even the flaring of a match might start an inferno. It seemed that the air itself could catch fire. Inside the stifling bungalow, she paced up and down, peering through the windows for signs of smoke, occasionally going outside to sniff the air.

Then came the Armageddon news via the ABC's emergency radio broadcasts. Fire. Fire disaster could strike in a range of ways. A lightning strike. A fire bug. A discarded cigarette butt. Today, the spark from a fallen power line generated the inferno.

A few strands of dried out grass had caught fire. The fierce wind caught the flame. Off it raced, across dried-out paddocks and the multi-lane Hume Freeway into the huge forested area north and east of Melbourne.

Soon she could see the evidence. The wind's direction took the massive fire on a trajectory well away from her but, from her balcony, she stared at the billowing smoke, black with carbon particles, turning day into night between *Wallumatta Farm* and Melbourne.

Hannah watched the television coverage of the fire racing up a hill, faster than anyone could outrun it. Flames leaping hundreds of feet into the air. The sky blacker than midnight. It stirred a primeval fear in her. She whispered to herself, 'Those poor people.' *Those poor animals too. Thank God I'm safe. Unless the wind changes to a southerly.*

Terrifying news filtered through from shocked water-bombing pilots and brave fire-fighters on the ground, news of a fire to end all fires devouring the countryside surrounding Melbourne. It burned so hot that anyone caught in the full fury of its path turned to ash. Glass melted. Roadways liquefied. Dozens of people burned to death in their cars. Native forests with resident wildlife, all incinerated. Hundreds of homes now piles of smoking ash and rubble. Whole towns gone. The full death toll of residents still unknown. Major highways closed. Every news broadcast brought worse news than the last.

She craved Philip's confident, competent presence. When he was around all felt right with the world, even a world as terrifying as this.

At 10pm a call came through. 'Hannah Stockton?'

'Yes, speaking.'

The person identified herself as calling from the local hospital.

'Hospital? Who—?' It was the last place she expected or needed to hear from.

'Philip Boulton has been admitted after being caught in the fires. He's asking for you.'

Fear engulfed her, worse than the hottest flames could generate. Hannah dropped everything and hurtled into town. *Philip needs me.*

She rushed to his bedside. It shocked her to see Philip lying motionless in his hospital cot, an oxygen mask over his mouth and nose. An intravenous drip fed liquid into his left arm. Her breath caught at the sight of this big, strong, virile man looking so vulnerable. Her racing heart slowed as her realisation grew that only his hands were bandaged. His upper body, shirtless, appeared intact and not swathed in bandages covering burns, as she'd feared. A white hospital blanket covered the rest of him without needing a cage to keep its weight off any injuries. His face looked no worse than a severe case of sunburn. His bloodshot eyes oozed liquid from their red rims. His eyebrows and eyelashes had disappeared.

His weeping eyes signalled his relief that she'd come. She longed to kiss him, out of pure relief that he was alive. Just in time she remembered her caretaker status and stopped herself. Instead she pressed a panicked hand on his right arm and blurted out, 'Thank God you're okay.' The pressure of her fingers on his arm increased with her agitation. 'Why, Philip, why? Why were you on the road today? You said you'd be down by the Bay.'

'Heard the news that an out-of-control fire had started north-west of here.' His muffled voice was gravelly, and he coughed into his oxygen mask. 'I was coming to be with you.'

*With me? Me?* Her eyes widened at his words and she gripped his arm even tighter. She gasped. 'Philip, it's so dangerous to drive through a fire zone.'

'I wanted to make sure you were okay,' he choked out.

*He cares about me? He cares about … me?*

'To help you defend the property if necessary.' His concern showed in his eyes, the extra stress forcing out drops of liquid. He dabbed them away with a bandaged hand.

'You could have died on that road,' she whispered. 'You could have died.' She dragged the visitor's chair over and sat down as close to him as possible. Desperate to show she cared, she returned her hand to his drip-free arm and began stroking it gently.

'I realise that now.' He groaned. 'I nearly did.' His voice faded into a hoarse whisper. 'The road from Melbourne wasn't an active fire zone when I left town. Had no idea that bushfires could travel so fast.'

She continued stroking his arm. 'No-one did. That wind! The fire raced like a bullet train.'

He shuddered. 'It bloody terrified me, even though I escaped the main path of the fire. Being on the fringes was bad enough, and I had shelter, of sorts.' He coughed with the effort of talking.

'Shelter? Where?' Her jaw dropped.

'My car! Luckily, I'd just picked up some dry cleaning, including a woollen blanket, and I had it in the car.' He coughed again and spluttered. 'I hid under it inside the car, as protection from the radiant heat.'

She stared at him and gulped. 'You mean the fire passed over you in the car.'

'Yep. That blanket was my saviour.' As if the meaning of that word had just sunk in, he stopped talking and inhaled deeply on his oxygen mask. 'No serious burns to speak of. Just my hands, contact burns. See.' He held up his bandaged hands for her closer inspection. 'It all happened quickly. After the fire front passed over, I managed to get out of the car and tried to clear some burning debris away from it.' He stopped talking for a minute to catch his breath. 'No luck. The firestorm had blown a lot of burning bark and red-hot cinders against my wheels and underneath the car. The fire took hold and the car's a wreck.' His voice faded into a wheeze.

She continued massaging his upper arm to indicate her relief and sympathy. 'So who rescued you?'

'I'd parked the car in a small clearing beside the highway when I saw the fire approaching. Afterwards, I walked out into the middle of the road, well clear of the burning car, with my blanket shield draped round me.' The stress of his memories seemed to exacerbate his shortness of breath and prompted more coughing. 'Dozens of CFA blokes were out and about. A CFA truck came along, stopped and brought me here.'

'Thank God for this town having a hospital.' Relief flooded through her.

The nurse hovering nearby and eavesdropping said, 'It's because we're surrounded by dangerous roads. We take road trauma in our stride. We're old hands at calling up the air ambulance.'

'I've noticed the helipad across the road,' said Hannah.

'Philip's a lucky man. We could treat him here. Anyone suffering serious burns today, anyone who actually survived those burns that is, has been choppered to the burns units in Melbourne.'

'I'm lucky all right,' Philip murmured. 'I saw hell today. I'm scorched a bit, that's all. My main problem is smoke inhalation.' He coughed again.

The nurse lifted his mask gently, held a tissue to his leaking nose and scolded him. 'That's enough talking.' She replaced the mask and turned to Hannah. 'Aside from all the toxic gases and fine particles of soot and ash he likely inhaled, we're monitoring him in case he has serious airway burns. That superheated air does a lot of damage if it's sucked into your lungs.'

Hannah recalled several episodes of windburn she'd suffered, affecting only her skin, a minor irritation by comparison. This damage to his respiratory tract had to be so much worse. How long would he take to recover? Who would look after him if he needed ongoing care? 'Should I call anyone for you? Your family?'

'No. No.' Another bout of coughing shook him. He shuddered and closed his eyes.

'Haven't you worked it out yet, he doesn't *do* family.' Pat charged in, a picture of concern. 'Are you okay, Philip? God, I can't believe it. You actually survived that inferno.' She glared at the sight of Hannah occupying the only visitor's chair and stroking Philip's arm.

He didn't open his eyes and feigned a sudden need for rest. Hannah could have sworn that a slight twitch of his mouth betrayed an expectation that the forthcoming exchange at his bedside would amuse him. She and Pat had unwittingly entertained him poolside a few weeks ago. Then he'd engineered it. This time it was coincidental.

Pat obliged him straight away with an angry outburst directed at Hannah. 'Why are you here? Shouldn't you be at home, caretaking?' She'd so busily focussed her furious eyes on Hannah that she missed seeing the second slight quirk of Philip's mouth.

Hannah spotted it. 'Philip asked for me.' No actress could have improved on the sugary sweetness of that answer. 'Who told you what had happened?'

'The sister-in-charge is a mate of mine. *She* rang me.' With fury in her eyes, Pat glowered at Hannah.

Philip finally opened his blood-shot eyes and choked out a few words. 'Pat, thanks for coming, but there's no need to stay.' He held up his bandaged hands again, an effort which brought on more coughing as he struggled to breathe. 'See … no hands at present, but overall my fire survival story is very tame.' His watery eyes closed again as he sank back against his pillows. 'I'll be back in business soon, and you'll be teaching me more of your farming tricks.' His voice faded out with the strain of talking.

Standing by his bedside, Pat seemed gratified at that and beamed with satisfaction.

Hannah had to admire his skills as a diplomat.

'Oh, okay. As long as you're okay. I had to see with my own eyes.' Pat turned to leave. 'You coming too, Hannah?'

Philip kept his own eyes shut but croaked out 'Not yet. Hannah and I need to discuss a small business matter.'

Pat leaned down to him and dropped a light kiss on a red cheek.

*She's determined to claim him!*

His skin must have been tender from the burns, and he flinched a little.

*I'm glad I resisted the urge to kiss him. He's hurting more than he lets on.*

As Pat left, she looked daggers at Hannah.

Hannah suppressed a V for Victory sign. 'So, what's this small business matter you mentioned? We should deal with it so I can leave you to rest.' She desperately needed to switch back to caretaker mode, a much easier role than competing with Pat for his affections.

'Plenty of time for rest. Got all night for that.' His eyes flickered open again and tried to focus on her. 'I need you to contact my office and tell them what's happened.'

'At this hour?' She checked her Fitbit. 'It's eleven o'clock at night.'

'In my line of business, we're used to it. I'm booked to head overseas next week. Can't go now.' The effort of talking made him puff a little.

'That seems clear. So, what do you want me to do?'

'Can you find my mobile for me? I can't use my hands because of these bandages.' He wheezed with frustration. 'Can't see properly either, through these watery eyes. I'll tell you who to call.'

'Sure. Of course, I will.'

She rummaged in the drawer beside his bed, where the staff had placed the contents of his pockets, and grabbed the phone. 'Why didn't you want good old Pat to do this for you?' She could have kicked herself. To refer to his friend in this sarcastic manner wasn't wise.

'Because country people like to gossip. I'm hoping you'll be more discreet about the numbers you'll find in my contact list.'

He'd ignored her "good old" barb. She liked him even better for that. She opened his phone. 'Passcode?' He whispered the sequence. She tapped in the number and scrolled through the stored names, a roll call of the nation's rich and famous. 'Hmmm. I see what you mean.' *It'd be hard to keep up the pretence of being a simple country boy if news of his mates got around the district.* 'So, who should I call?'

'Steve Johnson. We work together. He'll deal with everything.'

She selected the number and pressed the call button. 'Steve Johnson? Sorry to ring so late. I'm calling on behalf of Philip Boulton.'

A startled voice boomed in her ear. 'What? Why? Where's Philip?'

'In hospital. He's been caught in those shocking fires.'

'Christ! Is he badly burned?'

'No, some burns, but they're more worried about smoke inhalation. Hold on a minute, he can tell you himself. We're in the hospital so I won't put you on speaker.' She held the phone to Philip's ear with one hand and adjusted his oxygen mask with the other, so that the transmitter would catch his faint voice.

He listened for a moment. 'No, she's not the nurse,' he said. Philip gazed at Hannah, as if contemplating what to say next. 'She's … a friend.' A pause. 'Not *that* kind of friend.'

Philip's "fine, I'm fine" seemed to suffice as reassurance to the distant Steve about his basic okayness. "Yeah mate, defer it" dealt with the overseas business trip. Philip stopped to cough and promptly held his chest, as if the movement hurt. 'Can't keep talking, Steve. Once they let me out of here, I'll need you to come up and get me.'

Hannah continued to hold the phone to Philip's ear. After a few seconds he said to Steve, 'Because I can't drive at present.' Steve's next response prompted Philip to say, 'No can do, my car's a burnt-out wreck.' After more from Steve, Philip replied impatiently, 'Then come up the Hume, they can't close that indefinitely, you'll get through that way.'

Philip's "See you mate" signalled the end of the brief phone call.

Hannah retrieved the handset and pressed the red button to end the call. Steve hadn't sounded too resourceful. 'Who's going to look after you down in Melbourne, then? You can't do much with those hands.'

'The doc says I'll be kept here for a few days, and by then my hands should be much better. The skin on my hands should recover quite quickly.'

She could barely hear him. Too much talking. Not enough oxygen. She checked that she'd put his mask back correctly after the phone call. 'Should I alert your sister? You said you have a sister in Melbourne.'

He shook his head. 'Definitely not.'

'Does she have two heads, or something?'

'She can't help.' He shifted his position in the bed and winced, as if his chest had constricted. 'She's in hospital herself.'

Hannah gulped. 'What?'

'My unfortunate fair-skinned sister does constant battle with skin cancer. She's just had a melanoma removed but she's suffering a few complications. That's where I was last weekend—with her.'

'I'm sorry. I hope she'll be alright.' She reached out to stroke his arm again.

He made eye contact and gave her a bleary smile in return. 'So do I. She's all I've got.'

This admission made for sobering thought as Hannah drove home. Did it mean his sister was his only family member? Did it mean his sister was his only confidante? It must mean he had no permanent relationship. On the upside, then, Pat didn't count. On the downside, nor did she.

Next day, at the hospital, Hannah found him much improved and mask-free. He breathed more easily, his eyes wept less and his face was more pink than red. 'The doctor says I can go home at lunch time tomorrow, after they change the dressings on my hands.' He spoke more slowly than usual and his throat sounded sore, but the husky voice it generated sounded stronger and all the signs looked positive.

'That must please you. Hospitals are good places to avoid.' After his "all I've got" comment, she kept her reply restrained, pragmatic. This man excelled at sending her emotions on a roller-coaster ride.

'Exactly. You know, I've been thinking about how to pass the time over the next few days. My eyes feel a lot better. Would you mind lending me that book of yours, the one you wrote about the early days of Melbourne?'

She'd been in the process of sinking into the visitor's chair and nearly tripped on her own feet. To date he'd been so uninterested in her work. Well, strictly speaking, it was her *family* history work that seemed to threaten him. Otherwise, he'd always shown signs of intellectual curiosity. Her caution evaporated. 'Of course. I can get it now, if you like.'

'I'd appreciate it, if you can be bothered.' He sounded genuine in his interest.

She sprang back to her feet. She'd love his feedback on her book. 'Of course. I'll be back shortly.' If she were still a child holding her mother's hand, she'd be skipping down the hospital corridor.

Half an hour later she stood again by his bedside, her book in hand. 'Here it is, but how will you turn the pages when your hands are bandaged?'

'They'll slow down my reading progress, sure, but I'll figure something out. I'll return it next time I'm up here at the farm, if that's okay.'

'Fine by me. Take your time. Is Steve collecting you from here tomorrow, to take you back to Melbourne?'

'Yes, he rang this morning and the staff gave him the

pick-up time. For obvious reasons, I won't make it up here next weekend.' He tapped his head. 'My brain's been on holiday for a few days. Nearly forgot to tell you that the gardener will turn up soon for his regular booking, but you won't need to be there, he brings all his equipment and knows what to do,' He cleared his throat as he looked at her and a worried frown creased his forehead. 'Can you continue managing by yourself?'

'I'll do my best. That's my job, after all. Caretaking.' She made an effort to look and sound relaxed and breezy, as if perfectly content with the role of caretaker, even if a closer relationship with him tempted her more as each day passed.

His keen perception might have seen through her façade. 'Thanks,' was all he said.

Somehow, she survived the next few weeks without Philip. She missed his presence at his rural property more than she dared to admit.

Now that she better understood the risks of fire, she felt obligated to stay at the farm as its protector through the rest of the peak fire season. She even swallowed her pride enough to ask Pat to show her how to start the generator and attach the fire pump. The gardener came and went, leaving neat lawns and tidy garden beds behind. All she'd had to do was say "hello" and "goodbye". Even her offers of water had been declined with a "No thanks, I bring my own supplies". Philip rang from time to time to check on her progress as caretaker, giving her the chance to enquire about his health.

The weather cooled down after the bushfires, from the

forties to the thirties, and the cattle managed to survive on their scavenging among lean pickings. Pat had taken it upon herself to monitor their status and she opened all the internal gates, giving them roaming access to every paddock. Hannah appreciated being relieved of on-farm duties. For a girl still scared of large beasts, cattle patrol didn't come naturally.

Pat called in from time to time to provide progress reports on her self-assumed responsibilities. On one such visit, she arrived dressed formally. As usual she got to the point without sociable chit chat. 'Just got back from Melbourne.'

'The trip must have been important, for you to be away for the day.' Hannah made no comment on Pat's attire, dark from head to toe.

'A family funeral.' Pat shrugged her shoulders. No tears welled.

'Oh. I'm sorry for your loss.' Hannah meant it. Losing someone always mattered, even a relative too distant to engender tears.

'My great aunt. Very old, and sick. I think she wanted to go.' Pat allocated her great aunt a few moments of silence before her face brightened 'Called in to see Philip today,' she said gleefully.

Ah, the real purpose of Pat's visit. More one-upmanship.

'So, you know where he lives?' Hannah's curiosity got the better of her, fuelled by a stab of jealousy over Pat's familiarity with Philip's private life. Except *she* hadn't known about his sister.

Pat fired back her answer. 'Yes, Albert Park. Where so many bankers live.'

Did Pat claim superior knowledge of the city too? Hannah tested her a little further. 'I take it you reckon Toorak's out of fashion.'

Pat sniffed haughtily. 'It still has its aficionados. People who like mansions. Those places are too big for someone on their own. Anyhow, these days it's hard to beat Albert Park as an address.'

Hannah's hometown was Melbourne. Of course, she knew that … but she didn't know as much as she'd like about her current employer. 'Is the right address important for Philip?'

'Of course. Undoubtedly. He likes to keep up appearances.' Pat's confidence in her view showed in her dismissive reply.

'Really? I hadn't noticed.' Hannah had never sensed a scrap of pretension in him but saw no need to challenge Pat's assertion. 'Does he look all right, do you think? He tells me he's back at work.'

'Of course he's all right. He's no wuss.'

Hannah silently agreed. If one of her friends ever found out about Philip and asked her to describe him, the first word to come to her mind would be "manly". Followed by "sexy".

CHAPTER TWELVE

Hannah arrived in Melbourne for the day, intending to attend the monthly lunchtime meeting of her writing group at the local genealogical society. The members were a lot older than her, but they had valuable experience to pass on. Before the meeting started, she'd employ her time gainfully in the society's reading room.

She alighted the tram at the intersection of Swanston and Collins Streets and as she turned into Collins Street, where the society was located, she collided head on with a familiar figure. 'Philip!' She eyed off his immaculate business attire.

'Hannah!' He eyed her off in return—her informal clothing and the laptop slung over her shoulder.

Two different worlds clashed here but, as their eyes met, Hannah disregarded external appearances. We've been through "stuff" together. He's helped me conquer my fear of cattle. I've watched him overcome the nightmare of the bushfire. She hoped that the flash of pleasure she saw in his eyes signified a meeting of like minds.

She knew he didn't expect her to spend all her time at the farm, yet she felt the need to explain. 'Don't worry, I haven't abandoned my duties. I'm just here for the day.'

He nodded. 'I'm glad I bumped into you. I've been meaning to compliment you on your book. I didn't know that a story about Melbourne's early days could be so interesting.'

She hitched her laptop higher on her shoulder, pathetically gratified by his praise. 'You read it then?' She'd been desperate for him to see her as more than his caretaker.

'Avidly. It said a lot about you, you know.' He reached for her elbow and guided her across to the side of the pavement, out of the way of other pedestrians. His unexpected touch sent a little shiver through her.

'Me?' she squeaked. She hoped he hadn't noticed her body talk.

He gave a slight chuckle. 'Yes, you.' His eyes engaged hers. 'The way you look at things. What you see as important.'

'That's an insightful response to a history book. You'll have to elaborate.' *How can I even think when he looks at me that way?*

'Sure. Do you have time for a coffee?' He pointed towards her laptop and raised an eyebrow.

'Yes, of course. My research can wait. Authors always crave feedback. And I'd like to find out how you're faring.' She glanced at his hands, now bandage-free. 'I can't see any signs of permanent damage.' She beamed her happiness and relief at him.

Just then, a pair of very forceful hands grabbed Hannah

on the upper arm in a vice-like grip. 'I knew I'd find you eventually.'

Her skin crawled at the sound of Alex's voice. She shook off his clutches and turned to confront the man she'd hoped never to see again. What she saw repelled her. He had a semblance of good looks, but he appeared manic, and slightly dishevelled. 'I don't want to be found by you, Alex. I've moved on, remember.' Her icy voice should leave him in no doubt.

'To someone new?' He glared at Philip.

For a second she watched them both. *If Alex had to find me, I'm glad it happened when I'm in the company of a man who outclasses him in every way.*

'It's no longer any of *your* business,' she replied impatiently.

'I've changed, Hannah,' he said in a whiny voice. 'Give me another chance.'

'No more chances, Alex.' She spoke firmly, as if addressing a naughty child. 'A male chauvinist like you isn't … never has been … what I'm looking for. And I'm not interested in your possessive neediness either.'

'So I see.' He sneered as he looked back at Philip. 'You won't get rid of me so easily. I'll track you down.' His sneer morphed into a threat as he stepped closer to her.

'And then you'll have me to reckon with.' Philip spoke for the first time, in a very determined voice.

'And who are you?' Alex looked ready to throw a punch.

'Never you mind.' Philip's chin jutted out and he shifted his feet into the "getting set for action" position. 'Trouble, if you come near Hannah again.'

Grateful for his intervention, Hannah hoped Philip's

aura, his *presence*, had the same intimidating effect on Alex as it had on her, that first day at *Wallumatta Farm*.

Philip stepped closer to Alex, crowding his personal space. 'You heard the lady. You're out of her life now.' He backed off immediately and turned to Hannah. 'Come on, let's go grab that coffee.' Philip put a protective arm behind her and shepherded her away from the unpleasant encounter.

They settled themselves in one of Melbourne's countless laneway cafés and placed their orders with the waitress. Philip got straight to the issue at hand. 'What's the story with that Alex bloke?'

Embarrassed, she said, 'He's my ex-boyfriend.'

'So I gathered. Why ex? What did he do, specifically I mean, apart from being a general arse-hole?'

Eyes downcast, she mumbled, 'He was violent.'

'Violent? Did he attack you?' His voice rose in anger, enough to disturb the people at the next table. Their heads turned to check out the newcomers.

Reluctantly she raised her eyes to meet his. 'Not me,' she began to explain. 'My parents.' She tried to keep her voice low. The pair next door to them lost interest.

'What?' His eyes rounded in disbelief but this time he kept his voice down. 'Why?' As if lost for words, his voice trailed off.

She sighed loudly before huddling closer to him for privacy. 'They came one day to help me with some chores. Last year, before their seachange. A few things needed fixing. Dad loves his handyman role. I'd given them a key to my flat. I wasn't even there. I had some urgent research to do at the Library, to fulfil a deadline for an article.'

'So what happened?' His concerned eyes engaged with hers.

She warmed at the thought that he cared. 'They knocked on the door as a matter of courtesy, then used the key to come inside. Alex rushed down the hall at them and tried to slam the door in their faces, disregarding my mother's arm in the way. Dad managed to push the door back open and Alex then attacked him.' Her story revived unpleasant memories and to calm herself she looked away, towards the service counter, checking on the slow progress of their coffee order.

He said nothing but sat like a Buddha, radiating calmness and serenity, waiting for her to continue.

'Although Dad's a lot older, he knows a few self-defence moves. He grabbed Alex by the hair, manhandled his head down towards the floor and eventually managed to push him out the front door and pull the bolt across. Then he took Mum out the back door and called a cab to take her to the hospital. Her arm hurt a lot. X-rays showed she had a hairline fracture.'

'Nasty. Why on earth did Alex attack your parents? I don't get it.' He leaned back in his chair and looked at her, a puzzled look on his face.

'Because they *were* my parents, that's all. He blamed them for everything that was "wrong" with me.' It sounded ridiculous, she knew, but that was Alex.

'What? Wrong with *you*? The man sounds mad.' His indignant tone said it all.

'I think he was … is. Mad with jealousy. He couldn't cope with my independent streak and lifestyle.' She shrugged and gave him the palms-up gesture. Women like her could do with some help negotiating the world of men.

'Lifestyle? Are you a stripper on sabbatical?' His eyes twinkled.

She suppressed a wry chuckle. If only. From their dips in the pool, he knew she lacked the body for that. No boob jobs lurked in her past. 'Nothing out of the ordinary … for any professional woman, that is. My job *did* involve lots of interactions with men.'

'Really? You don't show that side of yourself at the farm.' He thought for a moment. 'Even in the pool.' He grinned.

Damn it. He was right. So far, she'd been on the back foot at the farm, in her role as the student. No wonder he hadn't seen her as an alluring female, or even as a professional to be respected. She heaved another regretful sigh. 'He imagined my every business lunch as an assignation of some kind.'

'An insecure type.' Philip the good listener had returned.

'Yes, very insecure. A coward and a bully. And I was stupid not to see it right from the beginning.' Her shoulders sagged.

He shook his head. 'Don't be so hard on yourself. Most people have to learn their lessons by bitter experience.'

'You're right, and bitter's the word.' Hannah tilted on her seat, making room for the waitress who was finally placing their coffees on the table in front of them.

When the waitress had scuttled away, she continued, 'Being used to passive, compliant women, he didn't respect my needs and wishes. If I asked him to do anything, he railed against "petticoat rule".'

He picked up his coffee and took a sip, keeping his eyes on her. 'But I bet he expected you to drop everything for him.'

She nodded. 'If he said *Jump*, I was supposed to ask *How high*? He didn't get it that, beneath my docile facade, I'm quite determined. I soon got sick of it all.'

'He didn't impress me as your type of guy.'

She'd never tire of Philip's dry understatements. She quirked an eyebrow at him, but he didn't elaborate. Who *did* he see as her type of guy?

In her own mind, only one answer popped up … someone more like Philip. Alex had hated the idea of looking after anyone, the way Philip did. He looked for someone to look after *him*. He begrudged the need to nurture, resented having to share his money with anyone else and resented any time away from what he personally wanted to do. Totally selfish, he wanted his outings and weekends away to be free of encumbrances and responsibilities.

She took a sip of her own coffee. 'I agree. Not my type of guy. It was truly a case of "Sleeping with the Enemy", being with him.'

'Sleeping with the enemy? An interesting turn of phrase. It says everything.' He finished his coffee and replaced his cup on its saucer. 'I reckon sleeping with a friend is much better.' He grinned at her.

Was he joking to cheer her up? Or making a pass … at last? She couldn't resist the opportunity he'd given her. 'Is that what you do?'

'It's definitely what I prefer to do. Speaking generally, naturally.' He grinned again.

She crashed her own cup into its saucer. The man was infuriating, such a *gentlemanly* tease, always playing such a straight bat.

He got back to business. 'Were the police involved in your Alex incident?'

'Briefly. After visiting the hospital, I went home, found Alex back inside the flat and called the police.' She bit her lip and looked down, remembering a step hard to take at the time and still painful to relive.

'The cops seem to be taking domestic violence more seriously these days. Did they attend?' His words conveyed his approval of her action. She took heart.

'Yes, quite quickly too. No complaints there. They spoke to me and then went into Alex's study to speak to him. Having taken this radical step, I wanted to press charges, but they said I had no grounds. It would have to be my parents.'

Philip rubbed his chin. 'I guess that's true. He hadn't actually attacked you.'

'The police must have decided he was trouble in the making, because they did say to me 'Madam, we'll wait with you while you collect your things, and don't ever come back without police protection.'

'Scary stuff. That's awful. How horrible for you.'

'Yep. I stayed with friends for a bit, until I had him evicted from my flat. Mum eventually had him charged with assault. It got into the papers. Then a few of his previous girlfriends came out of the woodwork and complained about some violent episodes. He ended up in a whole lot more trouble. He clearly has mental problems.'

Philip started with surprise. 'Not another one.'

Puzzled, she said, 'What do you mean?'

'Nothing.' He looked uncomfortable. 'Sorry. Please continue.'

'He's managed to talk his way out of trouble with the

law. I don't know how. He must have the right mates. Personally, I see him as dangerous.'

'I agree with you one hundred percent. And that's why you came to *Wallumatta Farm*. You wanted to disappear for a while.'

'Exactly. You won't give the game away, will you?' Her eyes engaged his and silently begged for his help.

'Of course not.' He answered her plea. 'He'd better not turn up at the farm.'

Since that's exactly what she feared might happen one day, she did her best to push that fear to the back of her mind while she enjoyed what was left of her few precious moments with Philip. 'I appreciate your support.' She thanked him by reaching across the table and placing her hand on top of his to stroke it softly. 'Enough of my woes. How are you faring? Fully recovered? Your hands seem okay, judging by the way you've been juggling that coffee cup. Any lasting respiratory ailments?'

'Nope, I'm fine now. It takes a lot to keep me down. Thanks for being such a help at the farm. At the time of the fires, and since.'

'It's nothing. Pat's done a lot more than me. She's very capable.'

A pensive expression flashed across his face. 'Ah, Pat, you're right, good old Pat.' His words ended on a down note.

She noted his unusual lack of enthusiasm and spoke wryly, 'Philip, the way you say that, you could be describing my grandmother.'

His eyes widened, as if he hadn't meant it that way. Next, he winked at her. 'Then your grandmother must be hot stuff.' He looked at his watch. 'Is that the time? Gotta fly.'

Hannah's shoulders slumped. Good old Pat was hot stuff? He'd confirmed her fears. Prim and proper Hannah would never attract a hunk like Philip when easy pickings like Pat surrounded him. Out of habit, she straightened up and pasted on a happy face. 'My meeting calls me too.'

He stopped beside the counter to pay for the coffees. She walked with him to the door. Briefly he brushed her upper arm in a token sign of affection. 'Take care, Hannah. I mean it.' He turned right and she turned left, each heading for their respective meeting.

As he strode up Collins Street to his office, Philip fumed. How could Hannah get caught up with such a looney? It was always the way—good girls, bad men. He envied her too. How could she be so close to her parents, when his family caused him so much pain? He suffered another pang of regret for his smart-arse remark about Pat, whose flaunting of herself had begun to annoy him. By trying to protect himself, he was making a mess of things with Hannah.

Her growing power over his thoughts and feelings scared him. She was reeling him in with her quiet dignity. He slammed his body into the revolving door of his office building, trying to hurry the door along and force out his discomfort.

After her meeting and long hours spent at the State Library, Hannah gave up the search for information and went in search of food. Eating out would make a pleasant change from another solitary evening, cooking for one at *Wallumatta Farm*.

It was late when she left Melbourne, hopefully too late for kangaroos to be hopping crazily into her path. She hated being on this so-called "highway" at night. In the section where the raging bushfire had jumped the road, and Philip had barely escaped with his life, her headlights illuminated an artist's nightmare. For kilometre after kilometre stretched nothing but black. Black bitumen road, black road verges, charcoal covered soil, blackened tree trunks. Skeletons standing like sentinels. No branches. No foliage. Weeks after the fires a slight smoke haze still hung in the night air. The unmistakeable smell of slow-burning eucalypt stumps and logs entered the car through the air-conditioning system. She could see a red glow in a few places. With nothing flammable left to catch fire and spread, these hot spots would be left to burn themselves out.

She was relieved to reach the river valley beyond the ranges, a valley calmly settled and fenced, where the countryside was more open. Cattle country.

She was developing a fondness for cattle. They were much gentler than she'd ever imagined and, as each day passed, they spooked her less and less.

# CHAPTER THIRTEEN

For the next two weeks, the vapour trails criss-crossing the stratosphere provided daily reminders of faraway Philip, overseas on the trip postponed after the bushfire. She reminded herself, over and over, *That's why you're here. Why he needed a caretaker.* Her reasoning didn't console her. She was mournful. She missed the buzz of anticipation that brightened up her Fridays, his normal date of arrival for the weekend. She missed his irresistibly masculine ways and his cheeky grins. Somehow, he'd burrowed under her skin. Without him, loneliness took hold.

Hannah needed to find another way to inject some life and passion into her day-to-day solitary existence. This morning, with no-one living close by she threw a city dweller's caution to the winds and indulged herself with music, played at the threshold of sound. Just as it had done to Bertie in 'The King's Speech' movie, Beethoven's Symphony No 7 on max overwhelmed her senses.

She had her back to the door and was marching in time, conducting with her hands and dum-de-dum-de-dumming in tune at the top of her voice, when someone tapped her shoulder. She jumped, her heart pounding.

Just as she'd always feared, Alex had found her hideaway.

She whirled to face the intruder. He couldn't have been more welcome … Philip, back from his trip a day earlier than she'd expected, looking tired, as if he'd driven straight from Tullamarine.

'Didn't mean to frighten you,' he yelled. The happy-to-see-you expression on his face was half-apologetic. 'I couldn't make myself heard above that orchestra. How've you been?'

She resisted the urge to shout back "Missing you".

He held out his hand towards her. 'I came over to return your book.' He handed over his borrowed copy of *Batman's Battlers*. 'Great read, as I told you before.'

'Thanks.' She dumped the book and turned down the volume.

'Phew. That's better. I could hear your concert at the front gate. Beethoven's seventh.'

'My secret passion,' she confessed with a contrite glance at him. 'Loud music. It's just like being in the concert hall.'

He nodded. 'I know what you mean. It takes you into another world.'

'One you're familiar with, if you recognised the music.' It secretly thrilled her to have that interest in common with him.

'I have a quiet passion for ABC Classic FM. Glad to see that you're taking *loud* advantage of an obvious benefit of low-density living.'

'You scared me half to death, you know.' Her mild rebuke was delivered with a note of joy in her voice. 'How was your trip? What are you doing back so early?'

'Attending to some other secret passions of my own.'

He quirked an eyebrow. Hannah's heart skipped a beat. His teasing words conjured up an image she did her best to reject, that she could be a secret passion of his.

Philip soon dashed her hopes. 'Actually, I was worried about the cattle. This never-ending drought's got me worried. I've organised the drilling of a bore, as a supplement for the water going into the main dam. It's going down too fast. Cattle need a lot of water. The bore will also supplement the water supply for the garden.'

It sounded like a wise precaution to her. 'Good idea, but where?'

'On the ridge line above the dam. The drilling team will be here soon. They're coming from Gippsland. The process doesn't take long.'

'Got time for morning tea before they arrive? You look like you need it.'

'I do. Was on an overnight flight from Hong Kong. It can be hard to sleep on planes.'

'Don't I know it! Are you hungry too? I can't offer much in the way of refreshments, but can do cheese on toast.'

'That would hit the spot. The cabin crew serves breakfast ridiculously early on overnight flights.'

'I know that too. It's a pain that we're ahead with our time zone. Our body clock from that part of Asia tells us it's about 3am when you first get the whiff of omelettes and coffee.' She turned on the electric griller to warm up as she rummaged in the freezer for her packet of sliced bread and found the cheese in the fridge. 'Cheese on toast coming up.'

She bustled around with the kettle and mugs. 'So you're

drilling a bore? You continue to amaze me, you know, with the complexities of running even a small farm like this.'

'I enjoy it. It's teaching me heaps.' He yawned slightly. 'Sorry. Tired.'

'Understood.' It would help him stay awake if she kept him talking. 'What else are you planning for the farm?' *This is nice. A companionable chat.* She sliced the cheese and positioned it on the bread still hot from her toaster.

He lounged against the doorjamb and watched her. 'I've decided to make it easier to hand-feed the cattle. Can't keep up the supply with the bales alone.'

She set the slices on the pre-heated griller tray and turned to him. 'I've been worried about the cattle going hungry. I haven't done anything about the hay. Pat's told me they've been fending for themselves, but only just.'

He shifted his position to a more upright stance. 'It's early autumn now. The break should come soon, if it comes. Even assuming the rains do arrive, there'll be no natural feed available for months.' His voice sounded gloomy.

'What else can cattle eat?'

A moment later he laughed. 'I once fed mine a trailer load of carrots.'

'You're kidding me.' She almost dropped the hot tray she was trying to push under the griller.

'Nope. Plenty of carrots are grown on the Ranges between here and Melbourne, and those not meeting the size and shape specifications for the supermarkets need a home elsewhere. I decided to try a few loads. I got some strange looks, trundling through town with my trailer loads of carrots, but the cattle loved their change of diet. I bet you could've heard the sound of crunching in Melbourne.' He laughed again.

'Amazing. I guess it makes sense, when you think about it. I like a bit of crunch in my food too.' She poured the boiling water onto the tea bags. 'I know how you take your coffee. Not your tea. Milk? Sugar?'

'A little milk, thanks. No sugar.'

He took the mug from her. 'Just what I need.' He inhaled the steam as he slouched against the door post. 'The carrots were a bit of an experiment, not on the permanent menu. I've ordered some rolls of hay to be delivered next weekend.'

She crouched down to check whether the food under the griller was burning or not. *All good.* 'You mean those huge cylinders, bigger than a small car?' She'd seen many of these lined up along some of the fence lines on the road to Melbourne.

'Yep. Trouble is, I won't be here. I'll be away next weekend.' He gave her a rueful look.

Again? She knew she'd miss him. The zap of energy he mysteriously created in her began to peter out. She slumped against the kitchen bench.

'Will you tell the driver to align the rolls the same way, along my fence line in the shed paddock?' He continued talking as if he hadn't noticed the change in her demeanour. 'He'll know what to do.'

'That's no problem.' Two could play the pragmatism game. 'How will you move them after that?' Those rolls could not be hoisted around like hay bales.

'With a tractor and a fork attachment. I've got both, up in the shed. It'll be a first for me. I haven't had rolls before.'

He tilted his head to sip the last of his tea. 'I'll have to be careful. They're heavy. With so much weight behind the big back wheels they can lift the small front wheels off the ground on these hills and tip the tractor up.'

He handed her his mug and she pulled a face at him as she took it. 'I don't like the sound of that much. Even in Melbourne you hear about all the tractor accidents on farms.'

'Don't worry. I'll take it slow, slow and steady.' He drawled out the words to make his point clear.

'Good.' She pulled out the griller tray and set the grilled toast on a plate. 'Here's your snack. Want to sit down, or do you prefer to keep leaning against the door jamb?'

He stepped across and took the plate from her. 'Thanks. I'm happy to stand. If I sit, I'll crash. I struggled to stay awake at the wheel, driving up here.'

Her mouth went dry. His admission didn't bear thinking about. That tricky road from the direction of the airport promised danger, even when fully alert. 'I'm glad you made it safely.' She congratulated herself on getting so good at offering him low-key responses, when her insides told her a different story.

'I had the aircon and blower on max. That helped. It was bloody freezing, but it did the trick.' He wolfed down the first of his grilled cheese triangles. 'Mmm. Tastes good. Thanks.'

'My pleasure.' She needed to distract herself. 'That hay you mentioned. Do you just dump the roll in the paddock and let the animals pull it apart?'

'Nope. You roll it out, like the runner carpet in a hall-way. I'm told there's an art with rolling out the bales.'

Another cheesy triangle went the way of the first. 'You must lift them onto the forks the right way, so that the bales will roll out once you're in position on the slope in the paddock.' He bit off, chewed and swallowed another mouthful. 'The strings are cut before you move off in the tractor. If the bale happens to fall off in transit, it could become a dangerous missile on these slopes.' He handed her his empty plate, along with an A-OK gesture, then continued. 'If it's not tied up, it will roll out. If it's still tied, it might keep on rolling, out of control down the slope.'

'You sound well informed on the whole process.' She loved how he explained things so well.

'Courtesy of Pat. Remember the story of my water tanks?' He raised a sardonic eyebrow.

'Ah, your favourite farming instructor.' Her voice faltered. *Why does Pat have to keep spoiling my every moment with him?*

'Favourite? Only, you mean. I don't have any others.' He gave her a sad-sack look. 'I do have a favourite farming pupil, though.' A cheeky grin lit his face.

He meant her? No other pupil came to mind. Her heart skipped a beat. 'I do my best to follow in Pat's footsteps.' *Where farming is concerned, anyhow.*

'There's no need to do that. I've been watching you. You have your own unique style. In every way.'

Her heart swelled. *Watching me? I have style?* Her self-confidence ticked up a notch.

He looked around him. 'Even here. You've made this place very cosy.' His arm encompassed the room in a broad sweep.

She realised he hadn't been inside her private space since

the tiger snake episode. She gave him a proper smile this time. 'It was cosy when I started. You set it up very nicely.'

'I see you haven't added lots of stuff. You're not a materialist. I like that about you.'

*He's noticed that about me? I impact on him too? It's not a one-way street?* 'True, I don't judge anyone's success by their material possessions. I prefer what's in their head.' She bit her lip. He'd think her crazy. 'Personally speaking, I love everything small and compact, like this' —she spread both arms wide to embrace her surrounds— 'so that I'm not a slave to cleaning and looking after possessions and can do other things with my life.'

'Still, you've made it a home, with your books on the shelf and your flowers on the table. You've rearranged the furniture a bit too.' He surveyed the room again. 'Your seating arrangements make more sense than mine did.'

'It must be the Cancerian in me ... we're home lovers.' She might not agree with the full profile of that star sign, but this one fitted. Crabs carried their homes on their backs and could duck back inside at the slightest sign of trouble.

'You go for all that astrology stuff, do you? I didn't expect that from a little fact-finder like you.'

She gave him a no-teeth emoji smile but this time her eyes crinkled too. 'Not really. It's a convenient short cut to explaining what I'm like. Most people know the connection.'

'Do you need a short cut? I'm quite enjoying taking the long way round to getting to know you.'

'You are?' Good heavens, she sounded like Maria in *The Sound of Music*, reacting to Captain von Trapp's confessions in the summer house.

'I am.' The tease in his voice faded away to a more casual tone. 'Which reminds me. Tomorrow. Doing anything?'

'Just sitting here, at my computer, staying out of trouble.' Her best low-keyness seemed advisable. This man never ceased to surprise her. What did he have in mind?

'I need to brush the cobwebs away. I'm going for a run up to Mount Buller. Haven't driven up to the high country for a while, and I want to go before the snow season starts.' He cleared his throat. 'Would you like to come for the ride, see the countryside? We'll have lunch somewhere along the way.'

'Of course. That sounds wonderful.' Her heart waltzed away, dancing straight to the top of Mount Buller. She dreamed that here was the real reason he'd hurried from the airport to her doorstep this morning.

CHAPTER FOURTEEN

Dressed in her best country-style jeans, shirt and jacket, Hannah relaxed in the comfort of Philip's new Merc. It replaced the old one, burnt in the fire. The kilometres zipped by. She enjoyed driving with him. Unlike the days with Alex, she had total confidence in Philip's driving skills. It seemed like a genuine date too, the only purpose for this outing being pleasure, not business.

They reached the sign for Lake Eildon and Philip turned off the main road towards a boat-launching ramp, with no water in sight. None at all. She turned to him, open-mouthed. 'Is it always like this?'

'Grim, isn't it. Lake Eildon normally holds about eight times more water than Sydney Harbour. Let's get out of the car, take a walk. You won't often get the chance to walk across land which is normally covered by 20 metres of water.'

They scuffed up the dust at the bottom of a bridge pylon and peered upwards at the water-level markings far above their heads. The lakebed had dried out and cracked, with not a blade of grass anywhere. It looked like a moonscape. They crossed to where a trickle of water ran through a furrow narrow enough for them to jump across. Some kilometres down the valley, it dribbled into the remnants of a lake of water once held back by a huge dam wall.

Open-mouthed, she slowly turned full circle, surveying the landscape. 'It's enough to break your heart.'

'I wanted you to see this. Come on, let's get out of here. We'll go from one extreme to the other today. You wait and see.'

Two hours later, replete with Thai-style pumpkin and ginger soup, roti bread and green tea from an amazingly sophisticated country café in Mansfield, they'd negotiated the endless bends zig-zagging up the mountain, parked the car and set off on foot.

He pointed towards the summit. 'We dignify this place with the name Mount Buller, but it's really only a hill by world standards.'

'Whatever, it's cold up here.' Hannah wrapped her scarf round her neck and pulled a cap down over her ears to ward off the chilly biting wind.

'Careful.' Philip took her hand as she scrambled over a narrow section of the rocky path leading upwards.

His gesture of taking her hand, though done on instinct, made her feel safe.

When they reached a broader part, he let go of her hand. She wished he hadn't. She consoled herself by admiring the native Brachyscome daisies poking their dainty mauve flowers between the rock crevices.

At the highest point, exhilarated by the steep climb, she knew what he'd meant back at Lake Eildon. Apart from the ski village perched on the ridgeline below, forest pretty much as far as the eye could see. One a complete contrast to the other.

They sat side by side on a rock, saying nothing. Hannah absorbed the scene, the vastness and emptiness of the landscape. With Philip by her side, she savoured being on top of the world. These heights reminded her of the position he held in her admittedly limited world of men.

After a while, into the silence, she said, 'I looked you up on Google, you know.'

He stiffened slightly but continued to gaze into the distance. In a low tone he said, 'I was worried you might. What did you find?'

'Lots of coverage of your career, of course. Impressive.' She talked to the sky, not to him.

'Proving that you're a nobody without a meteoric rise and a stratospheric salary?' He kept his eyes on the horizon.

'Others might think that. I think your rise is the result of competence and proven achievement.' She still talked to the sky.

'That's what I aim for, it's true.' He turned to her. 'Is that what you look for, too?'

She nodded. 'I'm not impressed with people's rank or title, only with their actual achievements, whether as an excellent garbage collector or an excellent brain surgeon.' She wriggled to find a more comfortable position on the rock where they sat, then added, 'I don't see houses, cars or any other material possessions as status symbols.' She shuffled her feet and kicked at a few pebbles. 'In the interest of full disclosure, though, I confess to a keen interest in *Wallumatta Farm* on that first day, my interview day. Your beautiful property did stun me and I thought your guided tour that day would be my only chance to see how the other half—sorry, top five percent—lives.'

He laughed. 'I'm impressed. By your priorities, I mean. In the finance sector I'm surrounded by fast-trackers, smart talkers, quite a few slick operators, some great pretenders and plenty of newcomers from other industries or other countries, who don't understand our specific cultural nuances. I sometimes wonder how long they will all last.'

'Banking may be a wasteland of shattered careers and a haven for hollow men,' she said, 'but you seem to be regarded as one of the exceptions. *A man of judgement*, said one article. Going far, said another.' She didn't add that the words intelligence, wisdom, foresight, guts and personal integrity had all been applied to him in various places. He might think she'd been stalking him on the internet. That word stalking carried such negative over-tones. She preferred to think of it as exercising her research skills.

He shrugged and looked up into the blueness overhead. 'I don't take much notice. Those journalists are always looking for a new angle. They usually swallow all the usual blatant self-promotions without question. They seem more impressed by clever moves than intelligent behaviour.'

'Well I doubt they would have made up their stories for a laugh, so it must be the way others speak of you.'

He returned his gaze to her. 'You know, that's one of the things I like about you. You see behind the façade, don't you? And home in on the nub of the matter. That's what I noticed in your book, too.'

'Maybe.' It was her turn to act nonchalant. Her focus of

attention in this moment was him, not her. 'I noticed something else about those articles.'

'And what was that?' He sounded wary.

'There was no mention of your family.' She hoped her expressionless voice would hide her interest in his response.

'Ah. Let's not spoil a special moment.' He stood up. 'The cold's getting to me. How about you? Time to leave?'

When they reached the car he said, 'Didn't mean to be abrupt up there.' He pointed towards the summit. 'My family's a sore point with me.' They buckled into their seat belts. He turned her way and said, 'I'm enjoying this. We have a few hours left in the day. There's no need to rush back. We can explore a little more, if you like.'

She answered with an enthusiastic 'Yes please.'

They retraced their route. At the bottom of the mountain, the road flanked an almost-dry creek running through a valley crammed with pines and deciduous trees in autumn leaf. The sight transfixed her, as it had on their upward journey to the peak. 'With the mountains looming above us and this vegetation, you can imagine yourself in Europe.'

He kept his eyes on the road ahead but said, 'I agree. We have so much flat or undulating country. It makes for an invigorating change of landscape.'

They passed the turnoff to Timbertop, the famous school in the bush once attended by Prince Charles and reached the sign for the Hunt Club Hotel at Merrijig.

'We'll stop here.' He turned into the car park.

Dusk was falling and Hannah was deliciously apprehensive about Philip's intentions, until she realised this simple country place served refreshments only, without offering accommodation. A small puff of deflation escaped her lungs.

*What's wrong with me, that he never takes our relationship to another level.*

He ordered a light beer; she ordered a pinot gris. Both ordered hamburgers with the lot. As they surveyed the panorama of Mount Buller from the front bar, Philip said, 'This place has icon status, Hannah. It'd be hard to get more dinky-di than this place, although the tourists are swamping the locals now.'

She twisted on her stool and looked all around her. 'It still has a "Man from Snowy River" feel about it. I love that poem, so of course I made a point of watching that old movie it inspired.'

'Strange you should say that. They filmed that movie in these parts.'

'How fascinating.' Her eyes rounded. 'It's a shame that particular part of our history has virtually disappeared. Banjo Patterson wouldn't recognise the land he wrote about in the 1890s.'

'History. You love it, don't you?' He gave her an affectionate look.

'It's interesting, but I don't need a full-time diet of it. There are other things in life. Like this.' Hannah waved her hand to encompass their drinks, him, the bar, the valley, the mountains.

Philip clinked his can against her glass. 'Exactly. Here's to a memorable day.' He tipped the can to his mouth, all the while maintaining eye contact with her. 'Up there,' he pointed to Mount Buller, 'you confessed to Googling me.'

'Sorry.' She flinched. *He does think I'm a stalker!*

'That's okay. Everyone does it. Our lives aren't private anymore.' He took a sip of his beer. 'What else have you discovered in your sleuthing? Relevant to you, I mean, your family, not me.'

'Plenty. You really want to know?'

'That's why I asked. And I don't want to hear about your great-aunt Susan.' His eyes twinkled.

'Hmm.' She thought for a moment. 'My grandmother, an unlikely feminist, loved to tell us that we come from a long line of strong, independent women. She seemed overly dramatic, but my research proved her right. I've discovered five generations of them down one line.'

'Do you see yourself as a strong, independent woman?'

'I'd like to think so.' She fiddled with the stem of her wine glass as her thoughts swirled. 'A very different one, of course. I'm almost their age, and childless.'

'By choice or circumstance?'

'That's what everyone wonders, for women of my age.' Even if she'd opened herself up to it, she didn't have to answer his direct question. She could keep her secrets too. A polite smile would do.

She continued with her original story. '*They* were all widowed in their thirties and forties, raising hordes of children, and survived well into their eighties and nineties. The genteel gentry of the family, they managed to endure a life of champagne tastes on a beer income.'

'You mean they were accustomed to the good life, before their husbands died.'

'Exactly.' She liked how he picked up the point so quickly. 'Their ways had the biggest influence on my own upbringing.'

'You like the good life?' His voice lifted in surprise.

'I wish!' Sarcasm dripped from those two words. She and

her immediate family had always lived a moderate lifestyle. 'I suppose I like the standards to which those widows aspired … a good education, good taste, proper behaviour, that sort of thing. I've never had "money".'

'Like me, you mean?'

He didn't sound at all suspicious of her intentions, just like his usual matter-of-fact self. 'Like you,' she agreed. 'However, you've surprised me.'

'How?' He shifted forward and leant on his elbow, rested his chin on his hand, and half-turned towards her as if keen to hear what she thought of him.

'The man in the street—that's me—sees clearly from media coverage that bigger salaries don't always correlate with higher performance, but the recipients of exorbitant salaries—that's you—usually take them as their due. Yet you seem to be very modest. You don't carry that air of entitlement with you.'

He sat up straight and grinned at her. 'Ah, but how do you know what I'm like in my other world?'

She directed her penetrating eye his way. 'I don't *know*, but I can feel.'

'So you're not after my money, then?' His eyes held a glimmer of amusement.

She laughed. 'I'm just your caretaker, not your girl-friend.' Their eyes met again, his with a flash of mutual recognition that her classification as caretaker might easily change.

'Money's not the test, anyway.' He eased the conversation onto safer ground. 'You've always impressed me as high-class.'

'That's quite a compliment. Thank you.'

'My pleasure.' He bowed slightly, aping an old-fashioned courtier before taking another swig of his beer. 'You said those strong independent widows represented one "line". What else lurks in your background?'

'Dare I mention the convict branch?' His expression sharpened with an interest that encouraged her to continue. 'Did you know I can trace my origins as an Australian back to the First Fleet?'

'You're full of surprises.' He remained quiet for a minute. 'You don't mind admitting to convicts in the family?'

'Not at all. It distressed my mother though ... if she'd been the researcher, she might have tried to hide it. However, I'm proud that my forebear, and hers, stood on the shores of Sydney Cove back in January 1788 as one of the founders of modern Australia.'

'Maybe that explains your pride—because good or bad, they achieved something great. And you like achievers, especially when they do great things. Unlike some people.' He seemed lost in thought.

'They weren't bad people,' she said. 'In fact, those early settlers of Australia were tough survivors, and the women in the convict and emancipist class didn't expect any favours from anyone. I must have acquired my pioneering spirit from them.' She directed a good-humoured look at Philip. 'I'm inspired to follow in their footsteps by helping at your farm.'

'The pioneering *there* is rather cushy, if you ask me, but I get your point. Plenty of women wouldn't venture beyond sipping cocktails in my gazebo.'

She laughed at the ironic tone in his voice. 'Maybe that's

another compliment. I'm not sure.' She angled her head, looking at him for verification.

He obliged. 'You can take it as such.' His voice lost its upbeat note. 'Don't take this the wrong way, Hannah, but it sounds like you're doing the usual thing, what always drives me mad with family history researchers, looking at your forebears through rose-coloured glasses.'

She shook her head. 'Not entirely. I've also discovered family traits I'm not so proud to confess.'

'Such as?' He raised an eyebrow.

'Apart from all the convicts? Alcoholism, for a start. And bipolar disorder, by the looks of it. There was definitely some crazy behaviour going on in some lines of the family, up to quite recent times. Genetics, most likely.' She suddenly remembered her wine and took a sip. Not so cold now. It served her right for being too much of a chatterbox.

'Do you ever worry that you'll be affected too?' He stared into the distance as he spoke.

His unwillingness to face her directly with this question aroused her curiosity. Did he have a crazy relative stashed away somewhere? 'No. I'd rather know the truth about most things.'

'You set a good example.' He still didn't look at her.

'Of what?' She resisted the urge to tug at his sleeve and draw his attention back to her.

'How to handle nasty surprises in your family.' He continued staring towards the distant mountains, in a reverie into which Hannah deemed it tactless to intrude.

His faraway expression bothered her. 'You okay? Am I boring you?'

He returned to her world and shook his head. 'Not at

all. Sorry.' His hazy look disappeared, and he said, 'You just reminded me of something I was trying not to think about today.' He shrugged his shoulders philosophically.

Considering it best not to pry, she said, 'Ah, so I'm a distraction.'

Fully paying attention now, he replied, 'Yes, but a welcome and pleasant distraction.' He grinned. 'Distract me some more. Tell me more about this family of yours. These genes you inherited.'

'The alcoholic and bi-polar genes have skipped me, but I guess I know why I look like I do. I've inherited a lot from my Celtic forebears. Part of Mum's family was Cornish and all of Dad's family settled in Northern Ireland around 1600.'

'You're lucky to know where you came from.' If anything, he sounded envious.

'Not lucky. Wrong word, my friend. It took a lot of work to find out.'

He tapped his empty beer can against the glass still in her hand. 'Point taken.'

'With the work done, it amazed me to realise just how Anglo-Celtic I am. Among eight generations of my ancestors, only one forebear did *not* originate in England, Scotland, Ireland or northern France. As I flinch from the skin specialist's spray can of liquid nitrogen, I readily understand and accept that my fair skin was never meant for Australian conditions, although my forebears here date back to 1788.'

Interest sparked in his eyes. 'My sister would agree with you.'

'You too? Irish in the family, I mean.' As she asked, the hamburgers were finally slapped down before them.

'Yep, but we'd better tuck into this food, before it gets

cold. We've had to wait an age for it to arrive and I'm hungry.' He neatly deflected the conversation from his own family ... again.

Hannah abandoned the effort to make conversation with him. Damn the man. Every time they edged emotionally closer, he closed up. It disappointed her. She found his touchiness difficult to understand. The panoramic view gave her a good excuse to gaze out the window as they munched thoughtfully on their hamburgers.

The days closed in rapidly at this time of year. By the time they'd eaten and returned to the car, darkness had fallen. An hour's journey lay ahead, but Alley could wait for his meal.

The car coming towards them meant Philip had to dip his headlights. On low beam, it was impossible to see very far ahead. A dark shape loomed out of the darkness, a rock-like object, exactly in the middle of their side of the road.

*Ker thump.* They ran right over the top of it. No way could they have avoided it, and no way the poor creature could have survived. Hannah pictured the blood and gore splattered all over the road, another bit of road kill on this busy road. She turned in her seat, watching as the car behind them flattened the kamikaze wombat's remains even further into the tarmac.

Their own car began making some ominous noises. Philip flicked a glance at his dashboard gauges. 'Damn. We're going to have to stop. Something's wrong. The temperature's beginning to rise. I'll have to nurse this baby along for a couple more k's, to where I can get mobile reception and call the RACV.'

He pulled over and got out to examine the damage. Hannah joined him. The front of the car had a large dent, down low, right in the middle. A loud hissing emanated from under the bonnet. 'So much for my brand-new car.' He sounded rueful, but resigned. 'We may have damaged the radiator. It sounds like she's just about out of water.'

Philip extracted his mobile from his pocket, his wallet from another. He consulted his RACV membership card for the roadside assist number, pressed the numbers and spoke for a few minutes, explaining the nature of the problem and their location. He put the phone back in his pocket. 'Let's get back in the car, Hannah. It's too cold standing out here. Autumn days cool down very rapidly once the sun goes down.' He opened the passenger door for her. 'It'll be a while before we're rescued. The car's undriveable and will need to go on the back of a flattop tow truck. They're trying to find one to send out here.'

Several hours passed. The traffic quietened and for minutes at a time, the road was as dark as only a country road can be. Except for the stars, dazzling on a clear night like this.

Philip and Hannah gazed upwards into the Milky Way's display, its glittering load of light always an inspiration to any city dweller deprived of its impact by the light pollution of an urban environment. Arranged just like the five stars on the Australian flag, the Southern Cross constellation swung across the night sky, its long axis always pointing to the point in the sky directly above the South Pole. By now, close to 10pm, the Southern Cross no longer tilted but stood almost vertically in the sky.

Philip disturbed their companionable silence. 'Do you see the pointer stars off to the left, Hannah?'

'Alpha and Beta Centauri? Yes, I see them. Can never remember which is which, though.' Hannah's voice trailed off as she marvelled at the panorama, humbled by the insignificance of her little life and the uniqueness of beautiful planet Earth in this enormous universe. 'With the heavens to inspire us,' she murmured, 'you can't believe that so many people adopt violence and destruction as a way of life.'

'I prefer the sentiment that we should make love, not war.' His warm voice in the darkened car conveyed a song in his heart, but he made no move towards her side of the vehicle.

As much as she might long for his lips to meet hers, she rejoiced in his sophistication. He didn't jump on women when the opportunity presented itself. This man invited her complete trust. It made him all the more desirable. She savoured that magic moment. 'For a banker, you're a beautiful dreamer, Philip.'

'Not always. It's the company I'm keeping.' He kept his eyes on the heavens.

'Thank you.' She loved his way of paying a compliment.

They lapsed into silence again and sat together quietly, at peace with the world. As her eyelids started to droop, she snuggled into her seat.

In the starlight, he watched her drift off to sleep. He resisted the temptation to tilt her his way, have her snuggle up against him. He doubted she'd be too impressed when she woke up. He'd been behaving in such an *on again, off again* way with her, suddenly shutting down conversations that most people would regard as normal chit chat, that she must be totally confused about him. He groaned inwardly. These last few months, he confused himself. It was silly to bottle it all up. She was obviously someone smart enough to understand, so why didn't he confide in her? Just habit. In his world, past and present, he could never let down his guard.

Philip thought about his recently acquired knowledge about his father. The truth had emerged at last, leaving him to process a life led as a lie until his mother's death last New Year's Eve. It had shaken his self-perception to its foundations. What a way to start the new year. The task of rebuilding his self-image was proving more painful than he expected, and slower too.

The chill in the crisp night air invaded the car. He shrugged out of his coat and draped it across Hannah, tucking it in behind her shoulders to keep her warm. She stirred a little. He gently smoothed his hand down the side of her hair and across her cheek. He whispered to her, 'One day, soon I hope, we'll do this when you're awake and needing me as much as I need you.'

She woke to the beeps of a truck's reversing lights, the glare of the revolving orange emergency vehicle lights blinding her sleepy eyes. She checked her Fitbit. Nearly midnight. Her stomach reminded her that six hours had passed since their hamburger meal. Her feet were very cold but Philip's jacket, draped over her upper body, warded off the worst of the chill. She luxuriated in the smell of his jacket. How typical of him, to be so remarkably considerate of others. She stretched and turned to thank him, but found him missing and his door wide open. Cold air seeped in and she shivered. He stood outside the car, waiting to confer with the tow truck driver.

Hannah scrambled out to join him, carrying his coat and her handbag, just in time to hear the driver apologise. 'Sorry for the long delay, mate. Had to attend to an accident further down the Highway. With several people injured, that job took priority. If I'd known in time, I would have called in the troops. At this hour, though, no-one wants to leave their warm beds and drive kilometres.'

Philip conceded that point with a nod. 'Appreciate you coming. The wait didn't bother me too much. I had my distractions.'

The tow truck driver noticed Hannah and she watched him give Philip one of those conspiratorial leers so familiar to women.

Philip turned to Hannah. 'You're awake. I thought I'd have to wake sleeping beauty with that famous kiss from the prince.'

He *was* a prince, in her eyes, but she ignored the kiss remark. 'Sorry to doze off like that. I didn't expect to be such boring company.'

'I can assure you, you haven't bored me.'

Her heart skittered but she maintained a polite distance.

'Thanks for the loan of your coat. You must have been cold yourself.' She offered it back to him.

'Keep it for now. We're about to take a ride jammed together in the front of this truck. I won't need it.'

The tow truck was the type to tilt down its tray and haul the car up the ramp before levelling the tray again. Its driver knew what he was doing and was soon ready to depart.

'Hop in.'

The two passenger seats to the left of the driver and his gear shift looked very cramped. Hannah assumed she'd be expected to take the seat between the driver and Philip and clambered up the step into the cabin of the truck. Philip climbed in after her and slammed the door. He moved left as far as he could but, shoulder to thigh, their bodies still pressed together. Her seatbelt was easy to access but she had to lift and tilt her bottom sideways to allow him to clip his seatbelt into position. As he pushed his buckle into its catch, his upper arm pressed against her left breast and a spark of sexual awareness zapped up and down her spine. She tensed up. He focussed only on his task.

At first she sat bolt upright alongside him, his coat resting across their laps. Two people squeezed into such a confined seating area proved awkward. When he raised his right arm and put it across her shoulders, their two torsos fitted better together. Perfectly, in fact. It made sense to snuggle into his warm body and rest her head back against his shoulder.

The little spark in her heart flared into a small flame and coiled itself around her lungs and beyond.

Except for an occasional change of pressure in his right hand on her shoulder, he behaved as if unaffected by her body restrained tightly against his and maintained a half-hearted level of male chit-chat with the tow truck driver.

Too soon for Hannah's liking, the front gate of *Wallumatta Farm* loomed in the headlights.

With both seatbelts released, Philip scrambled to the ground and turned to extend his hand to help Hannah slide out and down to the ground. The tow truck drove off with Philip's car aboard and they walked in silence down the darkened drive, together but apart, to the point where the security lights for the house activated.

Philip then spoke. 'You realise I'm going to have to ask a favour of you.'

His first words disappointed her, but she could play with a straight bat too. 'Sure. How can I help?' *Please let him ask me for a kiss.*

'It's Monday tomorrow.' He looked at his watch. 'Correction. Today. I have to be at work for an eight o'clock meeting.' He looked at her. 'But ... no car.' He nodded in the direction of the tow-truck's fading taillights. 'Would you be able to drive me to Melbourne?'

That pricked her balloon of hope. No good night kiss. Her shoulders sagged a fraction.

'I don't want to take my dirty old farm truck into the city,' he explained. 'You need it here. And if I *do* drive the truck, I'll arrive with my suit covered in hayseeds.'

*And looking like a country bumpkin will dent your image?* Her personal prince or not, she needed to test out the extent of his ego in his work setting. 'Um, well yes, I could, but isn't my old car a bit of a come down for you?' She thought about that other car space inside his locked garage. 'Don't you have a second car stashed behind that Roll-a-door?'

'No, I don't.'

*What, no Porsche or the like? He continues to surprise me.*

'Your car doesn't bother me,' he added. Wheels are wheels and the company will suit me.'

She thrilled to the sudden warmth in his voice, even if he kept his face deadpan.

'Trouble is, it'll be an early start.' His voice carried a warning note.

'Like six, at the latest?' She could do her sums too.

'Yep, 'fraid so.' He sounded quite apologetic.

'That's okay, I can manage that.' Of course, I can. Counting 'getting to bed' time, and 'getting ready in the morning' time, it gives me four whole hours for my beauty sleep. How much more does a girl need? 'I'll be idling at your front door just before six. Luckily, I filled the car with petrol during the week. You should make it, traffic jams permitting.'

'I'm sorry my schedule doesn't give us much time for sleeping.'

Matter-of-fact Philip. So infuriating. What's so wrong with me that he never attempts any intimacy?

They walked round to the back of his house, where he stopped at the store cupboard. 'I'll watch while you walk over to the bungalow. Make sure no bogey men get you.' He opened the cupboard door. 'I'd better stay here and feed Alley, although he's probably scrounged for his own dinner by now. The mice come into the hayshed at this time of year, looking for a warm hidey-hole.'

And I wish I could be in a warm hidey-hole with you.

He turned off the outside lights and retreated to his bedroom, keyed up with sexual tension. Two months he'd known her, and still no kisses. All this gentlemanly restraint was killing him. He knew that a restless night lay ahead, with sleep eluding him as he imagined what might have been. Two cold and lonely bodies slipping into two cold and empty beds, a hundred metres apart across a courtyard, would have found much more comfort and warmth sliding together into his bed—or hers. He held back only because she didn't seem the type for casual sex and he couldn't promise her anything else.

# CHAPTER FIFTEEN

The early morning mist made driving conditions dangerous. 'I reckon you take your life in your hands every time you drive down this road,' said Hannah.

Philip sprawled in the passenger seat. 'It had the worst accident rate in the state until the authorities started paying attention and made a few road improvements. The terrain it traverses doesn't help.' He stared at the road unfolding ahead of them. 'This mist will clear soon, but in winter the fogs through this valley can last for days on end.'

'You make the approaching winter sound so appealing.'

He laughed at her gentle irony. 'I like it myself. The variety. I'd hate to live in the tropics. The weather's so monotonous.'

Hannah drove obediently at the 100 kph speed limit. A motor bike chose the wrong time to thunder past, just as an oncoming vehicle loomed out of the mist. Hannah braced for the collision, but the bike chopped back in front of her, in the nick of time.

'And there you have it. The evidence.' He pointed

towards the bike accelerating away from them. 'The worst hazard of this road is its mix of traffic, ranging from the largest to the smallest, fastest to the slowest. Inexperienced P-platers like that young bloke on the bike take too many chances.'

'I've noticed quite a few bikes on this road.'

'Motor-cycle gangs treat it as a racetrack. They love the hills and bends. The road's a riding challenge.' He raised his hand to suppress a yawn. 'Not enough sleep.'

He continued where he'd left off. 'At the other extreme, you'll come around a bend and have to jam on the brakes because there's a tractor in front doing 40 kilometres per hour, shifting bales of hay.'

'Okay, thanks for the warning. So far I haven't met a tractor on this road. What other surprises are in store for me?'

'Interstate hauliers mixed with ski-traffic, trucks carrying cattle, vintage car rallies, Sunday drivers moseying along with their eyes on the scenery, not the road.' He ticked off his list on his fingers.

'Well I love to drive, so the challenges don't bother me.'

'Your driving skills are good. They need to be. Plenty of people come to grief along here.'

'That helipad beside the local hospital says it all.' She slowed as they passed through the speed-restricted area of a small settlement.

'Yep, accident victims often end up at the Alfred Hospital's Road Trauma unit in Melbourne.'

'The Westpac rescue helicopter sometimes flew over the top of my old home. Some of their mercy flights probably originated from this area.'

She accelerated back to 100 kph and drove on. The car was warm, the atmosphere between them comfortable. She bipped a warning horn at a galah dancing anxiously around its squashed mate, part of this morning's toll of roadkill. 'Sad. It reminds me that life is all about the survival of the fittest.'

'Despite their "silly galah" reputation, galahs are very clever birds. That one just got slow and heavy from gorging itself on grain dropped on the road.'

'I hated seeing that bereaved partner.' Her voice drooped.

'Me too. Broken bonds. Sad.'

She risked a quick sideways glance at her passenger. He looked thoughtful. Being with him, so much on the same wavelength as herself, filled her with confidence, a sense of comfort and a spark of joy. He understood her intent in almost every comment she made. Maybe she could risk a brief foray into his danger zone.

'That galah reminds me that our journey through life itself is full of risks.'

'Getting philosophical on me, are you?' His voice sounded wary.

No, not really. Just thinking about yesterday and what we talked about.'

'You mean all that family history stuff,' he grunted.

Out of the corner of her left eye she noticed his body tense and his knees lower as he braced against the car's foot well.

'Yes. The true essence of family history research is the journey … your own risky journey of self-discovery.' She'd better be careful. He seemed edgy.

'Why *risky?*'

'Because it can open up a can of worms.' *Yep, he's definitely nervous.* 'Let's start with the genes you inherited. I'm willing to bet that you know less about your genes than the genes of your cattle.'

'Hah, you could be right, there.'

She saw his tense body relax slightly. She'd identified some safer ground for him. He knew about cattle breeding. She could press on.

'You're not alone, being unfamiliar with your genetic background. You only have to watch one episode of "Who Do You Think You Are" for that fact to be obvious.'

'I must watch that show one day,' he grunted.

'When the cow jumps over the moon, you mean?' She gave him a quick sideways glance. It was clear he had no intention of ever watching that show. He responded with an embarrassed shrug.

'I'm curious,' she said. 'Do you know the backgrounds of your two sets of grandparents … just four people?'

'Come to think of it, Miss Persistence, no. I barely know their names. My sister and I never saw them. My grandparents lived far away, and it seemed normal not to see them, especially as my mother rarely acknowledged their existence.'

'Does that make you sad? As if you missed out on something important?' *I need to tread carefully here.*

He took a long time to answer. 'Kind of. I know I don't want that for my kids. If I ever have kids.' His voice sounded wistful.

'Are they on your agenda?' She kept her question light and casual, as if making small talk, even though he might think her too direct. He'd been the one to mention kids, not her.

'One day.'

His polite but non-committal answer impressed her. Some men would think her nosy and tell her to go jump. She decided it was safe to continue, with caution. 'Remember, if their grandparents are a mystery, they'll barely know anything about their origins on your side of the family.' She strove to keep the slightest hint of judgement out of her tone.

He took many seconds to reply. 'I think I see what you're driving at. Perspective.'

'Right. If we know only one story about our family's background, then that story then tends to dominate our thinking, as if it formed our entire identity.' She loved how he picked up logical consequences so quickly.

'And we forget all the other forebears who've contributed to who we are. Their genes, so to speak. I understand the concept, from my cattle breeding records.' He spoke with a little more enthusiasm.

'Exactly. If we set out to discover the full mix of ingredients in our personal cake, the journey might be risky, as risky as embarking on a new relationship, but the "ah hah" moments can be quite thrilling.'

He ran a hand through his hair. 'You're giving me a lot to think about.'

'I hope it helps. Knowledge of this kind is powerful, perhaps giving permission to break away from family expectations and burdens.' She tried not to sound too much like a counsellor.

'You obviously realise that family issues are troubling me at present,' he muttered.

'It's fairly clear … to me, anyhow.' She took her left hand off the steering wheel, reached across and gave his arm a quick pat.

'Thanks for being astute enough to notice. I can tell you're only trying to help.'

'You'd just rather I didn't.' She flicked a glance sideways to check the expression on his face. 'So I congratulate you for maintaining impeccable manners under duress.'

He caught her glance. 'Thanks. I'm tired and this morning I need a break from my personal woes,' he said. 'Do you mind?' He turned to stare out the window.

'Not at all.' She could tell she'd pushed him a bit too far. 'Want to hear the news?' Assuming his answer would be yes, she turned on the car radio. The news, the traffic alerts and the chatter from the breakfast host kept them entertained for the rest of the journey.

As they neared his office in Collins Street, he said, 'Would you be able to pick up the Merc when it's ready? The auto repairers told me it'll take about a week. Pat often goes that way on Fridays, to shop at the major supermarket. She'll give you a lift to the workshop. You'll need to drive it down to Melbourne and collect me.'

'Yes, of course. I'm at your service.' Her ready agreement made her think. Increasingly she found herself playing the role of a wife, not a caretaker. Apart from the bedroom department, in the role that tempted her the most … the lover role. What would he be like? She risked a sideways glance to feast on the sight of his gorgeous muscles and caught him glancing at her. When he quirked an eyebrow at her, she remembered what she'd just said. In farmland, cows are serviced by the bull. She burst out laughing. 'I didn't mean that literally.'

'Pity.' He grinned. 'Here's where I hop out. Thanks for the lift, Good Samaritan.' He reached across and lightly touched her hand resting on the steering wheel, patting it in farewell. For a second or two he locked eyes with her. 'See you next weekend. I'll come up in a hire car if I have to.'

She couldn't wait.

He slid out of the car and she moved off with the traffic, heading off to find food. Her 14-hour fast since that hamburger at Merrijig needed breaking.  After that, she'd drop by and see how her old neighbour Gracie was doing.

## CHAPTER SIXTEEN

It was crisp this Saturday morning, too crisp to sit for long on the balcony. Rugged up in her oldest trackies, a puffer jacket that had seen better days and her lambskin boots, she was glad Philip couldn't see her dressed for comfort, not glamour. She sipped her tea and watched the coils of mist down on Pat's river flats, where the cold air settled. She recalled Pat saying she'd soon need to move her cattle off her relatively lush summer pastures down there, up to higher ground, some degrees warmer in winter.

She smiled to herself. *Now I'm being just like Philip, citing Pat as my referral point at every opportunity. I'm beginning to see why he does it.*

Her former cosy existence in Melbourne, removed from the extremes of nature, hadn't prepared her for the last month of life experience, confronting life and death situations on a daily basis, getting a little dirt on her hands, literally and figuratively. *I have to admit, at last I'm really living.*

She wondered why she hadn't heard from Philip, asking her to go pick up his car, and then him. Almost immediately she saw him striding towards her balcony. She hadn't heard his car.

At her astonished look he said, 'Pat was down in Melbourne last night for a family celebration. She gave me a lift back to the repair shop this morning. They've replaced the front panel and the radiator's been fixed.'

Hannah deflated like a pricked balloon. The hope that she held a special place in Philip's life whooshed out of her. Pat was the one after all. *He didn't ring me to advise his change of plans, but all the while he's been making these arrangements with Pat.* It rankled.

She schooled her face to remain neutral in expression. 'That saved me a trip.'

'Yes, but I have a different favour to ask of you now. Not exactly a favour. Just a request.'

This time she would not make his "at his service" expectations easy for him to assume. She stood silently and waited for him to spit it out.

'I have some tree-planting to do. I'd like the pleasure of your company while I do it. So, it's your time that I'm requesting.'

A little air began to refill her balloon. *A date. A strange one, it's true, but a date. A crazy kind of date.* Her balloon continued to puff up, fuelled by relief and happiness. 'It just so happens that time is my friend at present. You mean right now?'

'Not today. I've yet to collect the trees. Doing that this afternoon. No, I mean tomorrow, around eleven, when the temperatures should have warmed up a bit. Wear your sunhat, regardless of the temperature. And your boots. And bring your gardening gloves, just in case.'

'Right. I understand.' An understatement, if ever there was one. *Hallelujah.* Tomorrow promised to be a day from heaven, in perfect company, tackling a project right up her alley. She wasn't sure whether he'd accept a suggestion from her. 'By the way, it'll help reduce transplanting shock if you soak your trees beforehand in a tub of water.'

He saluted her with a cheeky smile. 'Yes ma'am.'

Thank God he wasn't a "resist petticoat-rule" kind of guy. Thank God he hadn't batted an eyelid at her daggy clothing.

Next day, just before eleven, she heard the truck revving to ascend the steep slope between the house and the shed paddock. She cut through the gap in the hedge screening the sheds from the house and met him at the truck. He was loading four cylindrical columns of heavy wire mesh, the kind used in reinforced concrete, plus some star posts onto a box trailer hitched to the ute. Half a dozen large plastic pots containing young saplings rested in the back of the vehicle, along with a number of 2-litre containers of water and some strange metal objects.

She peered into the tray. 'Which eucalypts are we planting?' She inspected the nursery tags. 'Wonderful. Viminalis. Manna gums. Lovely trees.'

'Yep. For the koalas.'

'You're kidding me.'

'Nope. I've seen a few koalas around here. We're close to the Strathbogies, which hosts a large koala population.' He pointed to the distant range of hills across the valley. 'They're fussy eaters but they like these leaves.' He flicked the tender shoots on the saplings. 'I've got a few well-established trees in the paddock where we're headed. Come on. Let's go.'

They headed up the hill, along the ridge line and through the gate into the end paddock, currently free of cattle. Hannah breathed a sigh of relief. The idea of caring for cattle became easier by the day, at least in theory if not yet entirely in practice.

Cheerfully, she climbed back into the cabin after closing the gate. 'No sloppy cow pats here—they're dried out and a bit crumbly.'

'The cockies have helped with that.'

'Not my favourite birds.' She grabbed for the handhold as the truck bounced into the paddock.

'True, they're a pest, but when they descend on the place in swarms, looking for tucker, their sharp beaks can break up the droppings and they dry out quicker. The process speeds up the grass growing through again, aided by the recycled fertiliser.'

Her sunnies vibrated down and she pushed them back onto the bridge of her nose. 'So *that's* what they're doing! I've noticed hundreds of them on the ground sometimes.'

'Yes. They like the bulbs of the onion grass too, and they break up the hard crust of earth with their beaks, so rain can penetrate the pasture a little better.'

'Every cloud has a silver lining.' She marvelled at the way the natural world worked.

'Yep, those darned birds have some redeeming features.'

'Not for vineyard owners or orchardists—they must curse the cockies for the damage they cause.'

'They do. Graziers too, when they're reseeding a

paddock.' He changed gears and said, 'Hang on. This bit is steep.'

The truck tilted at an alarming angle as it traversed the hillside towards several trees enclosed in a protective ring of strong mesh.

He stopped the truck and pointed at the mesh. 'The security barrier between my precious trees and the ever-curious and ever-hungry cattle.' A crooked grin lit his face, which made her stomach somersault. 'Even when the paddock is lush with grass, you can guarantee that a newly planted tree will prove far more tempting a morsel than boring old pasture, especially when the cattle are saved the effort of bending right to the ground to chomp.'

He slid out of his seat, grabbed his wire cutters and walked over to the tree. 'I know I invited you here to watch, not work,' he called across to her, 'but can you help me to remove these two tree guards? I'm recycling these first, before I use the new pieces of mesh.'

She scrambled out to him and gazed doubtfully at the leaves waving six feet above her head. 'Surely you can't lift this guard over the top of this tree. It's too tall.'

'Ah, there's a magic trick.' Philip pointed to the twists of wire down the length of the first guard. 'I'm going to cut those strands and unwrap the mesh.'

She contemplated the work site for a moment. 'I see. Much easier.'

'Make sure that no bits of wire drop on the ground and get left behind.' He sounded serious.

'You like things to be tidy, don't you.'

'Yep, but that's not my primary concern. You have to be careful because if the cattle ingest bits of wire, it can prove fatal. I lost a cow once for that reason. After it'd happened, Pat told me why.'

There was a time when she thought she'd scream if she ever heard him cite Pat's advice again. More confident now that Philip also valued her, she could more easily let it go. Without the slightest hint of her usual sarcasm at every mention of Pat, she obediently asked, 'Why?'

'Years ago, a fencer who should have known better left some scrap ends of fencing wire lying around in a paddock. My cow must have disturbed the discards in her foraging, because she swallowed a bit of rusty wire.'

'Ouch. Did it pierce her insides?'

He shook his head. 'No, not that. Cattle have four stomachs. They don't pass food through one continuous intestinal tract and out the other end, like us. If they swallow something alien and non-biodegradable, it gets stuck inside. It blocks them up and they can't eat. They'll die of starvation without an operation to remove it, but you don't generally notice the obstruction until the problem is at an advanced stage.'

'You mean, when they've lost weight from not eating?'

'You're beginning to understand the ways of cattle. Great.'

His admiring look of approval bolstered her confidence.

'I noticed my cow losing weight but, as she was feeding a big, strong calf at the time, I blamed the calf for taking all her energy.' He bit his lip and waited to gain Hannah's full attention. 'You know how some women who are mothers of new babies get very skinny while others are very ... er ... well padded. In my early days of Collins Street farming I thought the same applied to cows.'

'No-one would blame you. It doesn't sound like an everyday problem. What happened to the poor cow?' She wanted to know how this story ended.

'Eventually she just collapsed in the paddock. It being a weekend, I asked Pat to come and take a look before I summonsed the vet on his day off. Pat figured out the problem and told me it was too late, nothing could save her, and why.' A catch in his voice betrayed his sorrow and regret.

'How sad.'

'Still trying to look after her calf, she died later that day. In hindsight, she'd taken a long time to die. Her heartbreaking devotion to her calf brought a tear to my eye, I can tell you. I was devastated.' He stared into space and blinked back his emotion.

'I had no idea that farming could put you through the wringer like this.' She wished she could give him a hug but held back.

'It teaches you a lot … about life, the universe, and beyond.' He gave her a wry smile.

They shared a comfortable silence for a moment or two before she withdrew her gardening gloves from her pocket and pulled them on. She wiggled her hands at him. 'Ready for action? I am. And for my next lesson, Professor. Knowing you, as I'm beginning to do, I guess these trees are part of your grand plan for the place.'

'Am I so transparent? Yep, these trees are part of my erosion control. This gulley was very eroded when I bought the place. My bulldozer mate—you know, the one who created Hamilton Island—built this new dam halfway down the gulley and then did a lot of ripping and earth moving to smooth out the erosion below the new dam. I'm planting the trees to help prevent future erosion.'

She eyed off the gulley. 'It's hard to picture it, with the weather so dry.'

'The dam's only half-full now, several winters later, but one day it will overflow, and water will once again pour down through this gulley, heading for the river over there.' He pointed across the flats. 'I get a buzz when I see the cattle having this new dam to drink from, with shady trees to laze under afterwards. Before I came, this part of the property was very inhospitable to stock.'

Once again Hannah noticed his consideration for the comfort of others—including animals. Television coverage more often featured other men treating their stock badly.

She walked over to inspect another of his manna gums, now unguarded, having grown tall enough to withstand hungry mouths and strong enough in the trunk to withstand the pushes and shoves from cattle. She looked up to admire the foliage and spotted a grey furry bundle. 'Oh wow, look at this! A koala.'

He rushed across to the tree and looked up. His face lit with delight. 'So, there's my reward. It's the first koala I've actually seen on my property. Told you. They love these manna leaves.' He gave her a high five.

Hannah contemplated the two round brown eyes, staring down at her. 'He looks decidedly grumpy. We've disturbed his rest.'

Philip continued to peer up at his special guest. 'He should be lifting his paw in salute, thanking me for my strenuous efforts to provide his favourite dinner.'

The koala gave a few grunts and slowly moved up into a higher fork.

'I'm chuffed though. He had to take his chances, crossing the paddock.' She looked to him for clarification. 'Koalas don't get much nourishment from their food, so they don't have much energy and can't move fast. The cattle would have trampled him if they'd spotted him. It's why I'm planting these trees not far from the boundary fence—so they don't have to traverse too much open paddock.'

'I'm still amazed that the koala knew these trees grew here. We're not in a forest.'

'Nature holds many wonders. It's another reason to love this farm.'

'As you clearly do.'

He nodded. 'Enough gawking. Let's leave this little fella alone and get to work.' Reluctantly they returned to the truck and he collected his tools.

He began the task with his wire cutters, freeing the mesh cylinder from its supporting star posts and then cutting the series of wire twists, binding into cylindrical form what was originally a flat sheet of mesh. She helped him pull the mesh away from the tree. It took considerable effort, as the mesh was strong and well moulded into its curved shape. They scouted around the tree site, making sure no scraps of wire had escaped Philip's careful snipping and fallen to the ground. He then wielded an ingenious metal contraption to prise the three star posts out of the ground.

They repeated the process with a second sturdy tree before they shifted the mesh and the posts to the spot designated for the next round of tree planting.

The ground was rock hard, set almost as hard as

concrete. He pounded the heavy crowbar into the unyielding surface and eventually managed to lever up a few large clumps of clayey soil, which he set aside on the edge of the hole. He continued hoisting and smashing down the crowbar, eroding the sides and base of the hole until he deemed it big enough. Then he grabbed the mattock and swung it vigorously to break up and loosen the clumps so that tender roots would have a better chance of penetrating the ground, allowing the tree to establish itself more quickly.

The sweat dripped from his brow and sweat also darkened the back of his shirt. The sight and smell of a man working hard and drenched in fresh sweat was an unexpected turn-on for her.

He laid the mattock on the ground and stepped across to the truck to hoist out one of the pots, a couple of the water containers and a clump of hay. Placing the items beside the hole, he pulled up the hem of his T-shirt to wipe the sweat off his forehead. 'Would you mind planting this tree while I take a break?' he asked. 'You've said more than once that you like to garden.'

'Sure. But first …' She picked up one of the containers and held it out to him. 'Is this clean water?'

'Nope. It's from the dam, via the garden hose.'

'Have you got fresh water in the truck? You look like you need a drink.'

He grinned. 'Yes, Mum.' He wiped away the sweat around his neck as he walked back to get his water bottle.

She turned to the job at hand. She clenched her feet around the base of the plastic pot and pulled the tree upwards to release it from its container. 'This root ball is nice and damp. Good.'

'I do believe someone told me to soak the trees.' He grinned again.

She laughed. 'I'm glad someone heeded the advice.' She rested the small sapling inside the hole and called, 'Do you have any fertiliser pellets?'

'In the truck. I'll bring them over.'

He walked back to her and handed her a large screw-top plastic jar. She opened it and scattered some of the pellets into the bottom of the hole. She also mixed some with the mound of earth waiting to refill the hole. She dropped a generous handful of hay into the hole before emptying one of the water containers into the hole, watching it soak slowly into the hard ground beneath the tree. Using her left hand, she supported the tree so that the top of its root ball was roughly level with the ground and she kicked with her boot to back-fill the hole under and around the plant, using her right hand to drop in the rest of the hay as she worked. The hay would add organic matter and help stop the clay setting hard again too quickly. She tramped the soil to remove the air pockets surrounding the plant and mounded up the surplus to create a saucer-like shape around the tree, before pouring the second container of water into the depression. The dry soil drank it thirstily.

Satisfied that her tender nurture would yield good results, Hannah picked up the empty water containers and the plastic pot and returned with them to where Philip had casually propped himself, swigging on his water bottle. She smiled at him. 'That saturated hay and damp soil at the bottom should encourage the roots to go down deep.'

'You know what you're doing, don't you.' His tone was admiring.

She shrugged. 'With plants, yes. With animals, no.'

'Now for protecting your precious baby.' He selected one of the used star posts, placed its point on the ground close to the tree and held it vertically. 'Can you hold that in that position for me? Keep your gloves on, and your hands down low.' Hannah was mystified, but quickly understood when he picked up a heavy rammer, a steel cylinder with two handles and closed at one end, inserted it over the top of star post and began pounding the post into the hard soil. The vibrations shook her gloved hands.

Once he'd rammed it a couple of times he said, 'The post no longer needs you to hold it. You can let go now and move away. I don't want to hit your hands with this rammer as the post is driven further into the ground.'

Hannah stood aside and took another opportunity to admire Philip's muscle power in action. His vigour was almost as sexy as ... his likely antics in a bedroom. She rolled that delicious thought around in her mind until he interrupted her daydream. 'Done. Two more to go. I need to bash in three star posts to support the mesh and give it sufficient strength to withstand cattle pushing against the guard. They like to use it as a scratching post.' He picked up another post. 'Can you hold again for me?'

The clanging echoed in the gulley for a few more minutes. Then he picked up the mesh guard being recycled. 'Can you help me stretch this mesh back against the posts? It's much easier with two.'

He was right. It took effort to pull back against the tension in the mesh coil and re-wrap the steel into its cylindrical form round the three posts. He refastened the two ends of the mesh by cutting short lengths off his roll of lightweight fencing wire and twisting them into place. Then he tied the mesh to the star posts and used his wire cutters to remove any sharp ends.

'Good. That's one new tree done and dusted. Let's get the next one into the ground.' He walked over to the spot where the second guard had been dumped and they repeated the process.

'How many more to go?'

'Four.'

'Good grief! We won't finish before dark.'

'Oh yes we will. I won't recycle any more tree guards today. I'll use the new ones in the truck. That will speed up the process. And we're in the swing now.'

The next ninety minutes rushed by as they crow-barred, mattocked, shovelled and watered, strained with heavy gauge mesh, snipped with wire cutters and clanged on star posts. Working together so harmoniously fed her soul. She liked to work and was by nature a builder, a creator, but she needed the sense of *togetherness* in her endeavours to experience her "magic moments". In the final analysis, she didn't like soloists, egomaniacs, super-stars. She didn't enjoy actors and singers talking about themselves all the time. She loved to watch opera stars singing a duet, disciplined in their teamwork, or to hear a choir, each member with a definite part to sing. With Philip she'd discovered exactly what she wanted in her own life—harmonious teamwork.

He stood back to admire their combined efforts. 'It's the right time of year for planting. So far, I've planted about two hundred new trees as shade trees in the paddocks by judicious use of these tree guards.

'It's very apparent how much you love this outdoor work.'

'I do. It's much more rewarding than the gym visits during the week.'

'You should have been a farmer.'

'No way. The work on the farm is a complete change from the bank and refreshes me. It's great fun and very good relaxation, all the more so since the property is so scenic. From every vantage point it's like looking at an artist's retreat. My friends love coming here. I've been a bit anti-social of late but you'll see. Various friends have given me trees and plants for the farm which remind me of them.'

'You'll have to point them out to me. The plants I mean.'

'Plenty of time for that. We've finished here.' He studied the darkening sky to the south-west. 'We'd better get back. A big storm is brewing.'

'I agree. The wind has dropped. It's gone very quiet. The air has that stillness about it.'

'You're becoming a genuine country girl.' There was a teasing note in his voice.

'Not entirely. You know full well it's the same in the city. You can tell when a storm is coming.' A storm already raged inside her—a storm of desire, for him.

They trundled back to the sheds. Hannah noted the heavy build-up of clouds to the south. Would these storm clouds be another disappointment and blow across the town to dump their precious load on some lucky place further to the north? Adopting the Boy Scout's motto of "Be Prepared", she decided to drive into town to grab a few supplies, in case the storm did hit.

'I have to duck into town. Need anything yourself?'

'No thanks. I'm going to have a shower and head back to Melbourne soon. I'm giving Pat a lift, so I'd better get organised.'

The tantalising image of Philip in the shower quickly dissolved, replaced by the vision of Philip and Pat in the car together.

As she drove the last kilometre into town, the sky became so black she needed to turn on her headlights. She'd got as far the café alongside the supermarket, carrying her loaded shopping bag, when the heavens erupted. Jagged cracks of lightning lit up the darkened surroundings, followed by earth-shattering rolling claps of thunder. Then the rain started, bucketing down, like standing under a waterfall. Everyone's joyous, upturned faces said it all … rain at last.

The gutters filled rapidly with water until the whole street, from kerb to kerb, resembled a river. It rose above the kerb and crossed the pavement, lapping at doorways. It was a double-pronged attack because inside the café, water oozed down the walls and leaked through the light-fittings in the ceiling, the downpipes unable to carry the flow of water off the roof. Staff rushed round with buckets and mops.

Fifteen minutes later, the storm ended as quickly as it started. Hannah took off her shoes and waded in ankle-deep water to her car. Luckily it had been parked during the deluge, motionless, so she hadn't splashed any water into the car's electrics while driving. The car started at first turn of the ignition key, and she drove slowly along the main road before turning into her dirt road.

She swallowed a mouthful of disbelief. The road was

now impassable. A tree had fallen across the road. A raging river thirty feet wide rushed down the long wide gulley and over the road as it headed towards the valley floor. Her eyes widened. The baked-hard earth repelled the rain. The paddocks may as well have been made of concrete. Maybe four inches of rain had been dumped by the storm, and all of it, across a wide valley, was running straight off the surface.

She waited for the flow to subside and drove gingerly off-road around the fallen tree, eventually reaching the farm. She'd left it maybe 90 minutes earlier, in drought, the dams nearly empty, the cattle looking set for the sale yard.

She stopped briefly at the main gate to digest a miracle. Lake Louise was full. That same torrent on the other side of the hill had flowed down this side as well.

She parked her car and rushed past her bungalow and the pool towards the vantage point of the gazebo, which overlooked the big dam. Philip stood in the gazebo, dressed in his city gear, gazing at the sight in disbelief. Hannah's jaw dropped too. From the big dam, which Pat had assured Philip would take three years to fill with normal winter rains, water streamed out of the overflow channel. A flash of exultant joy zapped through her. Pat had been proved wrong, for once. By a miracle. By a cascade of water funnelled from high ground through a parched gulley.

Hannah's eyes sought his. His sought hers. He reached for her with the high-five salute. She ignored it and flung her arms around him. 'It's wonderful. Marvellous!' She laughed with the crazy joy of it.

His arms embraced her too, at first as spontaneously as Hannah. Excited, like a puppy dog wagging its tail. Almost imperceptibly, the enthusiastic sideways hug morphed into a gentler, more aware kind of hug. His stance changed and he drew her around in front of him, pulling her closer to his body. Her pulse picked up pace. She inhaled the heavenly smell of a freshly washed male body.

He gazed down into her eyes. 'You're special … you know that, Hannah Stockton?' His head lowered and he pressed his forehead against hers and gently rubbed noses with her. His arms tightened round her, he tilted his head to the side so their lips could meet and he kissed her. 'Thanks for being you.'

Through her dazed reaction, the tingling in her thighs, the surge of heat to her belly, she mumbled, 'You're welcome.'

Again, he pressed his lips against hers.

'Where are you, Philip? We'll be late.' The call from the verandah shocked them both. Pat's car had arrived, and they'd been too distracted to notice. Reluctantly, their hungry lips unlocked, their sizzling bodies eased apart.

'Be right there, Pat.' His rueful look at Hannah reflected her own crushing disappointment. A perfect moment, spoilt. If only. He reached for her hand, squeezed it and walked away.

She lingered, elated and deflated in the space of a minute, watching the water still pouring into the dam and exiting through the overflow channel. One miracle had led to a second—his mind-blowing kiss. At last. A man who could rev her up sexually. She wasn't half-dead as she'd feared.

# CHAPTER SEVENTEEN

Philip had only been gone a day but it felt like forever, since that kiss had opened Hannah's eyes to the possibilities of a physically exciting relationship. Next weekend couldn't come soon enough.

On her way to feed Alley, she crossed the courtyard towards the main house. How many times had its secrets intrigued her? She'd resided at *Wallumatta Farm* for nearly three months and still she hadn't entered that house, like a dark fortress, always locked up with the blinds drawn when Philip was not present. The cleaner had turned up a couple of times midweek but did all her vacuuming, dusting and mopping behind those closed blinds. Did Philip realise that his cleaner did not air the house, or was she following his instructions? Even with Philip in residence, he kept half the house closed up, and lived at one end of the house, at the opposite end to her bungalow. She conceded that he did open the blinds and windows in the rooms he used.

He rarely had visitors himself. Why? She'd seen the list of contacts in his phone. She'd heard him mention a busy social life in Melbourne. He'd told her that his friends loved coming here, bearing plantable gifts. Why had he turned into a hermit, using his weekends as an escape valve? What *was* he escaping from?

———

Next morning, through her kitchen window, she spied the resident eagle circling in an unusual place above the boundary fence between *Wallumatta Farm* and Pat's place. Strange. What's going on there? I must take a look. She congratulated herself on her heightened observational skills. Her awareness of her surroundings grew daily with this self-imposed "Year-in-Provence"-type experience.

Out on patrol, she stopped the truck at the top of the rise onto the ridgeline. Her previous trips had taught her that the road along the ridge gave a clear view of the fence line for its entire length, except at this far end, near Pat's boundary fence, where she'd seen the eagle. She got out and walked back along the ridge to investigate that out-of-the-way downhill section.

The sloppy cowpats proved the recent presence of cattle in this paddock, but she picked her way around the glistening mounds with confidence. She didn't have to worry about facing up to a cow while on foot, as they currently grazed in the end paddock containing the newly planted trees. Philip had left the gate into that paddock open on their way back last Sunday, and she'd gone back yesterday morning to close it. Then, the cattle had been out of sight, far down in the gulley, near the dam and the new trees, and she'd been able to hop out and close the gate without fear that they would rush up to her.

All had seemed well, yesterday.

She reached the blind spot, on the other side of the hilly ridge visible from her bungalow. She halted, at first terrified and then horrified. A cow with a very swollen belly lay on its side with its legs jammed under a gate she never knew existed. She stepped gingerly towards the carcass, able to tell by the smell that it was dead. At closer quarters, she could see that the land sloped very steeply at this point. Gateways always ended up well trampled and the cow must have slipped in the mud around the gate, late on Sunday, after that freakish thunderstorm.

Heavily pregnant, she'd rolled so that her front legs ended under the gate. She'd been trapped and unable to get up. Hannah's eyes filled with tears as she thought about the cow's suffering. There being nothing she could do, she rushed back to the ute and headed back home to grab her phone and ring Philip with the bad news. 'I'm so sorry Philip.'

His heavy sigh preceded his sorrowful response. 'Animals die, it happens, but it's always upsetting. That's the second mother I've lost, although I've lost a few calves over the years.'

'What should I do?'

'I have a meeting scheduled for eight in the morning, but after that I can juggle things so I can come up for a few hours. It's not something that you or Pat should have to deal with, but you can help me.'

Chuffed that he now preferred her aid to Pat's, she replied, 'Of course I'll help, but how?'

'I'm getting to that. It's fortunate that the rest of the herd is already in the end paddock. She must have been the last straggler who didn't pass through that open gate. The gate where you found her, against Pat's boundary fence, is rarely used. Maybe she doubled back, looking for a quiet spot to have her calf.'

'It's so sad. And I feel so guilty.'

'Don't be. It's not *your* fault.'

'But I *do* accept responsibility,' she mumbled despondently. 'I should have checked more thoroughly yesterday morning.'

He mulled over that comment before replying, 'I didn't think the cows spent much time grazing down in that corner. So most likely it would have happened, even with me present.'

'It's shaken me up.' Hannah's voice trembled.

'I'm sure it has,' he said. His calm reaction eased her guilt. 'Not a pretty sight … and there's worse to come.' The line went silent for a few seconds. 'The fire restrictions have been lifted. It's cooler now and we've had that rain. We'll have to burn her.'

She flinched. 'Oh my God, you don't mean it?'

"Fraid so. Which means … there's one thing you can do this afternoon, to save me time tomorrow. You can climb through the fence into that empty paddock on the lower side of where the cow is stuck and drag any loose timber you find lying around into a pile. Branches are always dropping off the yellow boxes in that paddock.'

The penny dropped. 'You want me to make a funeral pyre?' She cringed at the prospect.

'That's the general idea. Not the heavy stuff, of course.

I'll use the chain saw on that. It will help if you create a pile of kindling for me.'

---

She spent the afternoon cleaning up the lighter debris which had fallen from the eucalypts in the far paddock, dragging the material and stacking it at the bottom of the slope where the land flattened out. Back at home and down in the dumps, she almost forgot to feed Alley. It was nine when she remembered to walk across to the store cupboard and get out the cat food. The loud and penetrating "kerk, kerk, kerk, kerk" calls of the plovers dwelling down near the big dam, mournful on the night air, perfectly reflected her mood.

Next day, well after eleven, she heard Philip's Merc cruise into the driveway. He stopped near his front door, disappeared inside the house, and soon emerged though the back door dressed in his oldest clothes.

She called to him across the courtyard. 'I've got the water on the boil, if you'd like a hot drink before we start.'

He gave her the thumbs up signal. 'Tea please. Can you bring a mug over here? I'll be back in a minute. I'm just going up to the sheds to collect what we'll need.' He hopped in the truck and roared off.

Tucking her work gloves under her arm and plopping her hat on her head, she carried a tray with the mugs and a plate of sliced fruitcake across. When he returned, they exchanged a glance acknowledging that things had changed between them, but no kisses. Their mood too sombre, they stood by the truck, companionably sipping and munching.

'Thanks for that. It's a long time since I ate, and the job ahead will take considerable time.'

'I confess that I'm dreading this afternoon.'

He nodded in agreement and changed the subject. 'I had to get the Council's permission to light this fire, you know. There's no wind today, and although the paddock's so bare of flammable fuel, we still have to guard the fire to make sure it doesn't generate sparks and spread.'

She left the tray near his store cupboard and joined him in the truck.

'The way you described it, that poor cow is actually blocking the gate, and the slope there is steep. She'll have to be dragged down the hill, so we'll have to use some different gates and come at this problem from the downhill side.' He drove out his front gate and along the public road, skirting the farm until they reached a padlocked gate. 'We can get in here. This is my back entrance to my land. I don't use it often.' He handed her the key and she cleared his path into the paddock. He stopped near her pile of twigs and loose branches.

'Thanks. That's a good start, to get the fire going, but I'll also need some heavy timber for this job.' Hands on hips, he looked around the paddock. 'It's an ill wind. It's been on my mind to clear this paddock of the heavy branches which the eucalypts shed in storms or when heat-stressed. I'll fire up the chainsaw.'

Petrol fumes and a puff of smoke from the two-stroke motor accompanied the distinctive eruption of sound as the chainsaw burst into life, alternately revving and burbling as he tested the throttle. He got to work, hoisting long branches into position across smaller logs to create a fulcrum and keep the chain out of the dirt. Fascinated, she watched his powerful display of muscle power … such an archetypal male activity.

The noise was deafening. No point trying to talk. She could help by dragging the chopped-up sections towards her existing bonfire site. Her contribution to the task would be her walking time. A generous stack of timber grew slowly.

An hour later the chainsaw stopped whirring and a sweaty Philip deposited it back in the truck.

'Now for the tricky part. This hill is too steep for the tractor and forklift. I'm going up to that gate in the truck. Don't come. It's gut-wrenching to do this. The sight makes you cry, and the smell makes you want to puke and you're still getting used to cattle.'

'I know all about the crying.'

'I know. I tear up too.' His quick hug around her shoulders consoled them both.

'How will you move her?' She couldn't see how he'd manage the task on his own.

'I'm going to rope her by her hind quarters, tie the rope to the tow bar on the truck and drag her through the gateway and down here.'

He drove slowly in a straight line up the hill and carefully manoeuvred the truck into position, rear end close to the gate, front facing downhill. She watched as he got out, tied a bandana around his nose and mouth, pulled on a pair of rubber gloves and busied himself around the dead cow, heavy with her dead unborn calf. At one point, he raised his shoulder and upper arm and lowered his head, as if wiping a tear away on his work shirt. It never failed to amaze Hannah that he could be a tough cowboy type one minute and then this caring human being the next.

He got back in the cabin and inched his way back down the hill, stopping with his load adjacent to the woodpile. He got out and untied the rope.

She got the whiff of the dead animal. Her stomach lurched.

'Stand back, Hannah. I'll do this.'

He collected some newspapers from the truck, crumpled a number of pages and placed them hard up against the carcass, heaping a large quantity of the kindling on top. He carefully stacked a few of the thinner timbers into a semi-circular tepee shape over the top. He turned to her. 'This helps create an updraft. Like a chimney.'

He tucked more newspaper in around the edge of the stack. Then he went back to the truck and returned with a can of diesel fuel.

'We have to ensure this fire gets going properly and burns really hot and fast. Once I've got enough heat generated with coals, I'll stack on all the rest of the timber.'

He poured the diesel over the cow and sprinkled some on the wood. Retrieving a box of matches from his pocket, he quickly set fire to each piece of newspaper poking out from the stack. He stood back as the flame flared up and reached the diesel. Black smoke billowed up from the pile. Soon a mini-bonfire wafted the smell of burning flesh into the atmosphere.

They stood back, side by side, watching, tears trickling down their faces. Her hand reached out for his.

'Have you done this before? With that other cow? The one that swallowed the wire.'

'Couldn't burn her … no fires were permitted. Couldn't bury her … you've seen that the ground here's too hard to dig a big hole. She died in a more accessible place. I used the forklift attachment on the tractor, and took her to the far part of the farm and left her for the scavengers. Foxes. That eagle up there.' He pointed skywards.

She nodded. The food chain in nature.

He continued his sad account. 'I kept the other cattle out of that paddock for a while. Her bones ended up on a fire when I was cleaning up that part of the farm.'

The carcase slowly burned down. Carrying his crowbar, he walked over to the offside of the fire and levered the cow's remains up, over on top of the hottest coals of the fire, then stacked more wood around all sides of the animal.

She watched with a heavy heart, glad she didn't have to perform this gruesome task.

He returned to her side. 'I have to wait here until this fire burns right down. You don't need to stay. Go home and have some late lunch. Come back for me in a couple of hours.'

'Lunch? No way. I couldn't eat after this. I'll stay with you, keep you company.'

'Thanks. I'd like that.'

They stood side by side, not speaking, focussed on the fire and the need to stay upwind of the foul-smelling smoke.

At last, a pile of smouldering coals and ash signalled the end of the cow, and their ordeal. Using the base end of the rake he pushed it all together into a high mound to intensify the heat and burn off the remaining fuel, and then used the pronged side of the rake to spread the coals into a wide circle, burning off the surviving grass tufts surrounding the fire. Once satisfied that a large patch of burnt ground surrounded the fire and only a few tendrils of smoke emanated from the ashes, he raked everything back into a small pile.

He returned to her side. 'It's safe to leave it now. There's nothing left to burn and no wind to scatter ashes. Let's go. It's been a gruelling day.'

Instead of getting into the truck, he walked down to the property's external gate and padlocked it before returning to her. 'I can't wait to get out of these stinking clothes,' he said. 'They reek of smoke. Yours do too.' He gave her a sympathetic look. 'For now, we'll drive home via that end paddock. I need to monitor the other cows. Losing that heavily pregnant cow showed me that some of them are closer to calving than I expected. It's caught me on the hop, as I haven't separated out the older calves yet.'

He drove carefully across the slope to the internal gate leading into the end paddock and she hopped out of the truck to deal with it, a confident pro now. He selected a vantage point and stopped the truck. They surveyed the scene for a while. The first of the cows scattered across the hillside, grazing, started to head up the hill in their direction. He took no notice but focussed his eyes on another animal.

'That cow down there near the dam is about to give birth.' He pointed.

She peered in the direction he indicated. 'How can you tell?'

'She's restless, pacing up and down. Lying down, getting up, lying down again.'

'You're very observant.' His range of competencies surprised her every day.

'I've seen it before.' He turned to her. 'Have you ever seen a calf born?'

'Of course not.' Instantly she regretted her rather abrupt reply, but she hated having to admit yet more ignorance of Mother Nature's ways.

'It's one of this world's miracles.' He revved the engine. 'We'll drive a little closer and watch.'

Ten minutes later, the cow lay down and they heard a few soft grunts and moans. Almost instantly, a slippery mass lay in the dirt behind the cow. She heaved herself upright to inspect what had slid out of her. She sniffed. Bent to lick the animal. Within minutes, the calf struggled to its feet. Very trembly, but upright. Minutes later, the calf wobbled around its mother's four legs, exploring. Under her nose. At her rear end. Within fifteen minutes of birth, it stood under her teats, sniffing. It only took a few more minutes before its head nosed at her underbelly and it began sucking.

A dormant internal bellringer suddenly yanked on Hannah's own maternal bell ropes. She'd never wanted a baby … not with Alex. Now, here, with *this* man, the yearning for his baby overwhelmed her. Her eyes filmed over with unshed tears. 'How beautiful, Philip. It's a privilege to have seen this.' She saw his eyes on her, watching her reaction, and she tried to disguise the direction her thoughts had taken. Death and new life. On the farm and in her life too. The death of her relationship with Alex, the start of something new with Philip. 'I had no idea that life on a farm could be so fascinating, so absorbing, so creative.'

'It's a bit of compensation for the ordeal we've just endured.' He reached across the cabin and took her hand. 'I wish I didn't have to rush back to Melbourne, but I told you on the phone I could only get up here for a few hours today. I've stayed longer than I should have. The joys of a business life … I'm meeting an important client group for dinner tonight, and there's another 8am meeting tomorrow. I'm looking forward to getting back here on the weekend … to you.'

She thrilled when he leaned across the cabin and, to heck with smoky clothes, finished the kiss he'd started in the gazebo, before Pat's arrival had spoiled their moment.

CHAPTER EIGHTEEN

She heard a car pull up in front of Philip's house. Her pulse accelerated in anticipation of seeing him again, after the emotional strains of two days ago, followed by the promise of that kiss and what their growing bond meant. For her, there'd be no holding back this weekend … she was raring to go.

She checked her computer screen for the time. Strange. A car door slammed too early on a Friday for it to be Philip. She hurried across to investigate. At the corner of the house, precisely where she'd first seen the pool and the bungalow, she bumped into the last person she ever wanted to see again. Alex.

*Oh no. This is a disaster.*

'I told you I'd find you.' His look of triumph rivalled an Olympic swimmer's after a win.

Her stomach roiled with fear at being caught here alone with him but she refused to let him sense her fear. *Offence is the best defence.* She glared at him. 'You're trespassing. Please leave.'

'No, I've come to see you.' He reached out for her.

She backed off. 'You know perfectly well that I don't wish to see you. Go away.'

'I don't want to go. I've missed you. I love you.' He took a step towards her.

She stood her ground, hands on hips, eyes blazing with the anger he was arousing in her. 'Rubbish. You don't know what love is. If you did, you wouldn't have treated me, and my family, the way you did.'

'I know. I'm sorry.' He whined an unconvincing apology.

'Stop that tired old mantra,' she shouted at him. 'I'm sick of hearing you say that.' She held up a hand warning him to keep his distance. 'You're not sorry enough to change your ways. You're like a racehorse … you wear blinkers and you only know one track to run along. It's time to find another girlfriend.'

'I don't want another girlfriend. I want you.' He tried to grab her wrist and she shook him off.

'I don't want *you*. I've already asked you to go.' She pointed at his car.

He looked around him and an unpleasant sneer replaced his petulant expression. 'Found yourself a sugar-Daddy instead?' He waved his hands at the spread.

She ignored his jibe. 'How did you find me?'

'Asked around. I knew from the neighbours that you'd left town. Martin claimed ignorance but Gracie mentioned your name in connection with Boulton's.'

She inwardly cursed herself for that bit of girl talk with Gracie on the day she'd driven Philip to town for his meeting. To explain her early social call, she *had* mentioned dropping Philip at his office. Nothing else. No place names. No details of her living arrangements.

Alex jeered. 'It wasn't too hard to track him down here.' He advanced towards her again, crowding her. She took a step back.

'If you don't leave, I'll call the police.' *Show no fear. Be firm.*

'Yeah? You reckon? Why? I've never harmed you.'

*But any minute now, you might.*

'You're pathetic, Alex. You *did* harm my parents, and you seem to think that not hitting a woman is the only condition necessary for achieving a satisfactory relationship.' She glared her fury at him.

'I'm not *that* bad.' He came too close, with a demented look in his eyes.

'Yes you are. Now, I said stand back. I'm going to call the police.' Surely he'd take that threat seriously. He wouldn't want more trouble with the police.

'How? I don't see a phone in your hand.' His stance shifted to that of a prize fighter, ready to knock her down with one blow.

She didn't carry her mobile here. No reception. She didn't want him to see her retreat to the bungalow to use the landline. She didn't want him to follow her there. Too isolated. He could do anything, and no-one would see.

She couldn't escape into the main house via the back door. She didn't have a key. She didn't want Alex to realise that she wasn't the mistress of all he surveyed. Her chest was tight, her heart pounded, and she struggled to breathe. What could she do?

It would be dark soon. Her first instinct told her to get

to the front gate, out near the road, in the open, where she could flag down the next passing car. She stepped sideways and tried to edge past him along the verandah. He grabbed her on the upper arms to stop her.

'Get your hands off me.' Her fury gave her the strength to shove him away.

'Make me.' He pulled her closer and tried to kiss her.

She reared back and tried to knee him where it hurt, but he ducked back. His avoidance move forced him to loosen his grip long enough for her to escape from his clutches. She ducked under the balcony rail, crushing part of Philip's front garden as she scrambled out onto the drive and started running.

He began to chase after her, thought of a better idea and ran to his car. She heard his engine start and her panic accelerated. She couldn't outrun a car along the public road.

She knew the layout of the farm. He didn't. She could run where cars couldn't go. He must realise by now that she was alone here. If she could make it back to the bungalow in time and lock the door, she could call the police on her landline and stall for time until they got here.

She ran up the hill into the shed paddock and ducked back through the gap in the hedge towards her safe haven. She could hear his wheels spinning on the gravel as he realised, too late, that the rise from the house to the sheds was trickier than it looked. She hoped that the few seconds it would take for him to regain traction would be enough. She rushed to her door, slammed it shut, locked it and ran to the other door to make sure it was locked too. She knew he couldn't enter through the windows. She generally kept them shut and locked in this cooler weather and simply opened the doors at both ends of the house to re-ventilate during the warmth of the day. She grabbed the phone and dialled 000 as Alex pounded on her glass door.

Relief flooded through her once her call was transferred to the local police station. 'Help. I have an intruder. He's trying to break in on me. *Wallumatta Farm*. You know it?'

'Yes, ma'am.'

'At the back. Behind the main house. The bungalow.'

'I'm on my way.'

She hung up and called through the door, 'The police are coming.'

'Liar,' he snarled. 'You're bluffing. You won't dob me in.' He tried to yank the glass door open. 'It's obvious there's no-one here but you and me.'

A deep voice contradicted him. 'That's where you're wrong, pal.' Philip had arrived. In his most intimidatory fashion, he marched right into Alex's personal space and shirt-fronted him.

Hannah sagged against the doorframe, overcome with relief. Philip could easily handle bullyboy Alex.

Alex was full of bluster. 'Get lost, Boulton. This is between Hannah and me.'

'And now me.' Philip growled. 'You're trespassing on my property.'

'You can bloody well mind your own business,' Alex yelled. Hyped up with frustration and aggression, he forgot the basic rule of unarmed combat. Size matters. Strength matters. Hannah watched through the glass door as he threw a punch at Philip, who retaliated in kind with a short sharp jab to the nose. Alex yowled with pain and bent over, clutching his face and trying to staunch the flow of blood.

'Police!' a gruff voice called out.

'He assaulted me,' whined blood-streaked Alex, turning to the cop.

'I arrived in time to see who threw the first punch.' The policeman shouldered Alex away from Philip.

'He started it. And while you're at it, charge him with trespassing,' Philip commanded.

'And I want an intervention order,' Hannah demanded as she slid open the door.

The police officer took out his notebook and jotted down a few words. Mobile phones didn't work here but he took a few photos. 'You two can come down to the station over the weekend and make formal statements. You'  he grabbed Alex by the arm  'come with me.'

Philip watched them leave and turned to Hannah. 'What a scumbag he is.'

Her heaving breaths were slowing.

'You're safe now.' He gave her a reassuring hug. 'We both need recovery time.' He sat her down and pulled up a chair beside her, reaching an arm across her shoulders.

Some minutes passed as both sets of breath returned to normal and then he spoke again. 'After all that unwanted drama … come over tonight.' He angled his head towards his house. He tightened his hold as he looked down at her.

Their eyes met. To her, his eyes promised everything she wanted and needed. She nodded.

He lifted a hand to brush her cheek and whispered, 'Give me 15 minutes. I need to do something first. It's a surprise.'

Hannah fizzed inside, as if a champagne cork had popped. Her entry to Aladdin's cave … at last. Not only his house, but him too. Tonight would be *the night*? All the signs were there. Last weekend's kiss, especially. She couldn't wait. If he didn't jump her bones, she might jump his.

She rushed to shower, to wash all the Alex taint from her skin, and changed her clothes before almost skipping across to Philip's back door. He greeted her with a happy smile but, oddly, kept his distance. 'Welcome. I've wanted to ask you over for weeks.'

*Darn, I just don't get him, he's still holding back. It's slowly, slowly, catchee monkey stuff. Two steps forward, one step back.*

She could play this game too. Keep him guessing. She pretended they had no previous "history" and simply smiled. 'So what stopped you?'

'Had things on my mind.'

She hoped she'd been one of the *things*, but knew other matters bothered him. He'd admitted as such, on that morning when she'd driven him to work. 'Well, your mind had better be clear for the next few hours.' She dredged up a cheeky grin to cover her uncertainty at his unexpected reserve. 'I'm here now, and looking forward to sampling your cooking.' *And hopefully, more of your kisses.*

'Cooking's not what I had in mind. Tonight.'

She thrilled to his undertones. He wanted what she wanted.

'Thought we could eat in town again.'

*Darn the man, why isn't he interested in sampling something other than food?*

He flicked the tip of her wrinkled-with-disappointment nose, teasing her. 'Can you smell something else that's good?'

*Apart from him? He always smells good.* She sniffed the air. 'How irresistible. An open-fire.'

He led her across the room towards the fireplace. 'That's my surprise. Already planned, after our dreadful day with the cow last weekend. I thought you'd like to enjoy a *comforting* fire. It's my first fire for the season. In your honour.' He draped his arm round her shoulders and drew her close as they stood side by side, gazing at the flames of the newly lit blaze.

She snuggled in to him. 'Thank you. What an alluring picture.' *And how alluring you are.*

He gave her a squeeze. 'Once the hot coals and ash bed form, they warm the whole room. It's very cosy.' He tweaked her nose again, playfully. 'You'll see, when we get back from the pub.'

She looked forward to sharing dinner with him and sharing the build-up of anticipation for what would surely come later. 'Is it safe to leave the fire burning when you're not here?'

'Very. For a start, you'll note nothing combustible lies close to this fire. And I can close this safety screen at the drop of a hat.' He toed the metal screen, currently drawn back from the fire. 'These fire boxes are great inventions.'

Being a girl from the city, where open fires were banned for air pollution reasons, she'd hardly ever seen an open fire. Standing by this fire, with him, she revelled in the warmth, the cosiness, the smell, the calming influence of the crackling wood and the changing colours of the flames. It touched a primeval part of her brain. She stood quietly, absorbing this unaccustomed pleasure.

'The metal box inserted into the fireplace is cleverly

designed to work on the convection principle. You know … hot air rises, cool air sinks. The room's cooler air at floor level is sucked in through that gap under the fire.' He grabbed the poker from the stand of tools on the hearth and tapped the gap. 'The air is warmed as it passes behind the fire and it flows out through the slot above the fire.' Another tap.

She had to laugh, even if inwardly. He'd grown so accustomed to her wanting and needing explanations all the time that he must imagine that's what she needed tonight too, an explanation of a firebox. How wrong he was.

Oblivious to the direction of her thoughts, he pointed to the metal screen. 'Open at present, for maximum enjoyment of the sight of flames and the direct radiant heat. When I'm out of the room, and overnight, I close the screen and clip it in position, just in case a rogue spark escapes or a log rolls.'

She'd prefer that sparks be flying between them as *they* rolled together. For now, she'd continue to play a straight bat as his rapt pupil. How long could she make this last? 'I don't like to douse your fire, but is this environmentally friendly? Burning timber? I have to ask … what about global warming?'

'Relax, Hannah. No need for concern. I know some might frown on this fire as an emitter of greenhouse gases, but it's actually incredibly efficient. I use the yellow box timber from the block, and that burns very cleanly, with minimum smoke. The firebox design sends most of the heat into the room, not up the chimney into the atmosphere.'

'So you're a greenie,' she said.

'It makes sense, here. I'd otherwise have to use electricity taken from the grid and generated by coal-fired power stations to run those wall panels.' He pointed to several heaters fixed to the wall of this large room.

She was having so much fun, keeping her straight face. 'What about solar cells?'

'I already have that for the hot water supply, with electricity back up.'

'Is that all?' Couldn't he stop being so serious?

No, he was intent on his man-splaining. 'I'll go further when battery technology improves. While I'm still in the throes of cleaning up all the fallen timber on the block, this arrangement remains most economical way of heating this end of the house, where I spend all my time.'

'I'm impressed. You've thought it all through.' She burst out laughing.

He finally got it and laughed too. 'You've been winding me up.'

'I hope nicely, not mean-spiritedly.'

He gave her a lop-sided grin. 'Sorry about getting on my soapbox. You do like my surprise, don't you?'

'I love it. You sure know the way to a girl's heart.' She put one hand to her heart, the other on his and fluttered her eyelashes in the best theatrical manner she could manage.

'You should go on the stage!' Wheels crunched on the drive. 'Bloody hell, who can this be?' Philip broke away and strode impatiently to open the front door as a car door slammed. 'Pat! What brings you here?' His annoyance at the interruption overrode his manners.

Hannah groaned. Not again. Pat sure knew how to pick the wrong moment.

Pat ignored Philip's abruptness. 'That police car, of course. Is everything all right?' Without invitation, she brushed past Philip and walked into the room as if she owned the place. 'A fire too! I saw the smoke trails wafting out of your chimney.' She spotted Hannah. 'Ah. A special occasion. Hannah's here.'

'As a matter of fact, Pat, it *is* a special occasion. Everything's okay but we have some private matters to discuss after the police visit so, if you don't mind, I'll catch up with you later on the weekend.' His arm barely touching her shoulder blades, he shepherded her back towards the front door.

Pat glared at Hannah as she departed. Her car roared off and Hannah laughed. 'Expertly done. Firm and effective. Polite at the end.'

He rolled his eyes. 'I get a lot of practice in getting rid of people at work.'

'She'll never forgive *me*, though! She wanted to hear all the gossip.'

'She can wait. You're more important.'

*More important than Pat? She doesn't hold the keys to his heart!* Adrenaline flooded through Hannah. She could jump over the moon.

He took both her hands in his, drawing her back towards him, his eyes searching hers, sending the message that *she* formed the centre of his world.

She trembled with excitement as his lips neared hers.

His home phone rang. He jerked away. 'Damn. What now. Sorry, but I'd better take that. I'm expecting a crucial call. My mobile doesn't work here.'

He grabbed the receiver. 'Philip Boulton speaking.' His face darkened. 'Oh. … Yes. … She's here.' Eyebrows raised, he handed the phone across to her.

'Hello? … Martin? … However did you get this number?' She glanced across the room at her frowning companion.

'Alex told you where I live?' Her voice rose in disbelief.

Philip scowled.

'This is very creepy. I'm sure this number's unlisted.' She eyed off Philip, nodding his head in confirmation.

'Ah, trust him to be able to work the system. It surely pays to have friends in low places.'

Philip's scowl deepened.

'I don't understand. How did *you* get it? … Alex? … He came to see you today? … You're ringing to warn me?' She chose her words deliberately, for Philip's benefit, to keep him abreast of the conversation.

'Thanks for thinking of me, but you're too late. He turned up here earlier this evening and had another brush with the law. … Yes, I'm okay Martin, it's all under control, no need to worry about me. Thanks. You're great.' She smiled into the mouthpiece.

'Sure, Martin, I'd love to catch up.' She listened for a moment. 'Here?' Across the room a very annoyed-looking Philip indicated what her answer should be.

'Actually, that's not a good idea. I'll be down in Melbourne again soon. I'll come round for a coffee.' Nervously she looked across at Philip, his face as black as thunder.

'Bye for now. And thanks for calling. It means a lot to me.'

She replaced the receiver. 'My old neighbour. Remember? The one who helped me when I left Melbourne.'

'*Former*, not old,' he corrected her.

That *should* have sounded like a teasing response but sounded more like a growl. She looked at him curiously. 'So you do remember?'

'Young, by the sound of him.' He snarled. 'Wanting to arrange a tête-à-tête?'

'Yes. He's a friend.' She stared at him. Uneasiness swept over her. Every skerrick of the earlier warmth between them had vanished. She'd never seen him acting like this before … jealous.

Surely he wasn't another man like Alex, unable to handle the women in his life having contact with other men and arranging to meet them. Surely not!

She had no room in *her* life for any more men like Alex. Her stomach plummeted. On this matter she had no right to challenge Philip … essentially her boss, not her lover. Fantasising about him in that role had been a bad idea. She must terminate her silly pipedreams. 'You're expecting your business call. I'll get going. I've got food over at my place.'

Philip watched her go. His hopes for this evening disappeared up his chimney with the smoke. Rage and anxiety had bubbled up in him during that phone call. An acute sense of loneliness too. He longed for her to talk to him as unreservedly as she communicated with Martin. What was wrong with him, that she seemed always to be on guard with him, holding back? He seethed with anger at himself. Where had these feelings come from? Why did she provoke them?

His mates down in Melbourne would never believe what a turn-on it could be with a woman like this. He'd have been hard to convince too, before she came into his life and proved that plunging necklines and tottery high heels weren't the way to this man's heart. He'd seen her dressed up, at the art show, and in her comfortable old clothes. He'd seen her in various guises: nervous, brave, happy, scared, content. He'd seen the passion in her eyes when he kissed her. She could be a real partner, in every sense of the word, but he was stupidly wrecking everything.

# CHAPTER NINETEEN

Saturday promised to be awkward. Last night had not gone well. With that phone call from Martin, all that electrifying promise radiating from Philip had vanished as quickly as a light being switched off. Her own buoyancy had vanished too. She'd crashed back to the wary starting point of their relationship, the day she'd first arrived at his front door.

She reminded herself that her caretaking role continued and work on a farm never ends, especially when cows are calving. Technically, he could perform his rounds alone, as he had before she arrived, and as she'd been doing all week, but she got ready for the call to join him. Just in case.

Her eagerness annoyed her. Despite discovering he had a jealous streak, she couldn't wait to see him.

He left her dangling in a state of uncertainty until mid-morning when he knocked on her door. 'Ready? We've got a lot to do before dark.'

She fumed inwardly at the ultimate pragmatist, so

matter-of-fact, standing on her balcony. His inscrutable face would have done credit to any card sharp.

They drove their usual route in complete silence. Though subdued, he made no apology for his angry reaction to that phone call from Martin. Stubbornly she declined to make small talk, to fill the conversation gap. What could she say? They had no acknowledged relationship and she couldn't chide him for a display of jealousy. She'd look silly.

She scanned the terrain as they bounced over the track and was the first to spot the cow in the paddock, agitatedly nosing a newborn calf lying on the ground.

'Over there.' She pointed. 'Look. A new arrival.'

He zoned in on the spot and frowned. 'Damn. Not what I wanted to find today. Something looks wrong. We'd better get closer.'

Philip drove the ute cautiously across, stopped a little distance from the pair and got out. 'I need to be careful here,' he said. 'She could charge me in defence of her calf.'

The mother watched Philip's cautious, measured approach, listened to his soft coaxing voice and, surprisingly, stepped back to let him look at her calf. The patches of discharge on the ground said it all. He called out, 'This baby's got scours, Hannah.'

He returned to the truck and rummaged in the cabin behind his seat, grabbing the plastic container of water and the bottle of Ribena that had always bounced around on the floor of the ute, mystifying Hannah.

As he walked backed to the cow and calf, he called over his shoulder. 'One of the old-timers told me what to do. You can come and help, if you're game.'

Hannah quickly followed in his shadow, across to the distressed animals. 'What's scours?'

'See that sticky yellow diarrhoea round its tail. Young calves exposed to new organisms in their environment often get that.' He set down the water and began unscrewing the bottle. 'I must get that calf up on its feet again, before it's too dehydrated from all that moisture loss. Lying down, it can't reach Mum's teat for a fresh intake of liquid.'

The cow stood guard on the other side of her calf, her huge brown eyes watching Philip's every move. She showed no sign of fear or distrust. Her calf was sick, and she sensed he'd come to help.

He poured a good dose of Ribena into the water container and swirled it around to mix it. 'This is a bit like the old 'flat lemonade' trick our grandmothers used to swear by.'

She nodded. It made sense. His endless capabilities never ceased to impress her. How could she resist such a competent *and* caring man? There must be a plausible reason reconciling his behaviour today with his behaviour last night. Her coolness towards him evaporated. 'What do you want me to do?'

'I'm going to straddle this little guy to hold him in position on the ground, then force his head right back with his jaws prised wide open. I want you to tip some of that liquid into his mouth. Wait a few seconds while he gulps down the big surprise, and then tip some more. We need to get quite a bit of liquid in, as much as we can.'

Hannah kneeled on the ground opposite Philip, with the protective mother hovering right behind her. Nervous of being kicked or trampled, but determined, she started to pour. Suddenly a large jaw bumped her shoulder and a raspy tongue licked at her ear. It should have scared her to death, but no fear erupted. Incredible. The cow trusted them to help and was thanking them. Of all the *Ah hah* moments she'd so far experienced on this farm, this surpassed everything. Philip had brought her a long way along the pathway towards her goal of engaging with real life.

A fair bit of life-giving liquid spilt on the ground, but a lot went down the calf's throat too. Philip waited for a few minutes, watching the calf respond. 'Now I'm going to heave him up onto his feet,' he said. 'He won't survive otherwise. He's small, maybe weighs 25kg. I should have no problems getting him up.'

He stood, straddled the calf, grabbed it round the middle and hoisted, steadying it in position once all four hooves made contact with the ground. The calf wobbled and seemed to be okay but toppled to its knees as soon as Philip released his grip.

As if to reassure both himself and Hannah that their joint efforts hadn't been futile, he said, 'I'll wait for a bit, then try again.'

He had more success the second time. The calf swayed a little, but stayed upright. Philip took a few paces back and let the mother come and sniff at her baby. She positioned herself so the calf could suckle. It astonished Hannah to see how quickly its energy returned.

Philip picked up the containers lying in the dirt, straightened up and looked at Hannah with a satisfied smile. 'We'll have to keep an eye on these two. We'll come back in a few hours to make sure he's not down again. We might have to repeat the process.'

Hannah returned Philip's smile. Triumphantly. Teamwork with this man for all seasons created a powerful attraction. In his company, she knew she could overcome all obstacles.

He high-fived her. 'I'm proud of you, Hannah. That could have been tricky, but you showed no fear. That anxious mother could tell, and trusted us.'

Hannah swore she must be glowing with elation. 'I'm thrilled that you … we … saved that little calf.'

'Me too. And that I've redeemed myself in your eyes … I hope.' He bit his lip as he eyed her off, an anxious expression clouding his face.

'You mean after last night.' *Is he seeking my forgiveness?*

'Yep. On reflection, I acted like the worst kind of jealous guy.'

Hallelujah for self-awareness in a man, but an unconditional pardon could not be his reward. 'I wasn't impressed with what I saw. Been there, done that, with Alex. No more jealous guys … ever.' Oops, her words implied the kind of relationship that didn't exist between them. 'Even as friends,' she rushed to add.

'It wasn't jealousy, my friend.' A shadow scudded across his face, like a cloud across a landscape. 'I had my reasons.' He stared into the middle distance of the paddock, as if debating within himself whether to divulge them. 'One day I'll explain.'

Hannah hid her disappointment that he categorised her as his friend, and not something more. 'I can see that something is eating away at you. It's usually better to let it out.'

'Soon. I'm getting there. It's a long story … kind of.' His voice trailed off and he turned to stare across the river flats.

'When you're ready, Philip.' She offered the supportive words of a friend.

He turned back to her. 'I feel that I *could* tell you, Hannah. You've got a heart. Intelligence too.'

'Thank you.' She'd end up with a swollen head if he kept this up for much longer.

'I often think about brainpower. You know, that's the thing about the cows out here in the paddock. The main difference between them and us is their grey matter.' He tapped his head. 'They're smart, in their own ways, but we're much smarter. And some people are smarter than others. Like you. You watch, you think, you learn.'

She shrugged away her pleasure at his compliment. 'I'm a writer, don't forget. Watching other people is part of what writers do.'

He leaned across and tweaked her nose. 'Sometimes I'm sure those gorgeous navy-blue eyes of yours can see right *through* me. With you, it doesn't make me nervous. Just simpatico with you.'

Simpatico. Music to her ears. 'D'ya know, I think we're two of a kind.'

'Sorry? You've lost me.'

'Maybe I lack the outgoing personality that the workplace must demand of you, but *here* we're both happy in our own company. We both need the solitude to restore our energy.'

Philip stared at her. His eyes widened and she could have sworn a torch bulb flashed on inside his head. He dropped his containers and grabbed her arm for a moment. 'You're right. I hadn't thought about it that way before.'

She leaned against him in a companionable way. 'I

reckon that's why we've been able to spend many comfortable hours together without needing other people.' Although being close to him thrilled her, she withdrew to her personal space to watch his reaction.

Another light bulb seemingly flashed in his head. 'Whereas Pat, for example, needs company and action all the time.'

'I've noticed.' Her eyes gleamed at him, projecting dry humour.

'Hmm.' His eyes gleamed back at her. 'I've enjoyed the interplay between you and Pat these past few months.'

She gave him her best "you naughty boy" look. 'I have a fair idea you engineered some of it.' They both laughed.

She held up a warning hand. 'Beware, Philip. People like us can be a relationship hazard.'

'Danger lies ahead? I'm willing to risk it.' He flashed her a cheeky grin.

'I think about a lot of things I don't talk about. From what I've seen of you, you're the same.'

'So, I might be surprised at what goes on inside your head?' He ruffled her hair for a brief moment. 'None of this what-you-see-is-what-you-get stuff.'

She resisted the urge to reciprocate, to touch him. 'Exactly. A mystery woman, that's me.'

'So you're a birthday gift, tied with a shiny ribbon, waiting to be unwrapped.'

Philip drew so close that he had to look down at her. 'I love mysteries,' he whispered. 'Are you going to give me a little clue?'

She lowered her chin and looked up at him coyly, doing her unpractised best to act the coquette. 'Maybe I'm not as prim and proper as you might believe.' *Flirting is such fun.*

'Show me.' They had no audience except the cows. He tilted her chin back up. 'Kiss me,' he murmured. 'Prove to me that you won't be shocked at what I've been thinking about you. Unshackle the real you. Have I seen it?'

The bedroom gaze in his eyes wooed her and she sighed with pleasure. 'Not yet … just the tip of the iceberg.'

'Then press your body against mine and melt a little.' He enclosed her in a fierce embrace.

Wrapped so confidently in his strong arms, she could have sworn she was floating in a bliss bubble.

Close by, the sound of the cow kicking the empty plastic water container as she fussed around her weak calf, brought them crashing back to earth. Philip had been pressing her ravenously against the bulge in his jeans. He slid his hands from her buttocks up to her shoulders, gripped her for a minute, squeezed and let go in a hurry. 'Forgot we might be in danger. We'd better get out of here.'

She stretched up and brushed her lips against his. 'More melting later?'

'I can't wait.'

He retrieved the container and the Ribena and they retreated to the truck.

She leaned across the cabin and teased him with another brief kiss. 'So what did you intend as my lesson for today? Before we were … distracted.'

'Something I should have done before this latest batch of calves started to arrive. Cull out the older ones. The mothers kick them away once they're feeding a newborn calf, but some of those older ones are persistent.' He pointed out the window at the calf they'd just saved. 'We'll leave this wobbly little man here with his mother, round up the rest of the herd and get them into the yards. Another new experience for you, Hannah.'

He drove down to the lowest corner of the paddock, opening and closing various gates near the stockyards, before they returned to the high ground.

'The trick is to get the herd moving down to that bottom gate, because beyond that gate is a fenced-in laneway which funnels the cattle up to the yards. We've doubled back to this cow because she's the most distant from that gate. We'll walk towards her, purposefully, yelling a bit and flapping our hats, to encourage her to turn tail and trot away from us in the general direction of that gate. She'll head towards one of her mates and her momentum should gather up the second cow. Once we get a few moving, and one of them sees the open gate at the bottom of the hill, they'll all get the general idea. The older cows have done this before. The calves will follow their mothers.'

It worked like a dream. Half an hour later Hannah found herself in the yards, up close and personal with heaving cattle.

By God, this was hard work. And dangerous too, in such an enclosed space. Yet somehow she felt safe with Philip as they dodged around with nothing for protection but a short piece of polypipe for thwacking at a cow's rump, a two-way gate as a shunt and a shield, and a pair of booted heels agile enough to power a scramble up onto the top rail of the fence. The cattle milled round in a frenzy, squirting poo in every direction, including Hannah's. She resisted the urge to wipe her face on her sleeve. So far her eyes and mouth had escaped and she was anxious to avoid smearing the excreta into them. Bit by bit Philip sorted the herd, swinging gates at the right time to send a mother into one yard, a strong calf in another direction, into a holding pen.

Hannah perched on the fence as Philip separated out the last of the animals. From her vantage point, she watched Pat crawling through the wire fence separating her property from Philip's.

Pat joined them at the stockyards. 'All that bellowing caught my attention. I can see these yards from my kitchen window.' She surveyed Hannah's filthy face and clothes. 'It's a long time since I looked like that! *I* know how to stay away from the back end of a cow. Hope you've got plenty of hot water at home.'

A stern voice interrupted. 'Leave it, Pat. Hannah's been a big help.'

For a moment Pat looked crestfallen. Then she said, 'How do you like our handiwork?'

Hannah was mystified. 'Sorry? Handiwork?'

'These stockyards.' Pat encompassed them with outspread arms.

'Oh … um, they seem to work well.' Hannah hadn't given this matter any thought. She'd been too busy avoiding being trampled and admiring Philip's moves.

Philip chipped in. 'It's no accident that they work well. Stockyards have been purpose-built for a long time. They're designed this way for a reason.'

'I've just seen the reason,' Hannah said.

'One of the reasons … for sorting out a herd.' He shunted the last of the cows through a gate. 'I also use them for ear-tagging, vaccinating and drenching, for treating an individual animal in that metal crush, and for loading the stock into trucks for onward movement.' He pointed to the ramp leading upwards beyond the crush. 'You'll see.'

'We worked from dawn till dusk over a number of weekends building these yards. They're perfect.' Pat lifted her chin and puffed out her chest.

Hannah asked, 'Were you the adviser?'

Philip shook his head. 'She inspired the project, because I was using *her* yards when I should have had my own. I worked out the actual design.'

'*I* was his "apprentice", as he put it. I helped him manhandle and position the timbers.' Pat seemed determined to gain credit for her role. Apparently justifiably so.

'You did that, Pat. Thanks. I couldn't have done it without you.' Philip turned to Hannah and grinned. 'The local farmers can't quite believe that a city boy like me does what I do here, developing the farm and getting my hands dirty.'

Pat nodded. 'They occasionally drive by on Sundays to see what he's up to. He's a tourist attraction.' She chortled.

A month ago Hannah might have been dispirited by the obvious bond between Pat and Philip. Now that his bond with *her* was becoming clearer, these days she tried to put herself in Pat's shoes. Pat lusted after Philip, but he showed no interest in her that way. Pat, jealous of her, kept trying to prove her worth to Philip. She could understand Pat's desperado behaviour.

Philip chuckled. 'Tourist attraction? A slight exaggeration there, Pat.' He took her arm and set her in motion towards her fence. As they walked, he said, 'Thanks for dropping by and all that, but we still have work to do.'

'Sure you don't need my help?' Pat dawdled beside him, clearly reluctant to leave.

Their exchange amused Hannah. *Eager beavers* had nothing on Pat.

'Not today, thanks. I hate to break up this party but it's a case of two's company, three's a crowd in the confines of these yards. I'm still teaching Hannah the ropes.'

'Then I'll leave you to it.' Pat slouched off, shoulders slumped.

A twinge of empathy flashed through Hannah. The boot had been on the other foot when she'd been excluded from Pat's dinner party. She brushed that thought aside to focus on the task at hand. 'What happens now?'

'We release the mothers back into the main paddock area, so they can give birth to their new calves in peace. Then we deal with these older calves.'

Hannah eyed off the heaving mass of animals frenziedly butting each other and the sides of their pen, frantic to re-join their mothers. 'Where do they go next?'

'I'm selling them. Until they go, I'll keep them in the holding paddock next to these yards. You won't get much sleep tonight.'

Her jaw dropped. Was this man for real? 'You have plans for me tonight, then?'

'I do, but not quite how that sounded. And not with you looking as you do right now.' He grabbed a rag from the back of the ute and wiped some cow poo off her cheek.

'Ugh. I need that shower.'

He laughed. 'You do. We both do.'

'But not together. Not when I look like this.' Washing

off this muck wasn't her idea of a romantic interlude with him.

'No need to rush anything. Relax, Hannah, I'm happy to go slow. We'll both enjoy it more that way.' To prove it, he gave her a lazy smile. 'For now, you can help me with these gates. Mothers first.'

Fifteen minutes later, she gave him the thumbs up sign as the last calf charged out of the yards into the holding paddock and they slammed the bolt shut on the gate. 'Job done. Now what?'

'Just you wait. Overnight the farm will resound with the bawling of incensed calves calling for their mothers, and the distressed moos from the cows as they pace up and down the fence line in their separate paddock.'

She watched the calves galloping down to the boundary fence separating them from their mothers. 'Do they ever push through the fencing wire? They're not as big and bulky as the cows.'

'They try, but that's a double fence line, with bushy trees planted in the gap between the two fences. It discourages them from trying to re-unite with Mum.'

'I see. Makes sense.' She looked down at her disgusting attire. 'I doubt my mum would want to reunite with me right now.' She shuddered. 'It's shower time.'

'Yep. Hop in, let's go.'

'Sure? You managed to avoid most of the squirts. My filthy clothes will mess up the seat?'

'No worries. It'll wipe off. It's only digested grass, after all.' He revved the ute and they bounced across the paddock towards the house.

Hannah didn't dare look sideways at him. Never had she

felt less sexy. She'd once hated the thought of even stepping in cow poo. Now she was covered in it. She stank.

They reached the parking spot for the ute and she scrambled out. Philip looked at her and grinned. 'I'll leave you in peace for now. When you're ready, bring over your soiled clothes and I'll bung them in the washing machine with mine. No need to soil the town's laundromat with them, although I'm sure those machines are used to it. We'll have a well-earned drink before dinner.'

She scuttled off to clean herself up, from her head to her toe tips.

An hour later she presented herself at his back door, carrying her bundle of washing. 'These items are wet. I rinsed them with the hose. The worst of the muck's on the garden bed.'

'Good. The laundry's down here.' He walked her along the verandah to another door at the end of the house and lifted the lid of the large top-loading machine for her to toss in her clothes on top of his. He set the washer in motion while she washed her hands over his laundry tub.

'We can relax now. Come on.' He led her back to his main living area, through the house this time. A guided tour was not on offer. 'Apart from my office, I don't use this part of the house much,' he said over his shoulder as he walked quickly past what she supposed were guest rooms and through the formal lounge and dining areas.

They reached the kitchen area. He lifted a bottle of Chandon Brut out of an ice bucket and popped the cork. 'A celebratory drink's what we need.' He picked up a fluted glass and looked at her. 'I know you like bubbly. The art show. Remember?'

She nodded. 'What are we celebrating?' She loved that he remembered that night.

He poured and handed her the glass. 'Us. Here's to us.' He clinked his glass against hers and each gulped down a gigantic mouthful.

The fizz hit her bloodstream. This is heaven, being with him.

'It's been a big day. Thank you, Hannah. We're a good team, you and I.'

They raised their glasses again and this time each took a leisurely, provocative, seductive sip, with neither taking their eyes off the other. A slow combustion stove caught alight inside Hannah.

He took both glasses and set them back on the tray. His eyes sought hers again. 'You take my breath away. Come here, Hannah. Let's finish what we started this morning.'

She stepped into his arms and their bodies pressed together. A fairy wand turned her smouldering internal stove into a factory furnace. 'I don't want to go slow, Philip.'

He backed her eagerly towards his bedroom, raining kisses every place he could reach.

She couldn't wait for him to explore the rest of her.

## CHAPTER TWENTY

'Wake up, sleepyhead. Breakfast time.'

Hannah dragged herself awake. She looked around the room. Where was she? The night's memories returned with a flush of pleasure.

'Sleep well?' Philip stood by the bed with a cup of tea in his hand. Something smelt good in the kitchen. Her stomach growled as she remembered they'd skipped dinner last night. There'd been no holding back. They'd both been ready to jump straight into the fast lane.

She pressed a hand to her mouth and yawned. 'The sleep of the exhausted.'

'Me too. You'll wear me out.' He plonked down the tea and kissed the top of her head.

'Sorry I slept in. It's not like me. I woke in the night and found it hard to get back to sleep with those mournful sounds from the cattle.' His sensuous body sprawled beside her hadn't helped either.

'It's distressing, I agree.' He pushed her across a few inches in the bed, sat down on the edge of the mattress and stroked his thumbs across her bare shoulders. 'Like that?'

She shivered. 'You have the magic touch.'

'You've been spared another sleepless night, my darling. Sleepless for that reason, anyhow.' He bent to kiss the tip of her nose. 'It usually takes about a week before the cows forget their calves and the mooing stops but those calves are being trucked away today. The cows won't be able to smell them, or hear them, and they'll soon forget.'

'When ever did you organise that?' She tried to focus her attention on what he was saying. His thumbs had moved down to her breasts and it was very distracting.

'Yesterday, while you busily showered away the evidence of your foray into the yards.' He grinned as she wrinkled her nose in distaste at the memory. 'It only took one phone call. I rang Rick, the local stock and station agent. He's coming this afternoon.'

Reluctantly, she pushed aside her masseur and wriggled into an upright position. 'I have to ask. What will happen to those calves?'

'They'll go to the store sale. Some other farmer with good pasture will grow them further over the next 12 months. Now, lazybones, drink your tea while it's still hot and come and eat your breakfast.'

<hr>

Rounding up Philip's calves for trucking to the saleyards proved to be men's business. Serious men's business.

The frisky young animals had no lead cows to calm them down and were in no mood to co-operate. As fast as Philip and Rick herded them into one corner of the holding paddock, aided by their shouts and the waving of their poly pipes, one would break away and gallop off in the opposite direction, spooking the others into following. Much cursing and swearing coloured the air. Running off the condition that would bring good prices at the market, the calves soon foamed at the mouth.

Hannah watched, mystified at the impatient ways of men. Philip had forgotten Pat's principal rule when handling cattle contained in manageable paddocks ... *be patient*. The ute happened to be parked in the middle of the paddock and it had a trailer load of hay bales attached, ready to deliver to the pregnant cows milling around in the adjoining paddock. Here lay the carrot, waiting to tempt. No need for the stick.

Pat emerged from her house, crawled through the strands of fencing wire and came over to join Hannah. Both women surveyed the scene with hands on hips.

Pat snorted. 'Men! They have no idea.'

The derision Pat directed at her hero startled Hannah.

Pat kept watching, and sighing.

Eventually, Hannah turned to Pat and gave her a friendly pat on the arm. 'It's time to do it your way, Pat.' Being more aware of Pat's insecurities these days, it cost her nothing to defer graciously to Pat's undoubted farming knowledge.

Pat looked surprised and grateful. 'I agree. Jump in the ute, Hannah.'

She obeyed and leaned out of the driver's window. 'What next?'

Pat walked over to the window. 'Move down to the bottom corner and angle the ute and the trailer facing up the hill, with the engine idling. Remain quietly in the driver's seat. I can see that the gate to the stockyard is open.' She pointed up the slope.

Hannah immediately understood Pat's intentions. The young cattle had been thundering past the ute, at a distance, with no chance to get a whiff of the hay. Next time the agitated animals headed in this direction and stopped for a rest, the hay would be in the right position to tempt them into submission.

Before Hannah drove off, Pat hoisted a bale of hay off the trailer and lugged it close to the stockyards, where she broke it up and strewed hay all the way into the inner reaches of the enclosure. She then positioned herself in the paddock so that she could head off at the pass any animals that might baulk at the gate and try to dash off sideways.

It worked exactly as Pat planned. With the trailer of hay to tempt him, the most rambunctious animal took a few steps toward it, then another few steps. His head dropped down to trailer level and hay stalks went flying. His half brothers and sisters got the message. Hungry after so much exercise, they started to move towards their prize.

Pat signalled to Hannah. 'Now. Not too fast,' she yelled.

Hannah engaged gear and crept the ute forward, pausing to check in the mirrors that the calves followed her. They had.

Like the Pied Piper, she drove towards the stockyards, just fast enough to stop the ute from stalling yet slowly enough to keep the cattle following behind, their tongues lolling. She positioned the truck at the stockyard entrance in such a way that the three humans on foot in the paddock would have no trouble shooing the cattle into the yards.

Which they did, thanks to the trail of hay carefully pre-laid by Pat.

From the truck, Hannah beamed at Pat.

Pat gave a happy thumbs up signal.

Philip turned to Rick. 'We should have listened to the ladies.'

'I'll never live this down,' Rick muttered.

'See ya, fellas.' Pat almost danced her jaunty way back towards her house.

Hannah remained in the ute while Philip and Rick directed the animals through the race and into the crush, one at a time, to clip on the electronic ear tag which would trace their journey from the farm gate. She thought about that little bit of camaraderie she'd just shared with Pat, who seemed to be less territorial about Philip today, compared with yesterday. It boded well for the future, if Pat could forgive her for intruding on her patch.

Half an hour later the cattle truck roared along the road and halted in a swirl of dust and the rattle of clanking metal. The driver backed up against the ramp, hopped into the truck to open all the relevant partitions and opened the gate between the ramp and the cattle race. Rick and Philip started shunting the animals down the race towards the truck.

Used to grass and dirt underfoot, the calves baulked at the concrete base in the crush and stopped completely when they reached the wooden slope of the ramp. Nothing would budge them. Just like an escalator full of people when someone hesitated to get off at the endpoint, the press of animals from behind threatened to topple the frontrunners to their knees. This would have injured them. Philip hastily slammed shut the gate in the cattle race to stop more animals pressing forward.

The truck driver had other ideas. Wielding his electric prodder, swearing and cursing, he forced the animals up the ramp and into the truck with repeated jabs. He treated the animals so roughly that Hannah winced. She could see anger written all over Philip's face. She knew he cared about his beloved babies, who deserved better treatment.

Once the truck had loaded and had driven away, Philip turned to Rick and commanded abruptly, 'Never again send that bloke to my property.'

Rick nodded. 'Okay. Okay. They're not all like that. He was in a hurry, I know, trying to collect all his loads before sunset, but he *was* over-the-top.'

Hannah wholeheartedly agreed. Philip was right to ban that carter from *Wallumatta Farm*.

It being Sunday, and getting dark earlier as autumn nights lengthened, Philip had to get back to town to fulfil obligations to his day job. She stood beside his car as he tossed his stuff into the back seat. He turned to her. 'I wish I didn't have to leave.' He brushed his hand down the side of her face, his thumb caressing her cheek.

'Me too. It's lonely when you're not here.' She turned her cheek to kiss his hand. Like two magnets, they snapped together into another feverish embrace.

Hannah regained her senses. 'You must get going,

Philip. Look at this fog rising up from the valley floor.' She turned him to face the fluffy white tendrils creeping over the landscape. 'Soon it won't be safe on the roads. I'm going to worry about you driving back.'

'I've got fog lights. I'll be careful.' He gave her another quick kiss. 'Please check the cows every day, Hannah. They're all in the paddock nearest you, the one you overlook from the bungalow. More calves will drop this week.'

'I'm a bit nervous about that.'

'Don't worry, these cows should have no trouble calving. Like that calf you saw born during the week. It's nature. Any problems, just call on Pat. And I'm at the other end of the phone line.' As he buckled up his seatbelt, he added, 'Oh, I nearly forgot. Expect me on Saturday morning. I'm guest speaker at a fundraising function for a charity on Friday night.'

He waved and drove off with a jaunty "bip bip" of the horn.

She stood rooted to the spot, weighed down by a sinking heart and leaden legs, wondering why he hadn't asked her to be his partner at the event.

## CHAPTER TWENTY-ONE

He strode straight from his car to her door, bearing fresh almond croissants and hot coffees from the café in town. 'Knock, knock,' he called out as he rapped.

She slid the door open, looked at him as if he were a door-to-door salesman, and eyed off his offerings. 'Just what I need. Lovely. Thanks.' With a polite smile, she took the coffee from him.

His joyous spirit sagged … confused, disappointed. No light shone from her eyes at seeing him, no bounce sounded in her voice when she spoke. She behaved as if last weekend had never happened. His heart sank. *She doesn't need me, as I need her.*

She warmed her hands on the takeaway cup. Very business-like, she said, 'You're here earlier than I expected. Keen for the progress report on the stock numbers, are you?'

'Keen to see you, more like it.' That got her attention. Her eyes engaged with his, at last. They gave nothing away.

She lifted her chin and continued as if he hadn't spoken

those words. 'Six new arrivals, including one a few hours ago. I was out on my rounds quite early.'

For all her fear three months ago, the spring in her voice proved she'd become as eagerly engaged with her new duties as a kid playing with a new toy. He'd ignore her cold shoulder treatment for now because he was hungry and he wanted them to drink their coffees before they cooled too much. 'Let's sit down here on the balcony. The air's still cold, but it's nice and sunny. You can fill me in as we tuck into our food.'

'Oh, of course, good idea,' she replied.

What's wrong with her this morning?

She tore off bits of her croissant and in between swallows she said, 'I've been watching these cows, Philip. They run a mother's club. Something else I've learned here. I had no idea.'

He rustled the packet as he reached for a second pastry. *Looks like I'd better stick to farm talk for a while.* 'Yep, they bed the new calves down in the paddock, in tussocks of grass, anywhere there's some cover, and then they spread out across the paddock to feed. One mother stays behind, on guard. She bellows if there's any trouble, and the others come charging back.'

She spooned the froth out of her latte and licked it off the spoon. He wondered if she realised how such a simple act could arouse him so much. When she caught him watching her, he said 'The froth's the best part, don't you think?'

He'd successfully disguised the direction of his thoughts because she just nodded and said, 'I love all the sounds the cattle make in the evening, as the sun's going down. Last night I rugged myself up and sat here listening to the newborns bleating for their mothers, and the cows softly mooing, calling to their calves.'

He watched as she licked her lips and set down her cup, keeping her eyes averted from him. *I don't know what's bugging her but if farm talk keeps her talking, I'll oblige.* 'That's when they're getting ready for the night. They all sniff round each other, pairing off. The babies sleep with their mothers for protection and warmth.'

Now she straightened up and looked directly at him. 'You know, I'm beginning to love these animals.'

*Great, she's beginning to forgive me, whatever I've done.* He smiled encouragement across at her. 'I hoped you would, eventually.'

She gave him a tentative smile. 'And this farm, Philip. Love it, I mean. Already.'

At last, a sign that he hadn't been mistaken about her as a human being. 'It sucks you in doesn't it. The beauty. The birds. The caring for the stock.'

She nodded. Switching her gaze from him towards the cattle, she said, 'They thrive here. Do you think they soak up the beauty too?'

He grinned. 'It's a lot more basic than that. Good food. Fresh water. Plenty of exercise. All of which are good for us too.' He tried to inject a flirtatious tone into his voice. *Don't you remember how we spent last weekend?*

She turned back to him without a flicker of reaction to his suggestiveness. Relentlessly she pursued her no-nonsense farm-based conversation. 'How come your grass looks greener than some of those blocks down the road? Did you have an eye for good food when you spotted this place?'

He knew when he was beaten. She clearly wasn't in the mood for flirting. 'Kind of. The agent told me before I bought my little bit of paradise that the pasture on these hills is regarded as above average in quality. I've also done my bit to improve the land. It's technical. I don't want to bore you.'

'Not at all. I'm interested.' Her eyes strayed from him and she gave a nonchalant shrug. 'Must have a touch of the scientist in me too.'

She sounded so clinical, so disengaged from *him*. Why was she keeping her distance, suddenly so formal and remote? He gave himself a mental rap over the knuckles. Ah! Last night. How could he have forgotten that hurt look of hers as he drove away last weekend? He must reassure her that last night's partner had been no threat to her.

He began by teasing her, reaching across the table to tweak her nose and attract her attention back to him. 'My home-grown scientific enquirer. The Madame Curie of *Wallumatta Farm*.'

She flinched back from his touch. 'That's over-stretching the analogy, don't you think?' Her reply was coolly polite.

'My sister would see you that way. I told her all about you last night.' He watched with amusement as her eyes rounded. 'Months ago she organised my role as speaker at a Cancer Council event. She's one of their ambassadors, having survived an advanced case of melanoma.'

He savoured the sight of the sun peeking through the clouds on her face.

He continued. 'She and I contributed our family's team effort to the cause last night. The function raised a lot of money. It made us the golden couple of the evening.' He chose that phrase deliberately, to make it clear who his partner had been.

The one-sided cold war ended instantly. 'Congratulations.' She radiated happiness. 'Thank you, Philip. For noticing that I was upset and for working out why. I spent a restless night last night, wondering whose hands you were holding at the function.'

'It took me a few minutes to twig, but I got there in the end.' He leaned across and kissed the tip of her nose.

'It hurt when I imagined a girlfriend down in Melbourne, with me a convenience to you here.'

Her downcast eyes conveyed an awkwardness, a sense of embarrassment, that he must clear away. 'I'm not that kind of man, Hannah.'

She directed a red-faced look at him. 'Now that you've told me, I feel bad for not trusting you more. You've always behaved honourably towards me. It's just that my confidence in my judgement took a hit over Alex.'

'I understand.' If only he could tell her that he too was having internal tussles, but not about her.

She pretended to squint. 'Your halo's blinding me, Philip, burnished by your good deeds with the Cancer Council on top of your good deeds as a farmer.'

He grinned, relieved that her apprehension about him had lifted so quickly. 'It's not just me, you know. Many farmers today are trying to leave their land in better condition than when they acquired it.'

'Okay, teach, you've successfully banished my insecurities. Today's lesson awaits. What *have* you done with your land, then?'

He loved that he could converse thoughtfully with her,

beyond normal banter. 'I don't till or cultivate the soil and, to avoid compacting it too much, I don't drive vehicles over it willy-nilly. There has to be good reason for me to get off the regular tracks. The cattle do enough to compact the soils, especially in winter when the soil is wet.' He dared to mount his hobbyhorse. 'So, one year I spread gypsum, just before the autumn break.' He waited for her attention to wander.

It didn't. Her eyes widened. 'That sounds dangerous, on these hills. Did you do that yourself?'

'Nah, no way, not me personally ... professionals. They're well practised and have the right trucks and spreading equipment.'

'How did you know that you needed gypsum?'

Good grief, she was equally as serious-minded as he was. 'Good old Pat.' He grinned at her again, now fully aware of the impact of that statement on her. 'Local knowledge. She knew gypsum hadn't been applied for a long time. The gulley erosion alerted me too. My bulldozer mate fixed that particular problem, as you saw when we planted those trees.'

'It's amazing that these everyday features in the land-scape tell such a story.' Her wonder sounded uncannily like that of Professor Brian Cox, who used exactly that idea to explain the formation of the earth and its solar system. It gave him a thrill, that she had these thoughts.

He nodded. 'I find it incredible too. The locals can also tell by the extent of muddy water in puddles and drains ... that too is a sign of dispersed soils that can be improved with gypsum. The surface of dispersed soil sets like a hard crust. It makes it harder for grass seeds to germinate and for new grass to grow.'

She laughed. 'In that case, your gypsum man must have

missed that rock hard area where we planted those new trees.'

He grinned at her. 'He didn't treat that part of the farm, but he covered most of the grazing area before my load of gypsum ran out.'

'What does this precious gypsum do, exactly?'

'It's all to do with chemistry, Madame.' His eyes twinkled at her. 'Gypsum adds calcium and helps improve soil structure by changing the way certain elements bind together.'

*Bind together.* Powerful words. Sexy words, conveying an erotic image. Did they resonate with her too? He gave her a lazy wink. 'Should I continue, Hannah?'

'Er, of course, professor. Your lessons are always, er ... memorable.' She looked at him with sultry eyes and licked her top lip.

'Where were we?' He suppressed his urgent desire to lick some other parts of her. 'Of course, gypsum.' *Who knew gypsum could be so fascinating as a line of chat?* 'It worked quite well at *Wallumatta Farm* because the hills are well drained.'

'You said you applied it before the autumn break, but for years we've hardly had enough rain to call anything an autumn break. Did it work?' She resumed the role of avid pupil.

'Surprisingly, yes. We had enough showers that year to dissolve the gypsum and let it soak in a bit. If we'd had heavy rain and runoff, my expensive gypsum would have washed away.'

'Beginner's luck, eh?'

He laughed slightly, in a self-effacing way. 'True. And

again the following year, when I employed a pilot to spray super phosphate from the air. Light showers of rain, no run off.'

Her eyes opened wide. 'You mean a crop duster? Here? With all these hills? And that almost invisible power line?' She pointed towards the single strand of wire strung across the valley.

'Yep. My nerves jangled, I can tell you. He came close a few times.'

'Rather him than me.' She cast her eyes across the surrounding landscape. 'I add fertiliser to my little garden, of course, but I've never thought about what it takes to keep grazing land in good condition.'

'Too much information, Hannah?'

'Nope. It's interesting. I hope you don't find me too nerdy.' Her slow smile begged him to say *No*.

He smiled back his total approval of all her traits, including the nerdy ones. 'I only have one more point to make in today's lesson. I used the bare minimum of super, as the run-off from widespread use of fertilisers is polluting river systems. Even the Great Barrier Reef.'

'You hear all this stuff on the news, but it's not until you live in a place like this that you understand what it means.'

He laughed. 'See. I've told you before, lots of times. This farm is teaching me heaps of stuff I need to know about at work. We finance many projects in the property, agriculture and renewable energy sectors. It helps to understand them at the grass roots level. My farm is my little incubator of practical insights.'

'Who would guess that a farm would become your mistress?' She waggled an eyebrow at him.

'That's where you're wrong. You're the big attraction. You're teaching me long-overdue lessons on the home front.' He stood. 'Come here and teach me some more, Madame Curie, before I jet off into that wide blue yonder up there.' He pointed skywards.

She started. 'What? Another trip?'

'Yeah,' he drawled nonchalantly. 'They sprang it on me yesterday. London this time.' *Will she miss me?*

Her face paled as she scrambled out of her chair. 'When? Your flight, I mean.'

'Early this evening. Actually, my bag's in the car. I'll be leaving my car at Tullamarine.'

Her jaw dropped. 'So why did you come all the way up here today, if you're jetting off to the other side of the world in a matter of hours?'

'To see you, of course. Why else?' *Surely she can see I'm crazy about her!*

She sighed. 'I'll miss you.'

*So she does care.* He pulled her towards him. 'And I'll miss you.' With both hands he smoothed back her hair and drew her face close to his, so that two eyes became one big owl's eye. 'I'll be thinking of you, my darling. Every minute.'

Hannah melted into his kiss, which signified less of farewell and more of *hello* to a bright new future.

As they drew breath he murmured, 'I've still got an hour or two.'

'My bedroom's only a few steps away,' she whispered.

## CHAPTER TWENTY-TWO

Two weeks later, she answered his knock at her door, and he rushed into her outspread arms. His kiss set a fire inside her and curled her toes.

His hands massaged her needy body as he pressed her close and murmured in her ear. 'I'm so glad to be home. With you.'

She ran her fingers through his hair, trailed them down behind his ears and thrilled as he shifted his stance to press her even closer against him. She clung to the vestiges of normality for just long enough to ask, 'The farm is home?'

'Home is where you are, my darling. You *feel* like home to me.'

Her eyes closed as she savoured his perfect response and abandoned herself to the simple but complex joy of loving him.

Twenty-four hours of bedroom bliss consumed them before Philip refocussed on farming duties. 'What's the latest here?'

'All the cows now have a small calf trotting at their heels.'

'Excellent! Then it's time to round them up, vaccinate and tag the calves and put rings on the bull calves.'

'I won't even ask what you mean by that last bit.'

He laughed. 'Let's just say I'm glad it won't happen to me.'

This time the cows and calves moved willingly into the laneway channelling the stock into the yards, thanks to the hay trick. It worked well with cows hungry from supplying milk to their calves, in paddocks suffering the usual autumn paucity of good feed.

Once they'd separated all the mothers from their calves and the bleating calves were lined up in the race, she sat on the fence and watched Philip in action. The calves jostled him, while their mothers bellowed their protest at the separation and heaved at the fencing rails, poking their heads through the gaps in the timber, their long tongues trying to lick the little bodies butting each other in the race.

He groped underneath the first squirming body to seek out its sexual organs.

'A bull calf.' She handed him the ring as he'd instructed and watched him grab the testicles, bunch them tightly together and force the slightly elasticised ring over. He grunted and swore as the calf kicked his shins and trampled on his boots.

She admired his strength and determination. 'Not an easy job.'

'I'll have a few bruises tomorrow.'

'How does it work?'

'The ring's already a tight fit. As the calf grows, the ring will starve the testicles of blood supply. They'll wither and fade away to create a steer. The calves grow fast. It doesn't take long.'

He gripped the squirming calf firmly between his knees. 'Quick. The tag.'

She handed him the ear tag machine set up with a numbered management tag, white for males, and he clamped it onto the right ear, piercing it just as some humans chose to do.

He moved on. More groping. 'A little heifer.' She handed him a tag, yellow for female calves.

When they'd finished, he said 'Now for the 5 in 1. Their vaccination. Same concept as for newborn humans.'

He walked over to the truck and retrieved a plastic bottle containing liquid. It was attached to a looped chord which he slung over his head. His height allowed the liquid contents to gravity feed through a narrow tube into the needle gun he held in his hand, like the IV driplines for hospital patients. After a quick squiz at the dosage setting and a trial squirt to get the vaccine moving, he walked along the race, injecting each calf in the neck area before pushing it past and behind him, making sure he didn't miss any of the animals.

He reached the end and turned to her. 'Did I get them all?'

'I think so.'

He gave her a satisfied smile. 'They're good to go now. Protected from the common diseases of cattle. They get a booster shot later.' He opened the race and released the calves into the holding paddock. They scampered off, kicking up their heels.

'Now to release the mothers.' He opened the necessary gates and shooed the cows through the yards and down the race towards the point of exit and their calves.

With all the animals back together. Philip took the clipboard out of his truck. 'We've yet to record the pairing of the cows and calves,' he said. 'This is my list of cows, Hannah, in numerical order of tags. We need to record which calf tag belongs with each mother, in case of separation. Also, I like to keep track, to see which mothers produce the best calves and get the best prices.'

'That sounds very scientific and business-like.'

'Nah, just curious. I'm not into serious breeding. If we sit on the top rail of this fence, we can watch them in the holding paddock. The calves are stressed at present, and have rushed straight to their mothers to suckle, making it relatively easy to match them up right now. If you've good eyesight, that is.'

'I think I can read the tags from here.' She screwed up her eyes to sharpen their focus.

'Just call out any pairings you see, and I'll write them down on this chart. I'll be looking too.' The job took a while, but the scene of happy cows and calves rewarded them as they worked.

The task complete, he jumped down from the fence and tossed his clipboard into the truck. 'Now we can let them go. Not much work for us for a while. We just let nature take its course. Mother's milk is the only sustenance for those calves at first, but gradually they learn from their mothers how to graze and drink from the dam.'

He stretched out a hand to help her down to the ground. 'You know, you've turned into a great partner.' He put his arm round her and gave her a hug.

'I've surprised myself, how much I enjoy this lifestyle.' She leaned against his chest, enjoying an all's-right-with-the-world moment. 'There's a challenge at every turn.'

'The busiest time in my … our … farming calendar ends soon. Winter is coming, the easiest time for farmers round here to take a holiday.' He sounded as carefree as a schoolkid at the end of term. 'The grass grows. The cattle grow. That's why grazing has always been regarded as a gentleman's occupation.' He grinned at her. 'It's the type of farming one does largely from the verandah, drinks in hand. Let's go.'

CHAPTER TWENTY-THREE

As darkness crept over the landscape, the crisp late autumn air warned Hannah to expect a double doona night. Normally she'd crank up her electric blanket. Not tonight. As she unloaded her shopping from the car, a thrill of anticipation shimmied through her. Tonight, she'd be warmed by Philip. She hurried inside to pick up her insistently ringing telephone.

She heard a stranger's voice. 'Is that Hannah? You'd better come. A head-on smash on the Melba Highway. On the bend approaching the bridge near Murrindindi Road. Philip ...' The line dropped out.

Her heart raced and her arm shook as she replaced the receiver. Her legs would barely support her weight. Philip should be on his way here for the weekend she'd been dreaming about all week, the one featuring him as her electric blanket. There'd be no survivors from a head-on collision impacting at 200 kph. Surely not her precious Philip. She grabbed her coat, her bag and her keys and flew out the door.

On the highway, an ominous lack of oncoming traffic signalled a road closure. She reached the tail end of the queue of stationary Melbourne-bound traffic. What to do? Ahead, maybe twenty cars queued in front of her. Beyond them flashed the red and blue lights of a highway patrol car, and the orange lights of the SES workers. She toyed with the idea of driving down the wrong side of the road to reach the accident scene, but that could be dangerous if one of the held-up drivers decided to take a U-turn and find another route. She might cause another accident. She pulled off the road to park her car on the verge and started running.

A scene of devastation greeted her as she panted to a stop at the end of the bridge. Behind a jack-knifed B-double oozing fumes and vapour, she could see a car no longer recognisable as any make or model, looking as if it had just come out of the jaws of a car-crushing vice. She clutched at her pounding heart. It was a blue car. Not Philip's. His smashed car lay twisted sideways beyond the first two vehicles. An emergency services worker charged with traffic control stopped her. 'Sorry ma'am. No sightseers. The public has to stay back.'

'I had a call. Was told to come. I live with the driver of that Merc.' She pointed across the bridge. If stretching the truth would get her there, who cared?

'In that case ma'am, wait here a minute.' He spoke into his walkie-talkie. 'They're sending someone across to escort you. It's dangerous over there. Fuel everywhere. Be careful. The air ambulance will be here any minute.'

A stranger wearing a helmet and a high-vis overall hurried across. 'I'm the one who rang. Come on. Hurry.'

'Philip ... is he all right?' she gasped as they ran.

'He survived. The first bloke didn't. The truck driver nearly didn't.'

'Oh my God. Thank God. How bad is Philip?' She panted her way around the wreckage and almost crashed into him, leaning against an emergency vehicle, a blanket draped over his shoulders, hugging his arms to himself and staring glassy-eyed at the ghastly scene before him.

He turned, ashen-faced, at the sound of her voice. 'I'm okay … I think.' His voice wavered. 'Shaken *and* stirred. Just the way James Bond does not like his martinis.'

His violent shivering betrayed his attempt at a joke. She collapsed sobbing against him and wrapped her arms around him and the blanket.

He whispered, 'I'm still here to tell the tale.' They clung together, trembling with relief.

He dredged up some more words. 'He was chasing me. Trying to run me off the road, I think. Tried to pass me several times along the way, the last time on that downhill stretch. Stupid.' Philip shook his head in sad disbelief. 'He ignored those double lines on the bend. The bridge lay ahead. That truck was on the bridge. Guard rails. The two vehicles had nowhere to go.' He shuddered.

'It's too awful. I nearly lost you.' She burst into tears and buried her face against his shirt, drenching it.

He continued to shake. 'I slammed on the brakes but couldn't avoid rear-ending him.' His strained words reverberated against the top of her head. 'He copped a double whammy, but the SES people said he would have died on impact with the truck.'

She angled her head up and lifted a hand to stroke his face and comfort him. 'How did you escape the carnage?'

Through his shivering and shaking, he managed to explain. 'The air-bags saved me. The seatbelt did its job too. Bruises, no doubt. My chest area is hellishly tender to touch.' He pointed at the crash scene. 'The car's a complete write off. Third time lucky, eh? The bushfire, the wombat, now this.'

She nodded through her tears of relief. 'Do they know who that driver was?'

He sucked in his breath. 'Prepare yourself, Hannah.'

She tilted her head in question.

He winced with obvious pain as he took a deep breath. 'It was Alex.'

Her face blanched. 'Alex? … Alex? … I know that's the colour of his car, but are you sure?'

He nodded. 'According to the cops, that's what the driver's licence says.'

'Oh my God, no!' She reeled back as the implications sank in. 'Do I have to identify him?'

He shrugged. 'I guess that will be the horrible job of his next-of-kin at the morgue.'

'His poor mother.' A tear rolled down Hannah's face.

'I've given the police my statement. You probably need to give them a statement too.' His voice gentled. 'It might help them if you take a look. Are you up to it, do you think?'

'I've never seen a dead body.' Her body shook and her voice trembled.

'It'll be hard on you, I know.' He groaned. 'You don't have to.' His quiet voice faded and he kissed the top of her head.

'I can do it if you come with me.' She gripped his hand.

It was icy. Shock. Together they approached a stretcher covered with a sheet.

'I'm Hannah Stockton. I used to live with Alex,' Hannah whispered to the police officer standing by the stretcher.

'Be prepared, he's totally smashed up and it's hard to recognise him,' came the reply.

'I won't need to see his face to know it's him.' Her face crumpled as she stared down at the stretcher.

The policeman folded back the sheet and she cringed from the sight of the battered head, the blood and gore.

She pulled the sheet down a little further and pushed aside a bloodied shirt collar. Her tears flooded out. 'Yes, it's him. It's Alex. He had that distinctive heart tattoo on his shoulder. My initials and his.' Uncontrollable sobs racked her body as the policeman replaced the sheet and jotted down a few words in his notebook.

Her sobs subsided as she buried her head against the comfort of Philip's chest. 'Oh, Alex had his problems, but he didn't deserve to die like this.'

Philip stroked her hair and murmured, 'I agree. Jealousy is a curse.'

She started at Philip's words. Now wasn't the time to raise the Martin incident. She re-gathered her wits. 'Where's the truck driver? I don't see him.'

'Still trapped.' Philip pointed towards the truck.

One of the SES volunteers overheard Philip and took a few steps towards them. 'Just so you know, the truckie's high cabin didn't take the full force of the impact, but his doors jammed. His seatbelt saved him, but he had no air bags and he was macerated by his shattered windscreen.'

'It's a miracle he survived. Will he be okay?' She peered towards the wrecked truck.

'The ambos have been busy trying to save him,' replied the SES man. 'They've staunched the blood, put him on an IV drip and wrapped him in space blankets, but he's in a bad way.'

'Is he a local?' asked Philip.

'No, but someone's in the cabin with him, keeping him company.'

Hannah watched the SES workers in action. So calm. So impressive. They'd been prised out of their daily life by the town siren, alerting them to the latest accident on the road. Their orange flashing lights lit the darkness, and their torch-lights danced like fireflies.

By the time the helicopter arrived, the risk of fire from spilling petrol and diesel had been dealt with, and access to the driver trapped inside the truck had been cleared. The medical team aboard the helicopter took over, working to assess the true extent of injuries and the safest way to extract the victim from the truck without causing him more damage. The dripline complicated the process of loading him onto the stretcher, covering him with another blanket and strapping him down.

A tear came to her eye, a lump to her throat, as the heli-copter lifted off, engines screaming and she braced against the turbulence of the *whop whop* blast from its rotors. The aircraft gained height and turned to make a beeline for the distant city. Hannah marvelled at the ingenuity of man, the level of technology enabling such sophisticated means of demonstrating man's innate humanity, its willingness to come to the aid of people in trouble.

With the chopper gone and Alex's crumpled body loaded into the only ambulance in the district, the police turned their attention to traffic control. The road had to stay closed while the Major Collision Investigation Group did their work, and all the cars banked up on either side of the bridge were turned back to find other routes to their destination.

The SES worker who'd called Hannah came over and said, 'I know you say you're okay, Philip, but you're still shaking.'

'And his hands are freezing,' Hannah added.

'Shock's setting in. You'll need to spend the night in hospital, under observation. You won't want to travel in the ambulance with the deceased. I'll take you.'

Hannah was desperate to help. 'I could look after him, at home.'

'Not unless you have nursing training, own a blood pressure machine and can stay awake all night. He may have internal injuries.'

'Oh! Then I'll sit by his bed while the nurses do their job. Can you please drop me off by my car and I'll follow you in?'

Changing vehicles, parking at the hospital and getting past the front desk tried her patience. By the time she reached him, Philip had been admitted and garbed in the inevitable hospital gown. She rushed to his bedside. 'What a night. I'm so glad you're here, and safe.' She bent down, pressed both hands to the side of his head and rested her cheek against his, breathing into his ear. 'Oh, Philip, what would I do without you?' she whispered. She withdrew, sat and grabbed his hands in hers. 'They're so cold.'

'Warm me up. I'm freezing. Come and lie down beside me.' He patted the mattress.

'Is there room for two in that narrow bed?' She leaned into him and kissed his cheek. 'First, I'll go get you another blanket.' She needed one too. The extra warmth might stop her shaking.

'No need, I've finally located what you both need.' A nurse bustled in carrying a standard hospital-issue cotton blanket for her and something special for Philip … a space blanket with a power cord dangling from it. The nurse wrapped it around him, tucked the end under his feet and plugged the lead into the socket on the wall. Warm air pumped out and bathed him in comfort.

He visibly relaxed and turned his focus to Hannah. 'No room for two now, with this contraption. Are you sure you're warm enough?'

'No. It's cold in this room. I can't stop shivering.'

'Put my coat on too. My clothes are stashed in there.' He angled his head towards the bedside locker.

How could she resist the idea of wrapping herself in his clothes, inhaling his special scent? Under the circumstances, it almost equalled being wrapped around his body. From the locker she fished out a beautiful, if crumpled, fine wool jacket and shrugged herself into it. The garment reached the top of her thighs and the extra shoulder width meant that the sleeves extended beyond her fingers, but she'd never felt more appropriately dressed. She hugged herself, her sleeve ends flapping and took a deep, calming breath. 'Perfect.' She exhaled, long and slow.

'It's the shock. Me. Alex. A distressing sight.' He clenched his teeth and shuddered slightly. 'He was a dangerous man all right, out of control. You had a genuine fear of him, and he proved you correct.'

His voice carried the no-nonsense tone of a newsreader, giving the facts. Hannah knew he spoke the truth. The sooner they both absorbed this fact, the sooner they could recover from tonight's shocking events.

The nurse returned with several tablets and a small cup of water that she handed to him. 'Swallow these. Painkillers for that bruising and a mild sedative. You need to rest.' Duty done for the moment, she scurried away.

Hannah pulled a chair close to his bedhead, sank into it, hoisted up one sleeve a little and used her freed hand to stroke his cheek. 'Alex has finally gone … I have you … Thank God you survived.' Stress forced out a few tears which trickled down her cheeks.

'Don't cry, Hannah.' The space blanket encased his arms, so he nuzzled his head against her hand and kissed her finger-tips.

'I'm okay. They're happy tears.' She raised her hand and swiped them away, smearing the cuff of his jacket with salty moisture.

'I'm happy too, that I survived. I'm glad I didn't die, before you knew why I've been so … moody.' He leant side-ways on the pillow and looked directly at her. 'I've done a lot of thinking lately. I had plans … to talk … to you … this weekend.' His voice slowed, his eyelids drooped.

Hannah's heart raced. At last, she might get some answers. She waited for him to continue.

Philip's eyelids closed and he drifted into a sedative-induced sleep.

CHAPTER TWENTY-FOUR

Within twelve hours of being admitted to hospital, Philip had passed all the overnight medical checks and Hannah was allowed to take him home. She helped him from the car to his front door, where he dealt with the locks and the house alarm.

He stepped inside, ahead of her. 'The house is cold. I'll turn on the electric heaters. It won't take long for the room to warm up.' He looked at her. 'Let's have some tea. I need to talk to you about something.'

'What you mentioned last night, you mean?'

'Yes. An explanation and an apology are long overdue.'

'All right. You turn on the heaters, then sit down and rest. I can find my way around your kitchen. I'll get the tea.' She headed towards the bench on the other side of his large family room.

Minutes later, she returned and placed the hot drink in his hands. He waited for her to take her seat in the armchair opposite him cradling her own tea.

He gazed at her thoughtfully. 'Where to start?' He stared

into the distance for a moment. 'I was raised in a single parent household. Mum, my older sister Cathy, and me.'

He had her full attention. Her brain willed her eyes to send out the right kind of signal, encouraging him to press on.

'Mum brought us up to accentuate the positives, act tough, and never breathe a word about any hint of scandal in the family. We had to appear to be perfect. But we weren't.'

Hannah remained silent. She gave him space to continue.

He bit his lip, took a deep breath and blurted out, 'Dad was a counterfeiter. He went to jail.' Philip slumped in his chair and stared at the floor for a few seconds. Then he straightened up, looked at her and said, 'Do something. Say something.'

Hannah sucked in her breath, eyes bulging ... then started to giggle. 'Sorry, I couldn't help it. Oh my, you never hear of that crime today. And here you are, with a senior role in a bank.'

'Yep. Can you believe it?'

His wide-eyed look prompted another giggle from her. 'It's not the background I expected of you, but I'm enjoying the black humour in your story.'

'There *is* that angle.' His glum face relaxed and a glimmer of amusement lit his eyes. 'I'm glad you're seeing the funny side of this. You're making me feel better.'

'But not happy, yet. Tell me, are you ashamed of him?'

'Not so much ashamed as embarrassed.' He shrugged and lowered his eyes.

'What do you mean?'

He looked back at her. 'Obviously, I know *I* didn't commit his crimes.'

'Right, so what's your problem? I still don't see why you are so hung up on this.'

'In business, you can't afford to show any chinks in your armour. I've spent a number of years toughing it out, keeping my own business to myself, and those old habits of mine are proving hard to shake. This news makes me feel exposed, vulnerable.' He bit his lip.

'So, having a convict in the family is a *no-no*?' Her disbelief showed in the rising inflection of her voice.

'In some circles, yes. You'd be surprised.'

'Why does this bother you so much, my darling? Convict forebears are the norm in Australia. They made our country. We can't hide it. The whole world knows it.' She gave a wry laugh.

'Convicts might be okay if they entered the family 200 years ago. Their genes are well diluted, and you can be proud of their resilience as pioneers. In today's world, it's not okay when it's your father. Would you want such a person in your immediate family?'

'It depends on the person and the circumstances. What was he like? Did you like him as a person?'

'I hardly remember him. Dad lived with us in my early childhood. Then he disappeared, never to be mentioned again. It made me sad. Still does. Mum was like that … tight-lipped.'

'That was hard on you and your sister.'

He nodded. 'I've always wished I had a father.'

Those longing words spoke volumes. Hannah began to see through to some of his emotional pain. Her heart ached for the little boy he'd been. She got up and squeezed into his armchair, beside him, and held his hand. She heard him swallow hard.

'He wasn't a big-time crook. It didn't make the front pages or anything. We moved to Victoria, away from everyone who knew us. No social media then, so the scandal didn't follow us. Mum went back to work. Described herself as a widow. Being so small, I thought it must be true. He *is* dead now. He died in jail.'

'I'm sorry.' She held his hand a bit tighter.

'That happened in my early high school days. That's why it came as quite a shock when Mum died last New Year's Eve and I discovered my father's conviction. She'd kept her secret for all those years. I've been angry with her, when I should have been mourning her.' His bottom lip trembled

'She damaged your trust. That's huge. Which is why you've been cautious about trusting me.'

'I guess. I didn't really understand what was wrong with me. I just needed time on my own, to digest Mum's lie to me ... and to my sister. My sense of identity, spinning evenly on its axis, went right off balance for a while. My emotions left me all at sea.' He held up his other hand and mimicked the up and down movement of a boat breasting large waves.

She linked her spare hand with his. 'You always seemed well balanced to me. Apart from your strange reactions to the word *family*, that is.'

'You helped me recover, Hannah.' He leaned his head against hers.

She snuggled into him. 'Me? How?'

'Just by being you. Natural. By giving me breathing

space when I arrived on weekends. By not being needy. By not expecting things of me. You're very different from all the women in my past life, other than my sister, of course. And nothing like my mum.'

She raised her head to look at him. 'Did she put pressure on you?'

'In a way. She wanted me to do well, make her proud. Now I understand what always drove her—she didn't want me to turn out like my father.' His eyes misted over.

She watched him will himself not to shed any tears.

'Being too late, unable to repair the damage to my relationship with my parents, sure does tear you apart.'

She leaned up to drop a kiss on his slightly damp cheek.

'Kissing me better?' he asked.

'I wish I could.' She kissed his other cheek. 'So, who told you about his dastardly deeds?' She hoped he'd accept her overly dramatic depiction as supportive, help him place it in perspective. His father had been a minor criminal, not an axe-murderer.

He shook his head. 'My aunt. Mum's sister. She told me and my sister at Mum's funeral.'

Hannah's teeth clicked as she clenched her jaw. 'Not the most considerate of timing.' It was the worst timing. She seethed with indignation at the aunt's insensitivity.

'She always knew about my father, but Mum had sworn her to secrecy. My blood boils even thinking about it. Family lies cause too much trouble.'

'Still, she could have waited to tell you.' Hannah squeezed his hand gently. 'It didn't have to be *that* day.'

'I don't see her much socially. Weddings and funerals, usually. I guess she wondered when the next opportunity might arise, and she couldn't wait to spill the beans. It's only recently that I've stopped feeling angry at my aunt.'

'Were you fond of her before your mother died?'

'I wouldn't say that. She's into family history research in a big way. She drives me nuts with her stories. My eyes glaze over.'

'She's boring, eh?' Hannah knew the problem. Some family historians affected her in the same way.

'Extremely. That's why I recoiled when I found out what you did.'

*So that explains his reaction to me, the first day we met.* 'Fair enough.' She laughed. 'Clearly this particular story of your aunt's was different … it made an impact.' She stated the obvious, hoping to keep him talking and opening up to her.

'How could it not? With my job, being the son of a counterfeiter struck a violent, clashing chord on the day of my mother's funeral.'

His sudden tight grip of her hand alerted Hannah to his ongoing tension. 'It was a rough start to this year, alright,' she murmured.

He relaxed his grip. 'You know, letting go of my big secret is proving much easier than I expected … with you.'

Hannah stroked his hand with her thumb. 'Once enough time's gone by, you might even be able to view this as a comedy skit on TV.'

'I'm glad you're seeing the funny side,' he mumbled. 'You're not like my aunt at all. She's deadly serious.' His voice grew stronger, more upbeat. 'When I met you, I thought you'd end up just like my aunt, regaling everyone with meaningless names, dates and places and nit-picking about the details—*now was it 1850, or 1849?* You get the picture, I'm sure.'

She winced in sympathy. 'Yes, there *are* too many people who think that their great-grandmother's date of birth, or the history of her special tea cosy, holds riveting interest for everyone else.'

'I couldn't believe that you could possibly like spending your days on anything as boring as family history research. It turned me off you—for a brief moment. Until you over-whelmed me with your other, er … attributes.'

She let that one go. It was important to gain more understanding of his strange switches of mood over the past few months. 'Boring? No! Family history gives you a new perspective on history.'

'Even I know that an interest in that field means you need to be more of a detective than anything else. That's why I became uneasy when I discovered your research interests. It worried me, that you'd find me out.'

She thought back to the day they'd met, months ago, when the gaping wounds in his sense of self were still raw and had not yet begun to heal over. 'Your story's not so shocking. You're doing well.' She leaned her head against his shoulder, and they rested like that for a few minutes, holding hands, soaking up togetherness.

He stirred and sat up straighter. 'It's not the story, as such. It goes deeper. I've been part of a cover-up pretty much all my life and I've been trying to hide the story since I became aware of it. I needed to grow up myself.' He stopped and stared towards the windows and the bright sunny garden outside.

She waited patiently and said nothing.

'I've done a lot of thinking this year, sitting here by myself in this house, and I can see all of that now.' His eyes flicked down and engaged with hers again. 'I needed to grow up,' he repeated.

She squeezed his hand again. 'It sounds as if you've made great progress. However, one thing does bother me personally.'

'What thing's that?'

'You've yet to explain that jealousy thing to me. You know, that phone call from Martin.'

'It wasn't jealousy. I was angry … with myself.'

'And that explains your black-as-thunder face?' She desperately needed confirmation that he wasn't another Alex.

'Yes. Your carefree friendship with Martin confronted me. With you I felt uneasy, I mean as a friend or lover. Our working partnership was fine. I wanted more but couldn't give you more. It hit me like a sledgehammer that night. That's when I really knew I had to change.'

Emotionally, this man of hers had come a long way in the time she'd known him. Full of admiration, Hannah leaned up and kissed him. 'And you have. Wise men say that we can't do much to impose order on the chaos of the external world, but it's possible to sort out the chaos within oneself. You've done extremely well to develop these insights.'

'I've worked hard on myself these past few months. Read books and stuff online. My sister's helped too. I hope it's sorted now.' He took a deep breath and immediately winced. 'Ouch, my ribs, I'd forgotten.'

'Shallow breathing, remember. Doctor's orders.' She

patted his hand. 'Tell me, did you think I'd disapprove of you, personally?'

'Not you, especially. I began to see that you uncover people, warts and all, and their past doesn't bother you in the slightest. I love that you can see the humour in all of this.'

'Well what, then?'

'People generally. I imagined that it would go against me, as a senior banker. I thought my colleagues would laugh at me behind my back and somehow my integrity would be called into question. It's the mantra I heard from my mother for many years.' His voice sounded despondent and faded away.

'Mantra? Your mother?' She encouraged him to elaborate without trying to press him.

'Men pick up a lot from their mothers.' His shoulders slumped a fraction.

'You mean it's not just fathers who try to train their sons to be tough?'

He shook his head. 'To give Mum her due, she tried to be mother *and* father. I recognise that in most ways she did a good job.'

'She certainly set you up for a successful future.' Hannah squeezed his hand in encouragement.

'Yeah. Be strong. That's what Mum always said. She was right. You can never show a weakness in the senior ranks of business, you know. We're all like bulls in a bullring. Strutting our stuff. Kill or be killed.'

She jabbed him playfully on his arm. 'Well, now you know different. Sure, you don't need to brag about it at dinner parties, but people are much more accepting of differences now. A triumph-over-adversity story always resonates. You've done your family proud.' She gave him another playful jab. 'I bet you're so trusted that you'll be running your bank before too long.'

He smiled at her joshing. 'You know, you've given me a great gift. I've learned to laugh at myself a bit more. Now I think I could even cheerfully admit to the irony of a senior banker being the son of a counterfeiter—a fox put in charge of the hen-house. How absurd.' He grinned. 'In the right company, of course.'

'You can bet it's happened before. The scary bit is that many bankers today *aren't* to be trusted, are they? We're always hearing about various forms of financial skulduggery. You exude integrity. No-one would doubt you, Philip.' This time she wasn't joshing, she was deadly serious.

'Thanks for that vote of confidence.'

'I meant it. I've always seen you as a fine, upstanding man. A real man … all substance, no image. I admit to being a bit scared of you at first—you carry that aura of being above the pack. I soon realised how responsible, smart and caring you are. Quite irresistible.'

He gave her a wolfy grin. 'Then come even closer, sweetheart.' He tried to lift an arm to wrap it around her shoulder but flinched with the pain.

She pulled back. 'Careful. Your ribs are bruised and we both need to rest.' She'd been awake most of the night while he slept with the aid of painkillers. Exhausted, she needed to clean herself up, from top to bottom, including her headspace. Truly listening to him had demanded a big effort from her. She needed to process his story. Plus Alex's death.

He nuzzled the tip of her nose instead. 'I'm not in the mood for resting.'

'But *I* am. You slept all night. I'm just about dead on my feet.' She wriggled forward from their squashed togetherness in the chair, stood up and blew him a kiss. 'I have to be strong about this. So do you. I'll leave a glass of water and another painkiller beside you in case you need it.' She passed him the remote control for the TV. 'Do you need any other help before I go?'

He conceded defeat with a mock grimace. 'No. Thanks. You *do* look tired. A few hours of sleep will do you good.'

She bent to kiss him goodbye.

'You won't get much rest if you stay here,' he murmured.

She put a finger across his lips to silence his temptations. 'I know you're a Superman but even he needs some down time. Shout if you need me.'

He grabbed both her hands. 'Come over for dinner tonight, darling. We've a lot to celebrate. No more worries for you … Alex has gone, may he rest in peace. Plus my survival of another near miss … first the bushfire, now the car crash.'

She raised an eyebrow. 'My cooking will provide no cause for celebration.'

'You undersell yourself, but you don't need to cook for us tonight. Even if my ribs do hurt a bit I *could* do the cooking if necessary. The truth is, I have another surprise for you! Already organised. I intended including you, and I'm not going to cancel it.'

She watched his eyes crinkle with pleasure. Whatever he had in mind, he clearly looked forward to it. 'That sounds intriguing.'

'So will you come over for dinner?'

'It's a date. I can't wait.' She blew him another kiss as she skipped out his back door.

---

The sounds and smells of activity over at the house filled the evening air. Car doors banged. Smoke curled from the chimney. Hannah prepared herself for the night ahead, keen to bask in the admiration of her storm-eyed handsome man. Other than at the art show months ago, he'd never seen her wear anything but jeans.

The late autumn evenings now held the promise of frosty mornings to come, so what should she wear? Her choices were very limited. She donned her one and only dressy evening jacket, a simple button-through garment of classic style. Made of royal blue velvet, with long fitted sleeves and a high round neckline, it went perfectly with her favourite choker necklace. Slim-fitting matt black pants and black court shoes with a touch of shine completed her outfit. She surprised herself as she got ready. *I've remembered how to be "girlie".*

As she approached the house, Hannah noticed Pat's car parked alongside the ute. Her heart sank. So much for her great expectations. She'd have to share Philip with Pat this evening. Had she completely misread him? She prayed Pat wasn't the cook ... a prospect too much to deal with. She thought about scurrying back to her quarters but that would be rude, and she was better than that. She could tough it out.

As she tapped morosely at the back door, she heard a

second car approaching along the driveway. Through the kitchen window, she spotted the signs of a modest dinner party. She did a double take. Was this the surprise he'd mentioned? On the kitchen bench, platters lay covered with plastic kitchen wrap beside a small pile of dinner plates. Four of them. Beyond the kitchen doorway, in the formal part of the house, she spied a dining table set with four places.

Philip opened the back door to her just as the front doorbell rang. She tried to smile brightly, act nonchalant and be practical. 'You're a busy man! Go answer the door. I'll wait here in the kitchen.' She set about gathering her scattered wits and restoring her equilibrium. He'd been in a serious car crash last night … a fatal car crash … and here he was, hosting a dinner party? Her mind boggled.

He returned accompanied by a man carrying an overnight bag. 'Hannah, this is Steve Johnson. You spoke to him on the phone on the night of the fires.'

Steve shook her hand. 'I remember it well.'

At that moment, a woman emerged from the dining room and she greeted Steve like an old friend before turning towards Hannah with a welcoming smile.

'Hannah, meet my sister Catherine. We call her Cathy.'

The family resemblance was strong but unlike her brother, Cathy radiated extraverted, easygoing charm. 'At last. I've heard all about you.' She ignored the polite handshake routine and went straight for a sociable kiss on each of Hannah's cheeks.

More genuine than an air kiss. Very friendly. Hannah liked her immediately, even as she wondered what Philip had told his sister about her.

Four settings at the table. Four people were now in the room. Disoriented, Hannah asked, 'Where's Pat? I saw her car parked out there.'

Philip laughed. 'That's what happens when you drive a generic Japanese sedan. Mistaken identity. Cathy drives a car just like Pat's.'

***

Philip returned from showing Steve to the second guest bedroom. Nervous about how this evening would pan out, he eyed his guests. He'd confessed to Hannah about doing a lot of thinking lately but acting on his conclusions tested his resolve. It had taken courage during the week to ring his sister and Steve Johnson, inviting them to come for dinner and stay overnight. He'd restricted the guest list to them alone, as he trusted them. Why let the minor … major … complication of a car crash interfere? He planned to make a big move this weekend and they needed to be a part of it.

He shepherded his guests over to stand near the comforting warmth of the fire. 'Let's all have a drink before we eat. *I* need one, that's for sure.'

'I'll do that,' Cathy said. 'You need to rest after your accident. I can't believe you didn't cancel these arrangements.' She bustled round, preparing everyone's drink orders.

Philip raised his glass. 'Let's drink to Lady Luck, who looked after me last night. Cheers.' They all rushed to clink his glass. 'And to trusted friends.' He quickly touched all three glasses. 'And to the future.' He clinked Hannah's glass and looked deep into her eyes.

Cathy obviously noticed that look and turned to Hannah with interest. Cheekily, she asked 'Does your mother know you're living here with a hunk like Philip?'

'Steady on, Cathy.' Her brother chided her. 'Aren't you jumping the gun a little? Hannah lives over in the bungalow.'

Hannah's eyes sparkled. *It'll be fun to keep Cathy and Steve guessing.* 'You don't tell your mother everything. Mothers have a tendency to fuss.'

'So you do have a mother?' asked Cathy, who would surely earn another rebuke from her brother if she didn't soon curb her curiosity.

Hannah replied, 'She's alive and kicking … down the coast. With my father.'

Cathy glanced at her brother. 'Sounds nice and conventional. Not like us.'

Philip smirked at his sister. 'Maybe convention applies to her parents. I'm not so sure about Hannah.'

Hannah smiled at both siblings. 'I'm not particularly concerned about conventions, but I don't deliberately flout them either.' *Let Cathy and Steve make what they will of that remark.*

The oven timer began dinging. Philip took a step towards the kitchen, saying, 'Phew. Hannah, saved by the bell from Grand Inquisitor Cathy.'

They all laughed.

'I'm serving the meal, Philip. Remember?' Cathy spoke firmly. 'That's why I brought it with me from Melbourne. You're injured. You sit down with the others and relax. Listen to your sister! You're off duty.' She shepherded everyone to the dining table.

Hannah's curiosity about Philip equalled Cathy's obvious curiosity about her. As the first spoonful of soup slid down her throat, Hannah seized her opportunity. 'Steve, you work with Philip. How about spilling some beans about him on the work front?' Behind her dinner party gaiety lurked serious purpose. What kind of a man was he in his weekday life, away from his weekend retreat? People often commented on her penetrating eye, but had she sized him up correctly?

Philip groaned. 'Does he have to?'

Cathy laughed. 'Oh yes. It's all good. You'll be impressed, Hannah.'

Philip protested again. 'Give me a break. I enjoy my escapes from that world. Banking's such a soul-destroying business these days.'

'Don't worry, mate, the wheel will turn full circle again.' Steve gave him a consoling look. 'Banking's been around for five hundred years.'

'Do you reckon you and I can wait that long?' said Philip.

Steve chuckled. 'Philip, you know damn well we can't. Greed has taken over. Macho men in their thirties and forties, obsessed with their own personal bottom line, have forgotten about the bottom line for their customers.'

Hannah interjected. 'I've never picked up that vibe from Philip. That he's like that, I mean.'

Steve raised his glass to salute her. 'How astute of you. Philip might fit the age profile and might look the part, but he's different.' He reached across and slapped Philip on the shoulder in a congratulatory way.

Philip flinched. 'Ouch, steady on.'

Steve smacked a hand to his mouth. 'Hell. I forgot your bruised ribs. Sorry mate.'

Hannah wanted to learn everything she could about *her* man. 'In what way do you think he's different, Steve?'

'Very few of our colleagues see our job as providing the essential lifeblood of the country. Philip does. He's a big picture kind of guy.'

Cathy laughed. 'My brother's so old-fashioned. Always has been. He treats the bank's money as if it's his. He looks after it, doesn't he, Steve?'

'Yeah, he doesn't splash it around on his mates' silly ideas. He looks hard for worthwhile business ideas that will benefit the country.' Steve grinned across the table at his host. 'I'm proud to work with you, my friend.' He gave the thumbs up signal.

Philip raised his glass at Steve and laughed. 'Anyone would think I'd paid you an advertising fee.'

Steve returned his focus to Hannah. 'Just so you know, he's an anomaly in the current banking climate. He stands against the conventional *unwisdom* of our times and sets us all a good example.'

'He's never wanted to be like all the others,' Cathy said. 'Even as a child. He's always set his own high standards. He's the epitome of *I Did it My Way*.'

'You two make me sound like a paragon of virtue.' Philip harrumphed.

Steve laughed. 'Don't worry, mate, people respect you for it. Don't change. We need a few more like you.'

Steve turned towards Hannah. 'He doesn't look after Number One either. I mean, look at this place. It's his bolt-hole and beautiful, I agree. But it's quite modest in size, by farming standards, and nearly everything he does here has the purpose of teaching him something useful for work.'

'I've noticed that characteristic in him. I like it.' Hannah couldn't resist adding, 'He's taught me a lot.' It was fun to watch Steve and Cathy exchange knowing glances.

Philip winked at her from across the table.

She knew exactly what he'd taught her … and what she'd taught him.

'So now you've heard from these two somewhat biased individuals that I'm bound to go far in this world, do I pass the "good catch" test, Hannah?'

She sweetly parried with, 'It's how people make you feel which is important, not who they are, or what they've done in life.'

Cathy beamed. 'Way to go, Philip. I think you've met your match.'

---

With the empty dessert plates about to be removed to the kitchen, Philip leaned back in his chair and said, 'Now that we're all full of fine food and wine, thanks to Cathy, and you've all had your fun embarrassing me, I have some serious men's business to discuss.' Three pairs of eyes swivelled towards him.

'What!' Hannah said. 'You mean Cathy and I are banished to do the washing up, leaving you and Steve to enjoy your port?' *Mock outrage is fun.*

Philip's eyes twinkled. 'Childhood conditioning.'

She gasped. 'Come again?' Surely he's not that old-fashioned in his other life.

'Relax!' he replied. 'My family's not part of that upper-class British tradition. Quite the opposite in fact.'

Cathy said, 'Mum was born of Irish immigrant parents. If you don't mind me saying, Hannah, your colouring looks a bit Irish too, like mine.'

Hannah nodded her agreement that she too carried some Celtic genes, but she had no wish to be deflected to this conversational topic. What Philip had said earlier interested her far more. 'How's your childhood conditioning connected to your *outrageous* "men's business" remark, Philip?' She adopted her best teasing tone to minimise the possibility of the dinner party talk veering off into the feminist minefield. She sensed that Philip had something important of his own to say.

It took Philip a few minutes to respond. 'Looking back, as I've been doing recently, I realise that my childhood did have a lasting effect on some of my attitudes, to women especially.' He scratched his chin. 'I confess I've been a bit suspicious of them as non-rational beings, because Mum was so full of her superstitions.'

Cathy said, 'She warned us endlessly about stuff that brought bad luck. That included certain people.' Cathy must have guessed her brother's conversational intentions because now she started to back him up. 'Mum didn't encourage family ties. She cut us off from our father's family and displayed no curiosity about any of our relatives.'

She eyeballed Hannah, as if checking she was paying close attention. Hannah nodded and Cathy said, 'Sadly,

Mum liked to pretend that things were different from what they really were, not liking to face the realities of her own life or of those close to her.' Cathy shrugged and stopped talking.

'Whereas I took to logic at high school. Maths. It took me into the finance world.' Philip continued his sister's background briefing. 'It's still a man's world, although it's changing rapidly now.'

'As you said, serious men's business.' Hannah probed his beliefs again, tongue-in-cheek. 'Not for the likes of Cathy and me.' Would he recognise her ribbing tone?

'No, no, quite the opposite,' he spluttered.

She watched a rueful grin spread across his face as he added, 'It's my serious men's business that I've been girding my loins all night to confess.'

Cathy clapped her hands. 'Congratulations, darling brother. You've always been too bottled up.' She turned to Hannah and Steve. 'He makes a show of being a "life of the party" guy, which might go down well in his career, but deep down he's very reserved and doesn't reveal much about himself at all.'

Philip sat up straight in his chair. 'That's all going to change, as of now. Just with you three, for a start. Well, actually, you and Steve. I've already begun peeling off the layers with Hannah. It's about my father. Who he was. Who I am. My identity crisis.'

A stunned silence descended upon the group. Philip began to talk.

Late on Sunday, Cathy and Steve prepared to return to Melbourne. Philip and Hannah escorted them to their respective cars, everyone busy with their effusive thanks and farewells.

Cathy steered her brother aside and gave him a carefully targeted hug, not too tight out of respect for his ribs. 'You did well last night. Showed us all another side of you. And gave us the chance to meet Hannah at last.' She said, 'I noticed she didn't sleep in the bungalow last night. We'll do fine as sisters-in-law.'

'Aren't you getting ahead of yourself? I haven't even asked her.'

'It's obvious that you two are ideal partners. I forecast that you'll make a long-term couple. I'm happy for you. At last you've found a soulmate.' She gave him another sisterly hug. 'I'm glad you revealed your perspective on Dad too. Since Mum's sister dropped her bombshell, I've tried to talk to you about it down in Melbourne, but you've always switched the subject back to my health.'

'That's what worried me more. I'm so glad you've beaten that cancer.' Gingerly, he returned her hug.

Steve interrupted. 'I've just remembered your wrecked car, Philip. You coming too? I'll give you a lift.'

'Not now. In the morning. I'll get Hannah to drive me.' Philip edged closer to Hannah and casually rested his arm across her shoulders. Cathy and Steve exchanged knowing looks and smirked.

The guests drove off in a swirl of gravel, a waving of hands out the car windows and a bipping of car horns.

Standing beside him, Hannah savoured her all's-right-with-the-world feeling. 'That visit went well, Philip.'

'Thanks to you.' He turned to her, tipped up her face so that her eyes met his. 'In just four months you've taught me a lot. No more bottling.'

'Excellent. Letting it out's not so scary after all, with supportive people around you, is it?'

'Facing my family's history has changed me for the better. It's even added greater meaning to my life. Thank you.' He swept his arms round her, pressed her against his bruised ribs and whispered 'You've helped to unfreeze me. See … I'm hot. Burning for you.' His lips seared hers. His erection pulsed against her groin.

Her body heated in response. 'You can unbottle like this any time you want.'

They surfaced for air and he surprised her by saying, 'I have something to show you. To ask you. Come with me.'

He stepped towards his garage and clicked the button to open the Roll-A-Door on the left-hand side, the door that had always been closed. 'See this empty parking spot. I've been saving it for a special person to arrive in my life. *The one*. You. Will you share your life with me?' His lips claimed hers again.

Before the fire took renewed hold, she spluttered her answer. 'Yes. You're the one, the man that I want.'

Next time they came up for air, she cheekily prompted him. 'You'll need a new caretaker. I'm coming with you when you're in Melbourne.'

'You're coming with me all right. I'll place an ad for your replacement this week. Maybe Pat will hold the fort temporarily. Or I could pay Horace a retainer for the time being.'

'Why didn't you go for Pat?' She enjoyed joshing him.

He slid his mouth round and murmured in her ear. 'Chemistry. Pat and I were never "an item". From the moment I saw *you* on my front verandah, I was hooked.'

She shivered with the pleasure of his compliment. 'You hid that reaction well.'

He whispered, 'I could barely restrain myself.' He renewed his clinch and his passionate attention to her lips. His kisses drove her wild.

With her unerring timing, Pat drove in the front gate at that moment. Philip refused to budge from his stance, making his affections and intentions perfectly clear.

Pat jumped out of her car and sauntered over. 'I knew you two would get together in the end.'

Philip turned to her and smiled sympathetically, while maintaining his close hold on Hannah. 'No hard feelings?'

She shrugged. 'I'm a realist. Hannah's always been too much competition for me. She's part of your world.' She grinned. 'I've been seeing Horace through new eyes lately. He's not a bad bloke. A country girl could do worse.'

# ACKNOWLEDGMENTS

*Retreat into Paradise* is a work of fiction but, in some cases, facts have inserted themselves. The story fulfills a promise once made to the real Pat Drysdale, an old-timer, to write a book about her. She was my neighbour at our farm near Melbourne. She had a great sense of humour and I wish she was still with us to enjoy this fictional twist on her farming lessons. She also introduced me to a memorable character named Horace who I couldn't resist using in this story, also with a fictional twist. Thanks for everything, Pat.

Otherwise, the characters are fictional, the usual eclectic mixmaster blending of all the hundreds of people a writer meets in life.

This book would not exist without the help of several people. My friend Pauline Johnston, another writer, was an early reader and encouraged me to finish the book and have it edited … although she's not a fan of Australian rural life!

My sister Cathy Gillespie-Jones has a Fine Arts degree and lives on a farm and I'm grateful to her contributions as a reader possessing English language and farming skills … although she's not a fan of the romance genre!

Serena Sandrin of Serena Sandrin Editing Services applied her expert editing skills to help me give up my non-fiction writing habits. Becoming a fictional writer is a work in progress but you have to start somewhere and I hope my first novel won't disappoint its readers.

Finally, the publishing whizz Sylvie Blair from BookPOD provided her technical expertise to get my Word file into the hands of Kindle readers just before Christmas in 2019.

More recently, the amazingly tech-savvy Melbourne author Ebony McKenna has done a marvellous job of re-formatting this book for all online *and* print readers. In the process I corrected a few minor glitches in the layout and punctuation of the 2019 edition, and modernised the cover, but otherwise I am republishing the same book.

I hope you enjoy it.

# ABOUT THE AUTHOR

Louisa Valentine, an Australian author, has long-since waved goodbye to her multi-faceted career in finance & economics and returned to her teenage passion for history, mystery and romance.

Her first novel 'Retreat into Paradise', an Australian rural romance of the old-fashioned variety and set close to Melbourne, was first published as an e-book in December 2019.

Her second novel, 'Trading Secrets', introduces a little mystery to a family story set in the Sydney financial world.

Louisa Valentine lives a double life as an author. Her former married name of Valentine became the perfect pen-name for an author of women's fiction. As Louise Wilson she has also published nine non-fiction books (in print format only). These bring previously untold aspects of Australia's fascinating history to life in well-researched and award-winning historical biographies and family histories.

She lives a double life in the real world too … a tale of two cities. One minute she's home alone, writing at her desk in Melbourne. The next she's driving up the Hume Highway to Sydney.

There, on Gran duty, she helps her daughter in a busy household containing two sets of twins born 14 months apart … completing the double theme!

https://www.louisewilson.com.au

# WANT TO READ MORE?

Thank you for reading *Retreat into Paradise*. If you liked the story, you should enjoy my book *Trading Secrets*. Here's a brief introduction:

Nicola Pearson is a new recruit to the Federal Bank in Sydney, hired to upgrade the system for managing the trading risks of the bank. It is the mid-90s and she has to prove herself professionally and intellectually to win over the dealers, especially their boss Tom Forrester. He has recently returned from a three-year stint in London to run the Federal Bank's financial trading operations.

Nicola has been left in the lurch by her ex-husband and does not trust men, lacking confidence in her judgment of them although she is confident of her workforce skills. She lives quietly, keeping her private life to herself and worrying over a secret.

Tom is also divorced, following a marriage experience which left him very disillusioned. The world sees him as living in the fast lane and Nicola is not his usual 'type' but something about her calls to him. He gradually recognises she is bottling up a secret. Does he hold the key to relieving her worries and changing her life?

Available in ebook and paperback.

BEFORE YOU GO

If you'd like to hear about future stories by Louisa Valentine, please 'Like' me on

www.facebook.com/LouisaValentineAuthor.

Or visit www.louisewilson.com.au

Remember, authors spend countless hours conceiving, drafting and perfecting stories in order to provide readers with a few hours of reading pleasure. Authors appreciate all assistance they can get with spreading the word about their book.

So please help in one or more of the following ways …
What is your rating for this book?
Share or Tweet that you finished it.
Tell friends & family if you enjoyed it.
Leave a review on your online sales outlet.
Leave a review on Goodreads.

Thank you for every bit of reader feedback.